THE BEST LAID PLANS

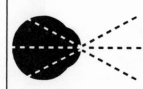

This Large Print Book carries the
Seal of Approval of N.A.V.H.

THE BEST LAID PLANS

JANET MAJERUS

WHEELER PUBLISHING

An imprint of Thomson Gale, a part of The Thomson Corporation

Detroit • New York • San Francisco • New Haven, Conn. • Waterville, Maine • London • Munich

THOMSON
GALE

™

Wheeler Publishing Large Print Cozy Mystery.

The text of this Large Print edition is unabridged.

Other aspects of the book may vary from the original edition.

Set in 16 pt. Plantin.

LIBRARY OF CONGRESS CATALOGING-IN-PUBLICATION DATA

Majerus, Janet, 1936–
    The best laid plans / by Janet Majerus.
      p. cm. — (Wheeler Publishing large print cozy mystery)
    ISBN 1-59722-348-4 (softcover : alk. paper) 1. Women authors — Fiction.
2. Divorced women — Fiction. 3. Murder — Investigation — Fiction. 4. City and town life — Illinois — Fiction. 5. Corruption — Fiction. 6. Large type books. I. Title.
PS3563.A38763B47 2006b
813'.54—dc22   2006019424

Published in 2006 by arrangement with Tekno Books and Ed Gorman.

Printed in the United States of America on permanent paper
10 9 8 7 6 5 4 3 2 1

To Bob who taught me to trust again

ACKNOWLEDGEMENTS

I must acknowledge the support of my friends and colleagues in The Three Rivers Writing Group in St. Louis who, when I said I couldn't write again, kept pushing me to try. Thank you for not letting me give up. And also my friends and colleagues in The Just Outside the Beltway Writing Group in Washington who took me the final step with their encouragement and critiques, especially Cliff Garstang, Susanne Stahley, Ron Seckinger, and Brian Neville. My deepest thanks and affection. And finally my agent Barbara Braun who made it happen.

CHAPTER 1

His eyes burrowed into my back as sharply as drill bits into a two-by-four. I sat perfectly still, pretending he wasn't there, but, as usual, it didn't work. I knew he wouldn't make a sound until I acknowledged him, but he also wouldn't leave until I did.

I stifled a sigh, hit the Save button on my computer, and slowly swiveled my desk chair until I faced him.

"What is it, Willy?" I asked through gritted teeth. So much for an uninterrupted hour of writing.

"I finished pinching the buds on the mums and got the wild strawberry out of the ivy." He stood in the kitchen doorway and twisted his hat in his hands. "Anything else you need doing?"

"No, Willy, that's all today." When he didn't turn to leave right away, I took a closer look at him. His usual sunny face was awash with anxiety. "Is something wrong?"

I asked, regretting it instantly.

"Please, Miz Schroeder, I need your help. You gotta talk to her. I'm afraid for her immortal soul. Please, please, it's really important."

"Calm down," I said. It wasn't like Willy to be so insistent. "Whose immortal soul are you talking about?"

"Miz Benson. You know, Miz Margaret over on Spring Street."

It took me a moment to respond.

"What in the world could Margaret Benson have done to endanger her immortal soul? I have never known her to be anything but a model of propriety."

"I don't know nothing about this prop . . . whatever that is," he said. "What I do know is the Devil's working on her mighty hard, and I'm scared she's gonna give in. She promised me she'd talk to you about it. I tried my best, but I'm not a person of the world like you are. You can save her."

"What is her problem?" I asked, hoping it could be handled with a simple phone call or a message delivered by Willy.

"I don't know. She won't tell me."

"She won't tell you?" All I could do was shake my head. "How can you be worrying about her soul if you don't know what's going on?"

"It's the way it's tearing at her. I've had enough run-ins with the Devil to know he's got a hand in it. And it's not just her soul I'm worrying about. She's real scared about something."

That made no sense. Margaret Benson had probably never even hurt a fly in her life. Her husband, Ray, had been a scoundrel, everyone agreed, but he'd passed away last December.

"How do you know she's scared?"

"She works her eyes that funny way people and animals do when they're scared, looking back and forth all the time like they fear something's sneaking up on them. And I know she's not sleeping 'cause the circles around her eyes are getting darker every day."

"Willy, are you sure she wants to talk to me? Or did you keep pestering her till she said yes to get rid of you?"

"Miz Schroeder, how can you say that?" He put on the hangdog face that he used to get his way with me. Usually it was an argument about what to plant in the garden. After two years of working for me, he assumed he was in control. The latest dispute had been over chrysanthemums — yellow versus lavender. He had won. A mass of yellow chrysanthemums sat in front of the

11

stone retaining wall. And I had to admit they were perfect.

"I know you're busy writing your stories at your computer all the time," he continued, "but please. Just this once."

"All right, Willy. I guess I can stop by on my way home from the family reunion this afternoon. Tell her it'll be between two and three. Now get."

I walked to the door and watched him ride away on that crazy bike that looked like something out of Dr. Seuss. Flags and reflectors bristled from every surface. At the end of the lane he turned and waved. As I returned it, I wondered what Margaret's problem was. I guessed I'd find out soon enough.

Three hours later I sat sweltering in the picnic pavilion of South Park in Riverport, Illinois. Rivulets of sweat oozed out of every pore as I listened to the droning voices of my female relatives gossiping away the afternoon. I didn't have proof, but I suspected the elders of my family consulted the *Farmers' Almanac* to find the hottest, most humid Saturday predicted for August before they scheduled the annual Schroeder family reunion. I know I am prone to exaggeration, but it must have been at least ninety-five degrees with humidity to match.

"Animals! That's what they are — vicious animals and that's how they should be treated." Aunt Henrietta, her generous body aquiver with indignation, reiterated last night's lead television news story, a bizarre ritualistic slaying in my former home, St. Louis.

"Sex, drugs, murder — thank the good Lord we don't have to worry about that here in Riverport. It's beyond my comprehension why anyone would want to live in that city." She glanced in my direction. "Oh, Jessie, I can't tell you how much easier we all sleep since you came home."

I wondered if Henrietta had placed her list in order of importance. Drugs and murder, I could definitely do without, but sex had been on my mind. I had to admit that I probably wouldn't be feeling those stirrings if it weren't for Gil Keller. Over the past several months he'd made a point to talk to me when he saw me around town and had stopped by the house several times. I was pretty sure he'd ask me out, and I knew I'd say yes. Wouldn't the back fence gossips have a field day if I started dating the Sheriff?

Actually, anything that ruffled the placid surface of life in Riverport would be welcome to me.

A brigade of ants formed a line to haul away the crumbs on the concrete floor, but I lacked the energy to do more than silently applaud their industry. My overheated brain threatened a shutdown, and I cast my eyes skyward, pleading silently, *Please, let something happen, anything, before I go mad.* It occurred to me later that I should have been more specific.

The young children had scattered to the playground. The older ones strolled around the park, sneaking sideways glances at the young people attending other family picnics. The men had drifted down the hill below the shelter to play softball and pitch horseshoes, leaving the women to circle their chairs in the pavilion. I would have preferred to join the men for softball but, at forty-two, I was expected to stay with the women. I tried to appear interested in the conversation, but failed. The subject of Margaret Benson and her circumstances kept recurring, reminding me of my promise to stop by her house on the way home.

"You know Ray didn't leave her anything," Aunt Henrietta said, "and I have it on good sources the house is mortgaged up to the hilt."

Nods of agreement all around the circle.

"Maybe Nancy Williamson can help her out? They're good friends and certainly there's enough money in that house," one of the woman said.

"Fat chance of that," Aunt Henrietta said. "You know Nancy's mother doesn't believe in helping the less fortunate, even those in her own family. She's more than willing to hold our money in that bank of hers, but giving back is another matter."

"What Margaret needs is to get married again," Cousin Frank's wife Mildred said. "She deserves a good man after all those years with Ray." Mildred shook her head. "Him and his get-rich schemes." Again agreement from the group, except Henrietta who heaved one of her famous sighs.

"Well, that's not likely to happen. No decent man is going to approach her as long as Willy Bachmann hangs around her house all the time." She directed a look at me.

I smiled, looking at no one in particular. Willy's character was a well-worn topic between Henrietta and me. She thought I was ruining my reputation, letting him work at my home. The last straw had come when I'd recommended him to Margaret.

"It's bad enough you let that bum come around your place," Henrietta said. "But to inflict him on that sweet woman, honestly

15

Jessie, that's downright sinful. How you could have done that?"

When I didn't come to Willy's defense, the conversation moved on to tomatoes. Everyone had a bumper crop, threatening to overwhelm even the most imaginative cook. "I'll bet it's because of that global warming they keep talking about," Mildred said.

I sneaked a look at my watch — one-thirty. How soon could I get away?

I had the strange sense I was caught in a time warp. I knew we were in the twenty-first century, but on days like this, Riverport seemed to doze in the 1950s. The founders of the beautiful old river town had chosen a site perched high on the bluffs overlooking the Mississippi, keeping the residents safe from the springtime floods. Maybe that's why people like Aunt Henrietta felt insulated from calamities.

My friends back in St. Louis could not understand why I stayed on in Riverport instead of returning to the city. Mom had died two years ago, leaving me the house and farm, and here I sat. Maybe it was inertia, maybe it was the comfort of family close by, or maybe it was because I didn't want to face St. Louis alone since Alec had taken a hike with one of his graduate students and the divorce had become final.

"Isn't that what I told you Friday, Jessie?"

Aunt Henrietta's question jolted me out of my reverie. I'd no idea what Henrietta had said or what she may have told me Friday. I looked in vain at the other women, but no assistance came. Chances were excellent that many of them were deep in their own daydreams. Some people resorted to booze or drugs, but not Henrietta. Solace came to her from a constant stream of talk, as if she'd cease to exist if she couldn't hear her own voice. She rarely spoke with malice, though she could have a sharp tongue. The family would surely vote Henrietta the most diligent among us, the quickest to arrive during a crisis and the last to leave. But I know they'd all agree with me: "If she would just occasionally shut up."

"Sorry, Henrietta, I wasn't paying attention. Too much good food has made me sleepy." I pried my body out of the lawn chair and stood up. "I think I'd better take a walk."

I hurried out of the picnic shelter before anyone could offer to keep me company. Exercise was definitely what I needed. I had missed my morning run. When that happened, it seemed I never got the cobwebs completely cleared out of my brain.

The family had thrown out veiled hints (and some not so veiled) that they thought it was unseemly for me to be seen running the streets and roads of Riverport and Spencer County. However, good old Cousin Frank had a different theory which he never hesitated to share with me. He claimed I used it to run away from my problems.

"Hell, Jessie," he had said. "You can't be enjoying yourself. Every time I see you, you've got this god-awful expression on your face, and you're always checking your watch. Besides, you wear those skimpy little shorts. One of these days some horny farm boy is going to give you a run you didn't plan on. You think you're invincible like that little girl you write about. What's her name, Elizabeth?"

"Emily," I had corrected him for the umpteenth time.

I had given up arguing with him. It made me feel good. Alec had insisted we take up running the year he turned forty and I turned thirty. I quickly became faster than he. Typical Alec. If he couldn't be the star, he wanted no part of it, so he quit.

A slight breeze whispered around the edges of the picnic shelter — just enough to tease but not relieve. I ran my fingers through my hair, but as fast as I pulled on it, the curls kinked back tight against my scalp. I was the only one in the family with red hair. Dad used to tease me and say that there must have been a tall, skinny Irishman somewhere in the family woodpile.

I resisted the temptation to walk over to the drinking fountain and stick my head under the stream of water. As delicious as that would feel, I knew the relatives would be mortified. Instead, I headed toward the tot lot, where Cousin Frank and Mildred's daughter Selma pushed her two children, Betsy and Joey, on the swings.

Frank and Mildred were only two years older than I and already grandparents, but that's what happens when you marry right out of high school. Their marriage plans had been accelerated. As Dad used to say, it's interesting how many first babies are premature while the rest always seem to go full term. But their marriage had worked.

I watched Selma with her children and, as always, admired her seemingly boundless patience. And not for the first time, I had to wonder if I would have been as good a mother. I stopped at a bench well short of the tot lot. Watching the children reminded me I owed them a story. I knew they would want to know what adventure *Emily Says* was up to, but I was having trouble coming up with a new tale.

The breeze had died and the air hung thick and heavy over the picnic grounds. Even the occasional shout from the softball field and the clangs of the horseshoes as they hit the stakes were muted. A peaceful, lazy Sunday afternoon, straight out of an old Norman Rockwell *Saturday Evening Post* cover, so why couldn't I just sit back and enjoy?

The persistent nag in the back of my head knew the real reason — a full-blown case of self-pity. If Dad were here he would say, "Jessie, it's time to piss or get off the pot."

"Jessie, please come play with us." The small voice jerked me back to the present. I sat up straight and bumped the little girl trying to climb up on the bench beside me and knocked her on her backside.

"Betsy, you startled me. Are you all right?"

Betsy giggled. "Me and Joey want you to come tell us a new Emily story. Mommy said you looked tuckered, but I said you're never too tuckered to tell a story."

I put my arms around Betsy and hoisted her to my lap. "You're both right. How about that? I am pretty tuckered, but not for you and Joey."

Betsy's tee shirt was streaked with watermelon stains and her whole body radiated warmth like an efficient convection heater. She twisted around to look at me. "Can Emily do something real scary this time? I promise I won't have bad dreams and Joey promises, too."

"I won't guarantee real scary, but go get Joey. Tell your mommy we'll walk over by the canna bed and sit in the shade. This sun is so hot I don't want you getting a sunburn."

By the time Betsy arrived back with Joey, I had it worked out. My comment about sunburn had given me an idea, but it turned out the story would have to wait. Their mother was right behind them.

"Sorry, Jessie, but we have to leave," Selma said. "No time for stories today."

Both children started to whine. I bent over and put my arms around them. "I'll make a promise. The next time you come out to your Grandma and Grandpa's house, I'll tell you about Emily and a little ghost named Sally Li Mahoney, who got a bad case of sunburn."

I walked back to the pavilion with them. It was time for me to leave, too.

"Aunt Henrietta," I said. "I have to go. Is there anything you need before I leave?"

"It's still early. Why go so soon?"

"Sorry. The muse is stirring. I need to get

21

home." I should have been embarrassed by my excuse, but I had discovered that a small town is quite often forgiving of writers. If people think you've had an inspiration, they'll stop traffic to let you get back to your computer. Even if what you write are merry little tales for children.

I collected my serving dish and headed toward my car, anxious to start the air conditioner.

Slowly, the car filled with cold air. Hopefully, I could deal with Margaret's problem quickly. Willy had been known to overreact to situations, especially since he had embraced sobriety and Jesus. Sometimes he took the charge of being his brother's keeper a little too seriously. Stop it, I chided myself. Sure Willy could be a nudge, but he was a good person. Mom's gardens would have gone to rack and ruin if it weren't for him.

The streets of Riverport were quiet, the silence so complete a person could almost reach out and touch it. Anyone with sense was sitting inside a cool house. I parked my car in the shade of a huge sycamore tree in front of Margaret's house on Spring Street and sat for a minute while I processed my idea about a sunburnt ghost. I'd never delved into the supernatural before with my Emily stories, but it just might work. It would be fun to see how Betsy and Joey reacted. Finally I cracked the windows and got out.

A walkway went around the house to the rear. Since I was expected, the door to use was the one off the kitchen. Only salesmen and the preacher came to the front door in Riverport.

The door to the kitchen stood ajar. "Margaret, you in there? It's Jessie Schroeder."

I took hold of the knob and pushed the door open. If she was as scared as Willy claimed, why had she left her door open?

"Margar . . ." I started to call again, but before I got the final syllable of her name out I knew she would not be answering me.

Margaret sat slumped over the kitchen table, her forehead resting in a pool of blood, and a coffee cup on its side in front of her.

CHAPTER 2

My feet didn't want to move. All I could do was stare at Margaret. My mind kept telling my body to do something, but the message was not being received. Probably only seconds passed, but it felt like hours before I could bring myself to step forward and take hold of Margaret's wrist to check for a pulse.

The only sign of life was the trembling of my own fingers. I gently laid her hand back into her lap, walked around the table to the telephone hanging on the wall, and dialed 9-1-1.

"Sheriff's Department."

"This is Jessie Schroeder and I'm at Margaret Benson's house on Spring. She's dead!" I heard my voice rise, and feared I was going to lose control.

"That's nine thirty-four Spring, correct?"

"How should I know? I'm visiting. Someone got here before me and smashed in her head." This time I did lose it, and I clutched the phone to my chest as I gasped for breath.

"Ma'am? Ma'am, are you still there?" The muted voice leaked out from the edge of the receiver.

I managed a weak, "I'm here."

"Listen carefully," the voice said. "I want you to hang up the telephone and go outside. Please don't touch anything. Can you do that? The sheriff and ambulance are on the way."

I nodded at the phone.

"Ma'am, can you do that?"

I started to nod again, but caught myself. "I'll wait outside on the back porch," I said, gently hanging up the phone.

As I started for the door, I looked around for the first time. Up to that point, I had been fixated on Margaret's body. The place was a mess. The kitchen cabinet doors stood open and the drawers were pulled out. I could see linens strewn around the dining room. A corner china cupboard lay on its side, oozing bits of china and glass. Someone had been looking for something, and he had been in a hurry.

The temptation to check the rest of the house was strong, but sirens in the distance stopped me. The phrase "interfering with a police investigation" came to mind, so I reversed direction and headed toward the porch. I couldn't keep myself from looking at Margaret as I skirted the kitchen table. The permed gray curls on the back of her head were divided in half by a swatch of blood that had made its way to the pool on the table. For the first time I noticed a second coffee cup. Someone had been with her. My stomach threatened to rebel, so I yanked my eyes away and stepped through the door. I remembered just in time to nudge it with my shoulder instead of grabbing hold of the knob.

Deputy Clarence Hockmeyer, gun drawn, came running around the house.

"Miss, please step down off the porch," he said, waving his gun toward the yard. "And keep your hands where I can see them."

"Do what with my hands?" I looked down, almost surprised to see them attached to the ends of my arms. "What do you think I'm planning to do with them? Whip out a six-gun and shoot?"

"Ma'am, please do as I say."

This was more than I could handle, but before I could speak again, Gil came tearing around the corner.

"Clarence, put down that gun. Jessie, what are you doing here? I got a call from Dispatch that Margaret Benson was dead."

All I could do was point toward the kitchen door. "I didn't touch anything except the outside door knob and the telephone." I had to stop and take a deep breath before I went on. "I did try to find a pulse, but there wasn't any. The house is a mess."

"Is that your car out front?" Gil asked.

I nodded again.

"Clarence, take Miss Schroeder to her car and then call Mitch and tell him to get over here. Jessie," Gil said, turning to me, "please, wait in your car. I'll need to talk to you after I check out the house."

A small cluster of people had already gathered out front, with more coming down the sidewalk from both directions. Several children on scooters made lazy figure eights in the street. The porches that had been empty minutes earlier were now occupied.

"Hey, Deputy. What's going on?" a man yelled at Clarence.

"Can't rightly say yet. But you folks stay there on the sidewalk. Don't be wandering around the house."

I was vaguely aware that people were pointing at me as I sat in the car, engine running and the air conditioning going full blast. I tried to sift through what had hap-

27

pened. Margaret dead. It made no sense. What the hell was going on?

I'd been with her less than two weeks ago at the church's summer Bridge-a-Rama, and she'd been fine. Stupid thought. Of course she'd been fine two weeks ago. She'd been alive. In fact, after she left, the other women remarked how much perkier Margaret was since Ray passed.

"It must be a mistake," I said out loud.

My thoughts kept darting from the past to the present. I felt strangely distanced from the murder. I was nervous and scared, but in an almost surreal sense, as if I'd just come out of a horror movie. Maybe reality hadn't sunk in yet. I couldn't shake the notion that something was crazy about the affair. Why would anyone want to kill Margaret Benson?

Probably any number of people would have been willing to do in Margaret's husband Ray, if half the stories Frank and Aunt Henrietta told about him were true. According to them, over the years he had managed to offend just about everybody in town, and more than a few had lost money on his get-rich schemes. He had done himself in when he blew an aneurysm last Christmas Eve. The townspeople joked he'd finally given Margaret a Christmas present she could enjoy.

Margaret was a different matter. I'd never heard a whisper of criticism about her. She brought cookies for meetings and stayed late to help with cleanup without being asked. I'd never heard her voice an opinion. Her smiling agreement to whatever subject was being broached could almost be an irritant at times.

As for a crime for profit, that didn't make sense either. The Bensons weren't destitute, but everything about them always looked slightly shopworn. Ray had liked to talk as if his pockets were lined with gold, but according to Cousin Frank, he rarely paid off his tab at Smitty's Bar & Grill. But the fact remained, someone had definitely been looking for something in the house. And then there was Willy's conviction that Margaret was scared of something or someone.

The second coffee cup on her kitchen table made the crime much more sinister. Margaret would never have invited a stranger into the house for coffee. It had to have been someone she knew well. An acquaintance would have been entertained in the living room. Only a person considered a friend would be invited to sit in the kitchen.

The ambulance came screeching to a halt in front of my car and two paramedics jumped out, grabbed a stretcher, and jogged around the house. Gil met them at the corner, said a few words, and then headed for my car.

He opened the passenger door and got in. "How're you doing?"

"Okay, I guess."

"Think you're up to answering a few questions? You've had a terrible shock."

I nodded and for the first time realized I was gripping the steering wheel so hard my knuckles were white. "Terrible shock is putting it mildly," I said. "First time I've been asked to come over to somebody's house, then find the person dead in the kitchen with her head bashed in."

"I'm sorry. Let's get this over with, so you can go home."

Slowly and gently he took me through the events of the day, starting with Willy's visit in the morning.

"And Willy had no idea what was bothering her?" he asked.

"None, but he assured me she would talk to me."

"And you saw nobody when you arrived? Not even walking on the sidewalk or driving away?"

I shook my head. "Nobody."

"I'll need to talk to you again, but this is enough for today. I'll get Clarence to drive you home."

I turned and stared at him. "Why on earth should Clarence drive me home? I'm not incapacitated. I can drive just fine."

"I'd feel better if Clarence took you home. And he can wait till someone comes over to stay with you."

He'd feel better? What was he talking about? I was the one who needed to feel better, and being treated like a child was not going to accomplish that.

"Thank you, but no," I said. "I'll drive myself home in my own car, and I don't need anyone coming over to baby-sit me."

"I'm afraid you're not thinking clearly."

"If there are no further questions, I'd like to go."

Gil looked at me briefly, then got out of the car. He must have realized he had pushed a little too hard. Still, I found myself fuming most of the way home. What did he think I was, a hysterical female who couldn't cope with adversity? I knew I was probably overreacting to him. Deep down, I felt he was genuinely concerned about me. By the time I arrived at my driveway, I was almost calm — calm, that is, until I saw Cousin

Frank's car parked at the head of the lane. Another man wanting to order my life!

"What are you doing here?" I asked as I got out of my car.

"What am *I* doing here?" he almost screamed. "You just discovered a body and you're asking what I'm doing here? When I heard what happened, I drove over here as fast as I could. What if someone had been waiting for you?"

"There *was* someone waiting for me, Frank. You were waiting for me. Now what do you want?"

"I want you to pack a bag. You're going to stay with Mildred and me."

"Thank you. I appreciate your concern, but I'm not going anyplace. I'm staying right here."

Frank's mouth snapped open, and I steeled myself for another reprimand, but he said nothing and shook his head.

Suddenly, he threw up his hands and said, "Goddammit, Jessie, why are you always so damned stubborn?"

I didn't answer. He looked at me, turned, and stomped up the walk toward the door. I could tell by the set of his shoulders that he had given up, and I felt a little ashamed of myself.

I grabbed my picnic basket and hurried after him.

"Frank," I said as I caught up with him. "I'll be fine. You know I'll call if I'm worried."

"Yeah, I know. If Jessie says so, it's got to be fact. Would it hurt your sensitivities if I checked out the house?"

I didn't turn down his offer. In the heat of our debate, I had been carried away with my brave front. I didn't want to enter the house alone.

"I'll feel better if you do," I said.

As we opened the door to the house, I felt I'd been away for a year instead of four hours, though nothing had changed. Even Genevieve curled up on the cushion on the kitchen chair. The same clock hanging on the west wall struck four, and the office niche I'd carved out for myself in the corner was as I'd left it, but somehow everything seemed different.

We made our way methodically through the house. Frank looked in all the closets, under the beds, behind doors, and made sure every window was locked. He even pulled the dust covers off the furniture in the storeroom and checked out the clothes hamper in the bathroom and the dryer in the laundry room.

"Please, Jessie, come home with me. Or Mildred and I will come stay here with you, if that's what you want."

I shook my head. "Just go. I'll be fine."

Frank sighed. "I'll check the toolshed and the barn, then I'll be on my way. Henrietta's going to pitch a hissy when she finds out I left you here."

Finally, he was back in his car. I watched him drive out the lane and up the road until he disappeared from sight behind the hill.

Maybe a cup of coffee would help clear my mind. A fresh pot would definitely be wasted, so I settled for warming up the morning's leftover. My brush with murder had left a metallic taste in my mouth. I set my cup in the microwave to heat it up and wondered if Margaret had made a fresh pot for her murderer.

Genevieve claimed a spot on my lap as soon as I sat down, nudging her head under my hand. I didn't particularly like cats, but there was never any question about Genevieve staying on after Mom died. Besides, I liked someone greeting me when I came home.

And what a different home it was from the condo Alec and I had shared in St. Louis. Empty space had been anathema to my mother. Where the condo was furnished sleek and spare, everything decorated in fashionable neutrals, Mom's decor could best be described as colorful, comfortable clutter. After she'd died, I recognized what a true reflection the house was of the woman herself. Always a little rumpled and disorganized, but open and warm. Mom had that rare capacity to make everyone feel special. God, how I missed her.

Her house was a big, rambling white frame with her kitchen the focal point. As large as many people's living rooms, the kitchen drew visitors like a magnet, many of whom never bothered to set foot in the rest of the house.

I had a sudden urge for a cigarette, even though it had been twelve years since I heeded the warnings of the Surgeon General and a persistent cough. The same summer, after many arguments, I'd let Alec convince me we should have no children. Maybe it was cause and effect, but less than two months later I quit my job and started writing full time. I had tired of the advertising game, touting products I would be ashamed to have in my own home. Why did we need the extra money if we weren't going to have a family?

"How could you quit your job without telling me?" he had yelled when I told him.

"You know all our decisions are joint decisions. And children's stories! How can anyone spend all her time writing children's books, for God's sake? Any idiot can do that."

It had taken two and a half years before the first *Emily Says* was published, and they kept coming. Five books in nine years, and one had received a Newbery Honor Award. The reviewers said my style was whimsical, refreshing, unpredictable, as much fun to read for the parents as the children, and I enjoyed every minute of it. My protagonist, Emily, was a child people loved reading about, but gave thanks they didn't have to raise.

The last two years had been a struggle, and I had written little of significance. A few reviews and pieces of fluff, but for the most part my computer sat quiet, taunting me from the corner of the kitchen. And now I had murder to contemplate and contend with.

Looking out the window at the garden reminded me of Willy. How could I have forgotten him? Had he heard about Margaret? I wished I could get in touch with him, but the room he lived in behind the Abundant Life Church didn't have a telephone. He wasn't due back to work for me until

Tuesday, though I was sure he would come see me as soon as he heard.

The rest of the family hadn't objected as vehemently as Aunt Henrietta, but they were none too pleased when I hired Willy. I couldn't convince them of the redemptive powers of AA and born-again Christianity. As far as they were concerned, "once a drunk, always a drunk." But if I was going to salvage anything of Mom's beautiful flower beds, I needed help.

One Sunday last January, Margaret had stopped me after church and asked if it would be all right with me if she asked Willy to do some odd jobs for her.

I hemmed and hawed and muttered something about his problem, but Margaret stopped me. "I think it's wonderful what he's done," she said. "Besides, even when he was drinking, he was never a menace except to himself. Not like my Ray," she'd said. "Ray had a tendency to get mean."

That was the closest I'd ever heard her come to criticizing anyone.

Willy had been pleased. He quoted Miz Margaret this and Miz Margaret that. They became friends. I teased him about the amount of time he spent at her house and asked if he was sweet on her. He had blushed bright red and said, "Miz

Schroeder, don't say nothing like that. A no-count bum like me got no right to think that way about a lady like Miz Margaret."

I jumped as the clock struck six and Genevieve leapt out of my lap like her tail was on fire. Nearly two hours had passed, and my coffee sat stone cold.

"The news, it should be on the six o'clock news." I hurried to the living room.

I flipped on the television just in time to hear anchorman Rex Montgomery say, "We'll be back in a minute with details on the brutal homicide that took place today in the town of Riverport," before his face was replaced with a herbicide commercial. The thirty-second ad seemed to stretch endlessly, but finally Rex Montgomery came back.

"The small town of Riverport, located sixty miles northwest of Springfield, was shocked today with the discovery of the body of long-time resident Margaret Benson, who had been viciously murdered," he said. "Special Correspondent Constance Naylor is on the scene, talking with Spencer County Sheriff Gil Keller and neighbors of the dead woman. Now, live from Riverport, here's Connie."

The scene switched to a young woman standing in front of the Benson house.

Several children were jumping up and down behind her, waving at the camera. Margaret's house looked forlorn in the late afternoon glare; peeling paint stood out in bold relief from the risers of the wooden steps leading up the porch. The brick bungalow was identical to its neighbors on either side. A weathered swing hung from the porch ceiling and double windows framed the front door, window shades pulled down to the sills.

"This is Constance Naylor, coming to you live from Riverport. With me is Sheriff Gilbert Keller. Sheriff Keller, tell us what happened." The reporter shoved the microphone into Gil's face.

I found myself distracted by his presence on my television screen. When I analyzed his features individually, they came up short, but something about the combination worked. The nose slightly crooked, the eyes set a fraction too close with crinkle lines around the corners, and eyebrows that usually looked like they needed a good grooming. His lips were full and sensual, almost feminine. He and Cousin Frank were both forty-four and former classmates at Spencer County High. Gil looked tired, but as I studied his face more closely, I realized that irritation, not fatigue, had deepened the lines around his mouth.

"Margaret Benson's body was discovered at two-thirty p.m. in her kitchen," Gil said. "She had been struck in the back of the head by a blunt instrument."

For a minute I was afraid he was going to mention my name. The last thing I wanted was the press pursuing me, but I shouldn't have worried.

"Do you have a motive or suspects?" Constance Naylor asked.

"I can't comment on that." Gil turned away from the microphone and walked toward the house.

The reporter took a couple of seconds to react, then she ran after him. "Sheriff, Sheriff," she yelled, "does that mean you know who did it? And what about the victim? Did she put up a struggle? Was she sexually molested?"

Gil didn't hesitate as he made his way through the crowd. He ducked under the yellow tape circling the house, and climbed the front steps.

The reporter shook her head as she turned into the camera. "There you have it. The details are sketchy at best. I'll have further developments and interviews with the townspeople at ten. This is Special Correspondent Constance Naylor, live from

Riverport where the brutal murder of Margaret Benson was discovered this afternoon. Back to you, Rex."

"Thank you, Connie. Now back in Springfield, we have a severe thunderstorm warning . . ."

I switched off the television and headed toward the kitchen. No more coffee for me. It was time for a gin and tonic. I would put off thinking about what Gil said, or rather hadn't said, until I was settled in the garden, but before I went outside I needed to do something. I walked over to the corner of the kitchen and turned on my computer. Leaning over the keyboard, I opened a new file and titled it: *"Emily and the Sunburnt Ghost."*

A slight breeze stirred the tops of the trees, but the air outdoors clung to my skin, hot and heavy. I thought I smelled a hint of rain in the air. Probably the storms reported on the news would come through Riverport before they hit Springfield.

The flowers drooped from the afternoon heat. What a blessing rain would be. Even though Willy and I watered the gardens diligently, I knew it was a losing battle unless it rained soon.

Genevieve had followed me outside. She stalked an invisible adversary at the edge of the garden. I tried to reconstruct the day, but the picture of Margaret slumped over the kitchen table kept intruding. Out of the corner of my eye, I saw Genevieve pounce on a dusty miller moth. Had the killer been following some basic instinct, like the cat? Maybe there was no motive, just the need to kill.

"Honestly, Jessie," I said out loud. "That is downright morbid."

I felt myself slipping toward the edge of panic and forced myself to lean back and take a deep breath. What in the world was I doing? Why was I sitting out in the open with some maniac running loose? I took another deep breath and tried to analyze what was going on. My reaction to the events of the day was all too familiar to me. Initial shock and paralysis, then calm reflection and analysis, but I knew I wouldn't be able to control the flashes of memory that popped up, unbidden. Even things I thought were long since buried often returned to plague my nights, clothed in every shade of gray imaginable. Why couldn't I learn to see things in black and white like my little *Emily* did?

The shrill ring of the telephone from inside the house interrupted my thoughts. I wanted to ignore it, but I knew that if it was

Aunt Henrietta and I didn't answer, she would call out the National Guard. In the good old days, I would have had my cell phone by my side, but now it stayed mainly in the kitchen drawer.

"Jessie, Jessie, have you heard?" Henrietta started talking before I could finish my hello. "Esther Holtzman saw the killer." Henrietta's sharp intake of breath rasped in my ear. "Oh my God, Jessie, it could be you dead."

CHAPTER 3

"What do you mean, Esther Holtzman saw the killer? I watched the news. The sheriff didn't mention a witness."

"Well, it's a fact," Henrietta said in my ear. "Lester Holtzman told your Uncle George. Esther saw him."

I had a bad feeling about what was coming. "Are you going to share your gossip with me or do I have to play 'Twenty Questions'?"

The events of the day were taking their toll. My aunt was the last person I wanted to talk to at the moment.

"Jessie!" Henrietta drew out my name as if she were talking to a difficult child. "It's not gossip. It's God's own truth."

I didn't say anything. Any comment from me would prolong her preamble.

"Oh, Jessie, I'm so scared." Henrietta's voice trembled. "I've worried constantly ever since you started having that Willy

Bachmann work around your place. I tried not to be a nag, but everyone knows he's a no'count, and it turns out he's worse. He's a murderer."

I was stunned. All I could do was stare at the telephone receiver. Willy Bachmann? Why was she talking about Willy? Surely no one could think Willy had anything to do with Margaret Benson's death.

"Jessie, are you there?"

I took deep breath and forced myself to speak slowly and distinctly. "That's ludicrous."

"It's not ludicrous. It's a fact." Her words came back quick and concise, unlike her normal circuitous conversational pattern.

"Willy would never harm anyone." I was sure of the truth of that statement. Willy may have had a rather unsteady past, but a murderer he was not. I'd put money on that.

"All I can say is Esther saw what she saw. I know you like to think the best of everybody, even that cheating husband of yours, carousing with that girl at the same time you were nursing your dear sweet mother through her final days. You know, the family never did think he was good enough for you. Only interested in himself. Everyone knew that except you."

"Henrietta, could we get back to Willy, please?"

The last thing I wanted was another harangue about my ex-husband. Keeping Henrietta on track wasn't easy, particularly when the subject was Alec.

"Oh, yes, Willy."

I could almost hear her shifting gears.

"Well, Esther saw him going into Margaret Benson's house a little before noon," Henrietta said. "According to both Esther and Lester, he's been hanging around her house a lot the last couple of months. And now no one can find him. If that's not proof of guilt, I don't know what is."

"That's definitely not proof of guilt." I tried to keep my voice steady. "Willy had a good reason to be at Margaret's. I asked him to go by her house and tell her I'd stop on my way home from the reunion. She had some problem she wanted to talk about. I've told this all to the sheriff."

"Jessie, please listen to me. All I know is the sheriff's looking for Willy Bachmann and that's good enough for me. You should be worrying about your own safety. He's on the loose, and he's already killed one poor defenseless woman. You could be next on his list."

I stifled a groan. "I am not some poor

defenseless woman." I felt my temper start to rise. "I can take care of myself."

"Well, that's neither here nor there." Henrietta suddenly turned brisk. "Main reason I called was to tell you to get your things together. There'll be no more nonsense from you about not going over to Frank's. After what you've been through today, you shouldn't be alone. Frank'll be over in about a half hour, soon as he gets the livestock penned. Looks like a bad storm is brewing."

God, now I had Frank to contend with again. I hung up the phone with more force than necessary.

"Dammit, wait a minute," I yelled. That damn cat was scratching at the door again.

She'd systematically worn a two-inch square of paint off the door with her persistent scratching. Should just get her declawed, but I knew I never would. She spent too much time outdoors. Besides, it wasn't Genevieve who'd irritated me. An occasional touch-up on the door was no big deal. *Willy Bachmann a murderer! Nonsense.* But I had a sinking feeling I was the only one who might think that.

Genevieve ignored my glare as I flung open the door. Instead, she proceeded to wrap her tail around my legs.

"Something's very wrong," I said, picking her up. "We know Willy didn't kill Margaret, but who did?"

I had found myself talking out loud to the cat more and more as the months went by. I guessed it was better than talking to myself.

Genevieve's only reply was a thunderous purr as she nestled deeper into my arms.

"Let's go back outside for awhile," I said, "and watch the storm come up."

The sky had darkened and the wind out of the west had picked up.

"We may be able to turn off the AC and open the windows tonight. Wouldn't that be nice, Genevieve?" I settled back in the lawn chair and took a sip from my now watery gin and tonic. "I wonder where Willy has got himself off to?"

The rumor Aunt Henrietta had passed on worried me. Surely Gil didn't suspect Willy. Dare I call him and find out what was really going on? I was sure he would want to talk to me. It seemed like recently it had not taken much of an excuse for him to call or stop by. But maybe I was reading more into his visits than I should. *No.* My instincts told me otherwise. Every time he saw me, his face lit up in that wonderful smile and his visits were getting more frequent. God, I felt like a teenager — does he or doesn't he? Will he or won't he? No impediment existed to prevent us from spending time together. We were both alone, and neither by our own choosing.

What a crush I'd had on Gil Keller in high school. He'd barely known I existed. Captain of the football team, captain of the basketball team, king of the homecoming dance. And how I'd hated that Christine Overmeyer, parading on his arm in front of the whole school, then dancing with him, her blond hair thrown back, laughing and looking in his eyes, cuddling into his shoulder. I would have sold my soul to be Christine Overmeyer.

But, instead, I'd been a lowly sophomore, relegated to the punch bowl, praying Gil would get thirsty during my shift. But that hope had been tinged with panic. What if I spilled the punch?

What a mess I'd been. Tall and skinny, oversized glasses that were forever slipping down my nose, hair that frizzed every which way in the humidity, and braces with those infernal rubber bands. I'd refused to smile for three years. Christine Overmeyer did not wear glasses and her teeth were perfect.

"Well, Genevieve, maybe I finally have a crack at Gil Keller."

As good as that made me feel, the thought of dating again after all these years felt bizarre. Would I remember how?

A snap of lightning lit up the horizon, bringing me back to reality. I couldn't believe I was sitting here thinking about Gil after what I'd been through today. Now it looked as if a major storm threatened.

Where had Willy gone? How absurd that anyone could think he'd killed Margaret. He wouldn't even kill the slugs that invaded the impatiens bed. I was the one who put out the saucers of beer and disposed of the carcasses. Then there was the debacle with the rabbits.

I thought we'd been invaded by a warren of rabbits. As fast as I put out bedding plants, they were nibbled to the ground. I'd asked Willy to trap and destroy them. Little did I know he was trapping one very pregnant rabbit over and over again, gently transporting her across the road, just a hop, skip, and jump from her feeding grounds. Then she'd delivered her babies in the irises, and he'd absolutely refused to dispose of them, even though he knew they would follow their mother's example and wreak havoc with the flowers.

"Please, Ms. Schroeder," he had said. "I can't do it. I can't hurt those babies. I can't

50

kill nothing."

"Jessie, Jessie, where are you?" Frank's voice came from the side of the house.

Before I could answer he came around the corner at a run, shotgun in hand.

"For heaven's sake," I said, "don't shoot me. I didn't hear you drive up. What in the world are you doing with that thing?"

"Why aren't you inside?" Frank demanded. "Murdering lunatic on the loose and you're sitting outside smelling the roses."

"Don't get yourself in a snit. Besides, I don't have any roses. I'm just enjoying the fresh air. You're here at your bidding, not mine, so don't go shouting at me. Sit down and tell me exactly what's going on. Your mother has Willy hanging by some pretty flimsy evidence. I thought people were innocent until proven guilty, not the other way around."

Frank lowered his gun and plopped down in the chair opposite me. "Evidence isn't so flimsy, Jessie. A wrench killed Margaret. Sheriff found it in Willy's toolbox. 'Sides, if he's not guilty, why'd he up and run away?"

All I could do was stare at Frank. What was he saying? Willy's wrench had been used in the murder? Willy had saved his money for over a year to buy a good set of tools, and no more than two months ago, he'd brought them by to show them off. He'd been so proud. "I didn't even buy 'em on lay-away. I saved up till I could walk right up to that counter, put down my money, and take my tools home with me."

"Sheriff found it on Margaret's back porch, sitting in the top of Willy's toolbox," Frank continued. "Lester saw it. Said it looked like he'd tried to clean it off, but it was still pretty gory. Sheriff's sending it over to the state lab in Springfield."

I tried to concentrate on what Frank was saying and not the vision of the wrench that trolled through my mind.

"I'll grant you Willy's not the sharpest knife in the drawer," I said, "but he'd sure have sense enough not to leave the murder weapon sitting in his toolbox."

Frank shook his head. "I admit it doesn't seem likely, but Jess, none of us knows what all those years of hard drinking might have done to his head. He used to do some pretty crazy things while he was still boozing."

"But did he ever hurt anyone?"

"Not that I know of, leastwise not since he's been in Riverport."

Willy had been on the wagon by the time I came back to town. Mr. Evans at the hardware store had told me what a good worker he was and suggested I talk to him. Advice I remained grateful I'd accepted.

Although Willy never gave me any details, once in a while, when I'd ask him how he was doing, he'd shake his head and say, "It's sweet Jesus saved me, Miz Schroeder, and every day I wake up without the tremors and shakes, I give thanks and rededicate myself to His good works."

And he had. If you could afford to pay for his labor, he'd ask, but for someone like Margaret, he'd undercharge or take goods instead of cash.

I looked at Frank. "Over the past year, Willy's been making restitution for bad checks and any other trouble he's caused people."

I'd helped compose the letter he had sent out. How surprised I'd been at his curiously childish signature and how out of place it looked with his name, Wilhelm Edward Bachmann.

"Besides," I continued, "the only reason he was at Margaret's house was because I asked him to tell her I'd stop by after the reunion."

"I can't argue with what you're saying, Jessie, but facts is facts. Maybe she said something and he snapped, I don't know, but things don't look too good right now,"

Frank said. "Come on, let's get going. Mildred's waiting at Mom's for us. She's afraid to stay alone for even a half-hour."

Thunder rumbled as we walked around the house, toward the kitchen door. "Looks like we're in for a gully washer tonight," Frank said.

I turned on the kitchen light and waited for Frank to close the screen before I spoke. The kitchen looked and felt as stark as an operating room in the artificial light. I felt more exposed inside the walls of my house than I had sitting in the garden.

"Frank, I'm not going home with you." I held up my hand to halt the protest that I knew was coming. "And I'm not going to argue about it."

"Why, Jessie? You know I'll worry. You shouldn't be alone."

"It'll be fine. I'll lock up tight, and I've got Dad's shotgun. I keep it cleaned and oiled, and if you recall, I'm pretty good with it. Besides, it's hard to miss with a shotgun. I'll even take it upstairs with me."

Frank muttered something under his breath.

"What did you say?" Not that I particularly wanted to know.

"I told Mom it was a waste of time to come here. But you know Henrietta. She won't take 'no' for an answer. I'm going to have hell to pay when I come back without you. Goddammed women. Can't live with 'em. Can't live without 'em."

I put my hand on his arm and gave it a squeeze. "Thanks, cousin. I promise I'll call if anything at all unusual happens, and I'll go get the shotgun right now."

The rain started before Frank's car reached the end of the lane, the scattered drops digging tiny craters in the dust. The sky to the west was a yellowish-gray and the tree branches whipped back and forth. Then the heavens opened and big, fat drops exploded on the windows. It turned pitch-black outdoors. A bolt of lightning streaked across the treetops. Good thing I'd let the people from the Conservation Department put a lightning rod in the top of the black walnut tree. They said it was a miracle the tree had never been struck, standing alone like it did in the clearing in the woods across the road, towering above the other trees. Going to be quite a night.

I kept the shotgun on top of a cabinet in the pantry, unloaded, and the shells on top of another cabinet. With Frank's grandkids in and out of the house, I was not about to take a chance. Which reminded me, I still owed them a story. Good way to spend the evening. I'd plot out the tale of Emily and the sunburnt ghost and let the rest of Riverport worry about Willy.

It took only a few minutes to check the gun and load it. I hadn't used it in over a month, since I had blasted away at the crows who were threatening my sweet corn. I only had a few stalks, but wasn't about to give any of those succulent ears to the crows.

Suddenly the entire sky lit up and a crash of thunder rattled the dishes on the shelves. Chances were good the electricity would go. I headed back to the pantry to get the Coleman lantern. Before I was halfway across the kitchen, another flash and roar of thunder rocked the house and the whole place plunged into darkness. The rain turned into torrents, sheeting the windows. Nothing to do but sit back down and enjoy the fireworks for a while.

Genevieve jumped into my lap and attempted to dig her way to safety. I grabbed her paws before she clawed her way through my skirt.

The trees groaned in the wind and branches whipped against the sides and roof of the house. Dad had told me that by counting the seconds between the flash of light and the thunder, a person could tell how close a storm was. By now there were no pauses between the lightning and thunderbolts.

I could just make out the outline of the barn when the lightning flashed. Suddenly my heart pounded so loud, it overwhelmed the thunder. Something was out there. Something had crossed the lot in front of the barn. I squinted to get a better look, but it was gone. I took a deep breath and put my hand on the shotgun. Probably an animal or a tree branch. *Nothing . . .* I stopped and forced the words into my mind. *Nothing or nobody would be out on a night like this.*

CHAPTER 4

My pulse raced. I squeezed Genevieve so hard she let out a yowl, scrambled off my lap, and disappeared into the darkness.

At times, people have accused me of having an overactive imagination. But I couldn't convince myself that my mind had manufactured the form I saw in the flash of lightning. Something had crossed the barnyard. Something too bulky for a branch and too upright for an animal.

Staring out the window, I felt so alone. Instead of feeling safe in my kitchen, I felt trapped, vulnerable. Why hadn't I gone home with Frank? The rain streamed down the glass, and the trees groaned in the wind. *Take a deep breath, Jessie. The house is locked, you've got your shotgun, and you know how to use it.* Even as I thought it, I knew it would take more than a simple pep talk to bring myself under control. Genevieve crawled back into my lap, making her customary circle before she settled down. My hand trembled as I stroked her fur. She must have sensed my unease because her skin twitched and she made a rumbling noise in her throat. Her signal to me that she was dissatisfied with my efforts.

I should move, get up, do something, recheck the doors and windows, anything, but generalized paralysis had set in. Maybe if I practiced my yoga breathing techniques. Fat chance. I'd tried yoga once and failed miserably. While the rest of the class meditated on a rose, I had reviewed my dinner menu.

The instinct of self-preservation finally proved better motivation than yoga. I needed a flashlight. No sense having a gun if I couldn't see what I was protecting myself from.

I eased my way across the kitchen and retrieved the flashlight from the drawer. I resisted the temptation to turn it on. If someone was out there, I didn't want to advertise my location. Back at the table, I picked up the shotgun and placed it on my lap. That made me feel better.

What would your friends think if they could see you now? A regular Annie Oakley. I remembered the furor that had erupted when Dad announced he planned to teach me to use a gun. Mom had had a fit. My folks rarely argued, but this time was different. They sent me to my room. They were strong believers that a child should be shielded from adult disagreements. As usual, I had sneaked back down and hidden around the corner at the foot of the stairs, praying all the time that Dad would win.

And he had, brushing aside Mom's claims that he would ruin me, turn me into a tomboy, and make it impossible to take my proper place in society.

I had proved an apt pupil. The shotgun had been almost as big as I was, so Dad let me prop it on a bale of straw. He had been proud of my prowess, but the lecture never varied. "Never take off the safety until your target's in clear view and your mind is made up to shoot. And never point at anything you are not prepared to shoot."

Could I shoot another human being? I honestly didn't know. Blasting away at the crows raiding my corn patch was one thing. Shooting at a person was another. I never had, and I never wanted to. And what about Margaret? Would she have shot her attacker?

The rain slowed. Frank had been right. A gully washer. Quick in and quick out, but violent as it passed through. *Frank. I should call Frank. See if they've had any damage. I* knew that wasn't why I wanted to call. I needed to hear another human voice, the voice of someone who cared for me.

Thwarted. Nothing but silence when I picked up the receiver. The storm had taken out the phones, just like the electricity. My cell phone! I scrabbled through the drawer and pulled it out. Nothing again. The phone was as dark and silent as the room around me. I had forgotten to recharge it. I tried to put the specter that had crossed the barnyard out of my mind. The only logical explanation was the storm.

As I stared into the darkness, the feeling of helplessness deepened. Who was I trying to fool? Sitting here with my shotgun and flashlight, cut off from human contact. Certainly not myself.

I prided myself on being able to analyze a situation, make a decision, take action, even in a crisis. Then Alec had walked out on me. For the first time I found myself equivocating. Oh, there were many times in my life when I questioned little things — will the roast be rare enough, will the Yorkshire pudding flop this time, is this the right dress to wear, will the audience fall asleep during my talk? — but my core had been secure.

Maybe I had been lucky. All around me, when I took the time to notice, were people buffeted by deceptions, false promises, lies. People afraid to look another in the eye, afraid it might make them trust again. The remembered pain too much to bear.

I pressed my fingers to my temples. Why was I wasting time mucking around in the quagmire of my failed marriage? "Be honest, Jessie," I muttered to myself. "It's a lot easier than thinking about murder."

The rain stopped; the thunder no more than a faint grumble in the distance. I looked out the window into a black void. Was this what it was like to be blind?

Whoever was out there was surely long gone. If there actually had been somebody. My eyes had probably played tricks on me. I flicked on the flashlight long enough to see that it wasn't even ten o'clock, but for the life of me I couldn't think of anything to do except head upstairs to bed, a prospect that filled me with more fear than I wanted to admit.

I debated getting some candles so I could read for a while, but the book at my bedside was a P. D. James murder mystery. I'd had enough murder for one day.

Finally, I convinced myself to move and used the flashlight to trace my way through the dark house, clutching my shotgun. I thought about Willy and Margaret as I trudged upstairs. It made no sense. Margaret Benson as a murder victim and Willy Bachmann as the accused. The casting was all wrong.

What was that ungodly noise? I slowly opened my eyes and rolled over to look at my clock, but the sight that greeted me brought me to full consciousness — my shotgun leaning against the nightstand. *What the* . . . and then I remembered. The murder, the storm, and the shadow in the barnyard. I'd been sure I wouldn't sleep a wink. My twisted sheets made it obvious it had been an uneasy night. But sleep I had.

"Jessie. Jessie, where are you?" Frank's voice floated through the window, punctuated by the sounds of his fist banging on the door.

I pushed myself upright and swung my feet over the edge of the bed, carefully moving the gun to the floor.

"Jessie, answer me. Open this door or I'll break it down. Do you hear me?"

Frank's voice sounded scared and angry. I'd no doubt my door would be demolished if I didn't answer immediately.

"Hold your horses, I'm coming," I yelled back.

"What took you so long?" Frank demanded as I stuck my head out the window.

"For your information, I was sound asleep. What do you want? And what do you mean, you'll break down my door? You've a key. No need to act so macho."

I heard the crossness in my voice. Barbaric seeing another human being, much less talking, before I'd had my first cup of coffee.

"Come down and let me in," he said.

"Let yourself in. I'll be a few minutes."

Frank had carried a key to my house for as long as I could remember, but he wouldn't use it unless I told him to. Hence the reason that Aunt Henrietta did not have a key.

I wanted to stay angry at Frank, but it proved difficult. I remembered how frightened I'd been last night, but I couldn't help but be a little smug. The storm over, the sun shining, I hadn't gone running for help, and I hadn't been murdered in my bed.

"Do you realize it's only seven o'clock?" I asked.

Frank sat at the table. Genevieve cautiously circled his chair. Calculating. Would this be the day he'd let her jump into his lap?

"I don't have the coffee made yet," I

added, "so please keep quiet until I get it started."

Frank ignored my plea and followed me around the kitchen, talking all the time, as I set up the coffee maker.

"Looks like you got off pretty light," he said. "Few branches down out back, but nothing major. You know that big old soft maple next to Mom and Dad's garage?"

I mustered a small nod.

"Split right in half. Crushed the whole east side of the garage. Mom's lucky. That's the side she always parks on. In all the excitement yesterday she forgot to put the car away. It sat outside all night. Not a scratch on it."

I leaned against the counter and listened for the first soothing drops of coffee trickling into the carafe. It amazed me how much energy Frank had in the mornings. He looked his best then, too. He'd inherited the same tall genes as me, but whereas I was slender he tended toward stoutness. Early in the day he held himself straight and firm. As the day progressed, everything seemed to soften and slip downward. Even his shoulders appeared to narrow.

I couldn't believe how long the coffee was taking. I reached over and touched the pot. Stone cold.

"Lots of people were hit pretty hard," Frank said. "Willard Munson got through to the Sheriff's Office. They told him a twister touched down ten miles this side of Springfield. Flattened a couple of trailers, and one little girl got pretty badly hurt."

"I can't believe this pot," I interrupted. "Why isn't it working?"

Frank snorted. "If the world was coming to an end, I swear you'd refuse to prepare for it until you had a cup of coffee. The electric's still out."

I had to laugh at myself. "You got me that time, Frank. Now you know why I insist on a gas stove." I retrieved the old percolator from the cabinet, transferred the coffee and water, and turned the burner to high.

"Most of the phones are still out, too. Willard said the sheriff told him the bridge over McGee Creek washed out again. Doesn't surprise me."

"That's incredible. Didn't they just reopen it last month?"

"Yep," Frank said. "That road commissioner is a damned fool. Thinks he knows everything. Won't listen to anyone. We told him at that hearing last spring they were still setting the bridge bed too low. We warned him the first big storm would wash it out again."

The coffee smelled lovely. I never understood people who drink instant. Half the pleasure of coffee was the anticipation. "Any word on Willy?"

Frank shook his head. "Everybody's pretty much occupied with the storm cleanup. Don't worry. We'll get him."

"Want some?" I waved a coffee mug at him.

"Just a half cup. I can't stay. I promised the folks I'd be back as soon as I checked on you."

Frank's words about Willy finally sank in. "What do you mean, you'll get him?" I asked. "You sound like some vigilante."

"Jesus, you can be insulting sometimes. It's not my fault the sheriff's issued a warrant for his arrest. And I sure as hell won't turn the sheriff down if he wants to deputize some of us. We'll find him in a couple of days and put him in jail where he belongs."

"Sorry. Everything's moving too fast. I'm afraid Willy's going to get trampled in the public's rush to justice." I took a closer look at Frank. He didn't appear his usual chipper self. His eyes were bloodshot and there were several spots on his face where his razor had missed his whiskers. "Are you all right?"

"Well, aren't you kind to ask?"

I was startled by the sarcasm in his voice. How unlike him. Sarcasm was my forte, not his, though recently I'd noticed he seemed to be getting more adept at it.

"Mildred had me up half the night chasing bogeymen. And I was worried out of my mind about you here alone." Frank started to say more, then settled for a shake of the head. "I've got to go. You stay inside and keep your doors locked. I'll call later."

I poured myself another cup of coffee and carried it back to the table. Frank rarely got irritated. I shouldn't have been so accusatory. Not his fault a warrant had been issued. But the thought of Willy as a fleeing felon was absurd. How could he flee with no transportation but that crazy bicycle of his?

Sipping my coffee, I looked at the barn. The longer I stared, the more convinced I became that someone had run across the barnyard last night. And the only person who'd think of taking refuge in my barn was Willy. He knew if I found him, I'd treat him fair.

The more I thought about the murder accusation, the more uncertain I became. Could I be having a knee-jerk reaction, defending Willy because everyone else said he was guilty?

I'd always had a weakness for the underdog, a trait fostered by my dad. We'd sit in the living room evenings after the news and he'd analyze the report of the day, railing against social inequities that the system heaped upon the backs of the less fortunate. "Beware the will of the majority," he continually warned.

As always, I'd taken his words literally and espoused some causes that made me blush. Like the petition drive I'd led in high school to have Everett Myers, the janitor, reinstated after he had been fired by the school board without public explanation.

I will never forget the night Dad sat me down and explained that Everett had been fired because he had drilled holes in the wall of the girls' locker room and sold viewing time to the football team.

"It's good to be for the underdog," he'd said, "but be careful. Sometimes he's nothing more than a dog."

And that was the question that kept intruding. What was it this time? Dog or underdog? I'd only known Willy for two years. True, he'd been totally honest and dependable in all his dealings with me. His almost childlike appreciation of the world around him fascinated me. But the episode with Willy and the rabbits didn't prove

much. Plenty of people have more rever-
ence for animal life than human life. Maybe
he was one of those.

However, the longer I analyzed my advo-
cacy, the more convinced I became that I
might just be manufacturing excuses to get
myself off the hook. Especially since I was
the one who had sent him over to Margaret's house. Well, I couldn't do that. At least
not until I had more information. How I
wished I could talk to Gil.

"Time to move," I said, lifting Genevieve
off my lap. I decided to take my shower.
Normally I would run and then shower, but
the rain had cooled things off enough that I
could wait till afternoon to run. Two show-
ers in one day wouldn't kill me.

I made it back downstairs about nine.
How nice to have the telephone out. For a
while I would be spared the endless speculation about the murder and the storm. I
decided not to break the shotgun down. It
wouldn't do me much good if I had to
explain to an intruder that he needed to
wait while I assembled my shotgun. Instead,
I put it on top of the cupboard in the
pantry, within easy reach.

The day was glorious, the air bright and
crisp. My angst of the night before seemed
foolish. Probably my imagination had cre-

ated the shadow figure in the barnyard. Not that it mattered. Willy was in danger no matter where he'd spent the night.

If only I could talk to him. I could straighten things out. I had purposely not told Frank what I had seen. It would have thrown him into a complete frenzy. I planned to check the barn.

I picked my way around the mud puddles dotting the driveway. The ground in the barnyard on the other side was soft and squishy. It had been years since there had been animals to churn up the dirt, and the lot sported a heavy thatch of grass and weeds. Like walking over a bog.

Suddenly, my pulse went into overdrive. The door I kept firmly latched stood ajar. Not much, but enough to suggest that someone had left in a hurry or — I took a deep breath — someone entered in a hurry and remained inside.

Okay, Jessie, let's think this through. Chances are Frank didn't secure the latch after he checked the barn yesterday. Whether that was true or not, it was clear I was acting the fool. All that hoopla last night over the gun and here I paraded toward who knew what, without protection. I abruptly turned and headed back to get the shotgun.

Gun firmly in hand, I once again forced

myself toward the barn door, pulled it open, and stepped back. A single shaft of sunlight shot through the middle of the barn, but the rest of the interior was left in gloom. The wooden flaps on the windows were closed, and the light seeping through the cracks did little to dispel the dark.

I ran my hand along the wall and found the crank that opened the shutter closest to the door. The hinges groaned in protest, but the heavy wooden shutter swung up, flush against the outside wall.

The barn had been cleared out and swept clean years before, but the acrid smell of manure still permeated the air and tiny motes of straw dust drifted through the beams of sunlight. Genevieve sat in the doorway and watched as I made my way around the barn.

It became obvious that there was no one but me and Genevieve in the barn, at least on the ground level, each stall as empty and undisturbed as the last time I had been here. I stood by the ladder to the hayloft, trying unsuccessfully to convince myself to give up my search.

It had been a long time since I'd been up the ladder, but the mud on the rungs had not been there before. Frank could not be responsible, because yesterday the ground had been completely dry. The temptation to abandon my search grew stronger, but it was too late. I would drive myself crazy with questions if I did.

As I got to the top of the ladder, I popped my head through the hole, doing a fair imitation of a turtle. The loft looked and felt empty. It, too, had been cleared out except for some bales of straw in one corner. I stepped into the loft, and saw nothing except the bales and a heavy accumulation of bird droppings.

"Anyone here?" I called softly, and heard soft coos from the pigeons perched on the rafters.

Muddy footprints led over to the bales. I could see several bales had been moved to make a hidey-hole for someone.

It took a minute for my eyes to adjust as I peered into the cleared space. At first it seemed empty, but then I noticed something crumpled in the corner. I poked it with the barrel of the gun and then dragged it toward me. Finally screwing up my courage, I picked it up.

A blue and white checkered, oversized handkerchief, the kind Willy always carried. So Willy had been hiding in the barn, but where had he gone off to?

I stuck the handkerchief in my back

pocket and started to leave when something else caught my eye.

"What's that?" I picked up a scrap of paper. It looked like the corner off a page with printing on it. The light was too dim to make it out. I tucked it in my shirt pocket, careful not to crumple it. I checked the rest of the floor, but nothing else had been left behind.

Back in the house, I took the scrap out of my pocket and smoothed it carefully on the kitchen table. A piece of heavy stock. The paper had a bluish cast with scattered specks of darker blue. It must have been thoroughly soaked, because the edge was feathered where it had torn. Across the straight edge was a series of letters and numbers.

I got out my magnifying glass, but what I read made no sense at first: SEG 5-SJ907-2, precisely spaced in a blue-bordered box.

Something tickled the back of my mind. I'd seen paper and notations like this before. It had something to do with Dad. Then it hit me. When I'd been in high school, Dad had served as Road Commissioner for the county. What I had in front of me was a corner off a sheet of construction plans. Why on earth would Willy be hiding in my barn with a set of construction plans?

CHAPTER 5

Thursday. Five days since Margaret's murder and still no Willy. And I hadn't seen or talked to Gil, even though he had said he would need to interview me again. Today I would find a way. Most everyone else in town, it seemed, had either called me or tracked me down. Since I'd discovered Margaret's body, I'd gone from a minor curiosity to a celebrity.

The prospect of going to a funeral this morning ranked right up with having a root canal. The heat and humidity had returned with a vengeance. I didn't begrudge Margaret a decent send-off. God knows, she deserved it. But I was skeptical of why people would attend. If she had died of a simple heart attack, possibly half the pews in the church would have been filled. Today the church would be packed, the TV cameras at the ready out front. Come evening, everyone would tune in the news to catch a glimpse of himself or herself.

"Being a bit of a hypocrite, aren't you?" I muttered as I pulled out my blue silk shirtwaist. "You're putting on your mourning dress and your navy and white heels and joining the crowd. And you know you're going to watch the evening news."

The Presbyterians rarely violated the sanctity of the August break, but the church had been reopened for the funeral. And Reverend MacDonald had interrupted his vacation to officiate. Thirty minutes before the scheduled service, all the pews had filled.

I was surprised how many people I recognized. I was becoming more a part of Riverport than I realized. More and more I thought of Riverport as home, not St. Louis.

The local politicians were out in force. Mayor and Mrs. Bernard Ellwood, along with the entire town council, occupied the bench directly behind the family pew, empty except for a small gray-haired woman. Even State Senator Arnold, his face flushed redder than the heat warranted, had made an appearance. He must be up for reelection soon. Riverport ranked low on his priority list, according to Frank.

How sad. Every seat filled, yet the one person who thought Margaret truly special didn't dare show his face. Poor Willy.

The temperature in the church rose dramatically, defeating the air conditioning. The paper fans donated by Fowler's Funeral Home fluttered back and forth. A steady drone of muted conversation buffeted my ears, resonating like a beehive that had been whacked with a stick.

"Who's the woman in the family pew?" I whispered to Mildred, leaning over Frank. As usual he had planted himself firmly between us. I didn't understand why he did that. Maybe something to do with keeping his harem under control or making sure he didn't miss any of our conversation.

"That's Margaret's sister from Ohio," Mildred said. "Esther Martin said they had a falling out after Margaret married Ray. Seems he swindled the sister's husband out of a lot of money. She was at the funeral home last night, first time she'd seen her sister in ten years."

"Will you two be quiet?" Frank muttered.

Mildred glared at him and sat back, but not before she mouthed the words, "I'll tell you about it later."

Even family hadn't been safe from Ray Benson's scams. An equal opportunity swindler. He must have been some kind of operator.

Our seats were toward the side and back of the sanctuary. I had a good view of the congregation. Aunt Henrietta sat right up front. "I don't know how she does it," Frank whispered when he spotted his mother. "She always has a ringside seat."

Was the murderer present? Despite the heat, I shivered. *Surely the killer wouldn't be here,* I thought, but abruptly changed my mind. The killer obviously knew Margaret well. Such a person wouldn't call attention to himself by not attending the funeral. I amended that statement as soon as I thought it. It should have been "himself or herself."

Grace Michaelson's labored organ rendition of "Rock of Ages" mercifully drew to a close. Many people in Riverport played better than Grace, but her family had donated the organ to the church. The question of who would play was moot.

The congregation shifted. All heads turned to the back of the church. The pallbearers gathered at the door, ready to bring Margaret's casket down the aisle. A huge blanket of red roses covered the top.

"You would have thought she was just taking a nap, she looked that natural," Mildred had reported in the car as we were driving to the church. "So at peace. I tell you, Mr.

Fowler is a miracle worker."

I firmly believed in closed caskets, willing to take the word of the person in charge that the right body was inside.

My interest in the service began to wane about halfway through Mayor Ellwood's eulogy. I had no idea how he had convinced Reverend MacDonald to let him give the eulogy. But judging by the number of articles and pictures devoted to him on the pages of the *Spencer County Argus*, he seemed to have a politician's unerring knack for getting himself in the middle of group opportunities.

"A good woman. A patient woman. A simple woman. A woman who moved quietly among us, never seeking recognition. A doer of good works, struck down in the prime of life by a villain's blow." The Mayor's voice rattled off the stained glass windows.

I couldn't argue with the Mayor's words about Margaret. But the force of his words implied an intimacy that irritated me. I'd bet he couldn't have picked Margaret out of a line-up if his life depended on it.

"This is a sad day for Riverport." The Mayor's voice dropped to a murmur. "There moves among us a man who took the life of this woman, this woman who trusted him, this woman who gave him a chance."

I could barely disguise my disgust. So much for innocent until proven guilty. Any hesitation I felt about taking on Willy's cause vanished. The Mayor had no right to talk like that in a public forum.

Bernard Ellwood had been elected Mayor the April before I came back to Riverport, defeating Henrick Bowers who had been mayor for years. Ellwood brought in a hand-picked slate on his "It's Time to Clean House" slogan. Not very original, but the voters had bought it.

Mom had sent me a running commentary about the campaign and election. I remember being bothered by the implication that something dirty had been going on at City Hall. Mayor Bowers had been a close friend of Dad's. I'd even been pressed into service to work on his first campaign. My God, twenty-four years ago.

Frank claimed the town needed a man like Ellwood, someone with the energy and vision to revitalize Riverport. I pointed out that results, not promises, would determine Ellwood's worth. As his time in office progressed, I saw little action, other than rhetorical.

I wasn't the only one bothered by the Mayor's oratory. Several people were squirming and shaking their heads and a cell phone rang somewhere in the back. Mildred rolled her eyes at me when I looked at her. It wasn't his puffery I didn't like. That I'd come to accept as a natural trait of politicians. There was something else I couldn't quite put my finger on. I tuned out the Mayor's bombast and concentrated on the people sitting around me, working my way across each row.

Bud Berry and his wife, Linda, sat across the aisle. Mildred said they were at the funeral home the night before. Frank had gotten angry when Mildred started in on what a sorry excuse for a man Bud was, how he had no right to strut around like someone important when everyone knew the only reason they had food on the table was because Linda was working nights at the nursing home. I had never understood why, but Frank seemed to take criticism of any man he knew as a personal affront. It certainly didn't make any sense in this case. It had been Frank, after all, who claimed the Berrys would probably lose their farm. Seems Bud had taken out a second mortgage on his land for some mysterious investment that Frank refused to elaborate on.

Linda's shoulders had that droop that comes when life is reduced to nothing more than a struggle for survival. I remembered what a bubbly and bouncy kid she had been. She was a Kilmer and their farm was a half mile down the road from ours. She used to ride her bike to our place and tag around after me summers, when I was home from college. Mom had sent me the account of the wedding, and even in the grainy newspaper photo, I could see that the little girl had grown into a vivacious young woman. But ten years married to Bud had changed all that. Grim lines pulled at her face and her eyes had lost their sparkle.

Damn that Bud Berry. Frank had never said, but I suspected that Ray Benson had been behind Bud's money troubles. Mildred said Bud and Ray had been thick as thieves.

Several rows in front of the Berrys were Harry and Nancy Williamson and her mother, Mrs. Pfeifer. Nancy Williamson was one of the few people with a legitimate reason for attending the funeral. She and Margaret Benson had been Bridge-a-Rama partners and good friends. Nancy was the one who had sat with Margaret the night Ray had died.

Nancy had been in my class in high school and Harry a year behind. We hadn't been teenage confidants. Nancy's day-to-day outlook on life was a little too stolid for my taste. However, in a strange way, we were friends. Still were, in fact. She had a quirky sense of humor that appealed to me, and no matter how outlandish a cause I used to advocate, she had been first in line to support me.

What a curious couple she and Harry made. Nancy stood above her husband by a good four inches. Harry reminded me of an oversized Pillsbury Doughboy, soft and pasty. Nancy could have posed for the illustration of the hearty frontier woman, splitting the kindling, hauling the water, and wresting tree stumps from the fields.

If ever a man deserved sainthood, it was Harry Williamson. Poor Harry must not have realized that "till death do us part" was a package deal and that where Nancy went, so went her mother. They all lived together in Mrs. Pfeifer's house. I'd be willing to bet Mrs. Pfeifer made them sleep in separate bedrooms. We had all referred to her as "the witch" when we were young. She had not mellowed with age.

"If I was Harry, I'd strangle that old biddy in her sleep," Frank had said at the church social after he watched Mrs. Pfeifer berate Harry for not bringing her a chair fast enough. But poor Harry never said a word. Instead he went to work each day in the bank Mrs. Pfeifer's family owned, and he ate. Every time I saw him he seemed to be munching on something. Even at his desk in the bank I had seen him surreptitiously reaching into the drawer for a cookie. He was beyond overweight and would surely be classified as morbidly obese. I couldn't help but wonder if he had decided the only way he could get out of the marriage contract was to eat himself to death.

Maybe some people are meant to be victims, I thought.

I could hear the muffled yells of a baby somewhere. When I leaned around the man sitting in front of me, I saw the Joseph family filling one entire pew, from the center aisle all the way to the side aisle. Why on earth would they drag all those children to a funeral on a day like this? The baby was trying to scramble over her mother's shoulder.

Otis Joseph worked for Frank during the busy seasons. With so many mouths to feed, Otis was always looking for extra jobs. "Never known a man to work as hard as Joseph," Frank had said. "Don't see how he has enough strength left at the end of the day to keep getting his missus in a family way."

I knew the Josephs rarely had more than

two nickels to rub together, but you would never guess it. Always a cheery smile and wave and the children, all six of them, scrubbed and tidy, their manners straight out of Emily Post.

Not fair that an obnoxious old crow like Mrs. Pfeifer should have more money than she could possibly spend, while good people like the Josephs had to scrabble after every penny. *God gets his priorities screwed up sometimes,* I thought.

On down the rows I went. Esther and Lester Martin, Margaret Benson's next-door neighbors. I had heard that Esther was repeating to anyone who would listen that she had seen the killer. I needed to talk to her. Next, Mr. Evans and his daughter Barbara from the hardware store. Florence Nevils, the librarian. Herb Springer, editor of the *Spencer County Argus.* Most faces were familiar, though I couldn't name them all. Then a couple caught my attention, sitting about two-thirds of the way up.

The woman wore a wide-brimmed hat. I couldn't get a clear look at her. I surmised she was young from the way she held herself in her seat and the firmness of the arm in her sleeveless dress.

The man appeared middle-aged, early fifties I guessed. He wore an expensive-looking gray pinstriped suit, much like my banker in St. Louis would wear, but this man would never be mistaken for a banker. Bankers always appear intense, focused, as if they are trying to assure us that their guardianship of our money is foremost in their minds. This man looked as if he dared the world to worry him about anything.

He sat sideways with his arm over the back of the pew, his fingers touching the woman's shoulder. The ring he wore sparkled in the sunlight that filtered through the stained glass. His hair was dark with streaks of silver and carefully coifed. A little too flamboyant for my taste, but I did have to admit he was rather handsome in a Hollywood sort of way. The longer I looked at him, the more I was sure I had seen him someplace before, but nothing clicked. Maybe Mildred knew.

After what seemed like an eternity, the eulogy ended. Mayor Ellwood looked surprised when he did not receive a thunderous ovation. He must have forgotten he was in church. Reverend MacDonald's benediction ran longer than usual, I guess, to make up for being moved out of the spotlight. But in fairness to the minister, his words were directed toward Margaret, and he asked for salvation, not retribution.

"Lovely service, wasn't it?" Mildred said

as Frank steered us out of the church.

I made do with a nod, though I was tempted to make a comment about the Mayor. "Who was that couple sitting on the other side, up toward the front? He looked to be in his fifties, but she much younger."

"Isn't he a looker? Almost handsome enough to be a movie star. That's Mr. Emerson."

"Mr. Emerson?"

Mildred gave me a funny look. "You know who Hap Emerson is. He's the man the Mayor's been working with to bring new business into Riverport. He's a big-shot real estate man from Springfield."

Of course. It had been all over the front page of the *Argus* last fall. Mayor Ellwood had announced the city had bought and annexed land on the edge of town for an Industrial Park and would issue development bonds to entice investors. Emerson was named project developer and probably given a substantial chunk of money up front, and commissions later. The four-column picture of Emerson and the Mayor wearing hard hats and grins would have done the Cheshire Cat proud.

Unless I'd missed something, all that had developed in the past twelve months was a large sign advertising prime industrial sites for sale, with Hap Emerson's name prominently displayed.

"Frank claims he's really a mover-shaker and it was a big feather in the Mayor's cap to get him involved. I'm not so sure. He's a little too slick for my taste . . ." Mildred paused and looked over her shoulder. "There are the folks. Let's go join them."

Mildred started toward Henrietta and George, but I stopped her. "Mildred, why would this Hap Emerson come to Margaret Benson's funeral?"

She shrugged. "I don't know, though Ray Benson was doing some work for him just before he died."

"I don't recall seeing him at Ray's funeral," I said.

"So what?" Mildred gave me a curious look. "Lots of people didn't come to his funeral. I sure wouldn't have gone, except out of respect for Margaret."

"It just seems strange, that's all."

"Wasn't that a wonderful service?" Aunt Henrietta's face was flushed and little rivulets of perspiration had worked their way across her powdered cheeks. "Margaret would have been thrilled. There wasn't a vacant seat or a dry eye in the house. And have you ever seen so many beautiful roses in a casket spray? Nancy Williamson sent it.

I can't even imagine how much it cost, but then she can afford it."

"I wasn't aware the Mayor was on such intimate terms with Margaret." I couldn't keep the sarcasm out of my voice.

"Now, Jessie, be charitable. Everyone knows the Mayor likes the sound of his own voice," Henrietta said. "But that's neither here nor there. It's the thought and the sentiment that matter."

I forced myself to smile. "Sorry, Henrietta. The heat has me in a sour mood."

Henrietta nodded. "It's okay. You're probably having a delayed reaction to your experience. Guess we know now why we usually cancel services in August. George," she said, turning to my uncle, "get the car and start the air conditioning. We'll all ride together to the cemetery. No sense taking two cars."

"I'm not going to the cemetery." The words popped out of my mouth.

They all stared at me.

"I've got things to do in town. I'll meet you back here."

"Oh, Jessie, do you think that's a good idea?" Henrietta frowned. "Think how it will look. What will people say?"

"No one cares whether I go to the cemetery, and it certainly doesn't matter to Margaret."

Henrietta opened her mouth to reply, but Frank held up his hand. "Now, Mom. It's no problem. We have to circle back here to pick up my car anyway. Jessie can run her errands and we'll meet here in, oh, let's say an hour."

He looked at me. "Is that okay? Will that give you enough time?"

I nodded, feeling foolish at my outburst. It occurred to me this might give me a chance to see Gil. He hadn't been at the funeral, and I doubted very much if he would go to the cemetery.

"I guess you know what's best for you, but if you ask me it would give you a sense of closure," Henrietta said as she turned and headed for the car, followed closely by Mildred.

"You all right, Jessie?" Frank asked.

"I'm fine. I've had all I can take with funerals today, that's all."

"Can't argue with that."

I waited while the procession made its way down the street. Directly behind the family limousine was a white Cadillac I had never seen before. As it drew abreast, I shook my head. I should have known. Hap Emerson and the young woman. Several kids on bicycles escorted the hearse around the first corner.

"Excuse me, may I have a few words with you?"

I jumped at the voice behind me and whirled around to find myself face-to-face with Constance Naylor, the Springfield television reporter I had seen on the newscast the evening Margaret was murdered. A man stood beside her with a video camera balanced on his shoulder, aimed at me like a gun.

"I understand you are the person who found the body," Constance said, "and I'd like to get your reaction."

I felt myself turning red. I hated television interviews. I still broke out in a sweat when I thought about the one my agent had arranged when I was in the running for the Newbery Prize. The little twit of an interviewer had joined me minutes before airtime and her first question to me had been, "So, what are you here for?" I explained I was an author, and she groaned and said, "I hate interviewing authors. They can be so intense. Promise me you won't be intense." It had gone downhill from there. Since then, I had been wary of television interviewers.

I thought about fleeing, but my feet seemed glued to the ground. All I could do was mumble, "I don't think so. I mean, I don't know what I could add."

Suddenly going to the cemetery seemed like a good idea, but it was too late.

"Just a few words," Constance said. "Sheriff Keller has asked that we not use the suspect's name since he is still at large, and we are respecting that request. However, just about everybody I've talked to seems to know who it is. Are you aware of who the suspect is?"

I found myself nodding. "I've known him for several years. He works for me."

Her eyes widened slightly. "Really? And your name is Schroeder, right?"

"Jessie Schroeder," I said without thinking.

The reporter looked over her shoulder at the cameraman. "Let's roll it," she said and turned back to me.

"This is Constance Naylor. I'm speaking with Jessie Schroeder who found the body of murder victim Margaret Benson. Jessie Schroeder is a former employer of the man suspected of killing Margaret Ben—"

"I'm not a former employer. As far as I am concerned, he still works for me and can continue to work for me as long as he wants. I don't believe the accusations against him."

"You're saying you don't think the man the police suspect is guilty of murder?"

"That is correct. He is a kind and gentle man, incapable of violence against anyone or anything. That's all I have to say." I couldn't believe I had talked to that woman. When would I learn to keep my mouth shut?

As I hurried away, I heard the reporter say, "In a surprising development, Jessie Schroeder, who found the body and is an employer of the murder suspect, says he is not guilty. She characterizes him as a kind and gentle man. This is Constance Naylor reporting from Riverport."

Well, Jessie, now you've done it. You've proclaimed to the world your belief in Willy's innocence. Looks like you're in for the long count. I suddenly felt overwhelmed with the responsibility. I was tempted to call the camera back and retract my statement, but something my father taught me many years ago overrode my hesitation.

"If you believe in something," he had said, "you must have the courage to speak out, even at the risk of being unpopular."

It had been good advice when I was young and it was still good advice, I thought as I walked off the church grounds.

Willy needed an advocate. Apparently, I was the only one willing to take the job.

Besides, it gave me a perfectly legitimate reason to see Gil.

CHAPTER 6

The Court House, built in the late 1800s, was a mad riot of curlicues, cornices, and cupolas. A bronze plaque by the main door proudly proclaimed its place on the National Historic Register. The wooden floors had been worn into gentle groves by generations of Spencer County residents seeking help in ordering their lives. The Sheriff's Office and adjoining jail cells occupied the ground floor at the rear.

"Jessie Schroeder! What are earth are you doing out so soon after that terrible shock you had? You should be at home."

Virginia Beckelmeyer sat perched on her stool behind the counter. Gil and his people shared the office space — and Virginia — with the Riverport and Spencer County Volunteer Fire Department.

"Oh, I'm doing fine," I said. "I just came from Margaret Benson's funeral. Is the Sheriff in? I need to talk to him."

Virginia shook her head. "I didn't hardly know Miz Benson, but folks are all saying what a sweet thing she was. Wouldn't hurt a fly."

"Yes, a lovely woman. If he's not busy, I'd appreciate a few minutes." Maybe by repeating my request, I could divert Virginia from a lengthy discussion of the murder.

"Don't know why not," she said. "He's just sitting in his office with his feet up. Been like that since late this morning. He didn't even go to the funeral. Hold on. I'll check."

I detected a note of disapproval in Virginia's voice. She probably didn't approve of people sitting around with their feet up.

Virginia punched a button on the console in front of her.

"Sheriff, Jessie Schroeder's here to see you."

I heard a muffled answer.

"Sure thing." Virginia clicked off the button. "Go right on in."

As I walked over to the door, I felt my face flush. What would I say to him? The thought of being in the same room with him made me strangely nervous. *Business, you're here on business,* I reminded myself as I hesitated at the door, unsure whether to knock or go right in.

96

But before I made the decision, Gil opened the door.

"Jessie, come in. How are you doing?" he said, taking my arm and leading me over to a chair that faced his desk.

I repeated my assurances that I was fine.

"Now tell me," he said, settling into his own chair, "is this visit business or pleasure?"

"Business, I'm afraid," I said, wishing otherwise.

"Well, I'm sorry to hear that." His countenance turned serious. "What's the problem?"

"I saw you on the news Sunday night. You looked quite handsome."

Oh my God, why did I say that? Well, why not? He had looked handsome.

"Handsome, huh?" Gil pulled himself up straighter in his chair. "I wasn't feeling handsome. Half the town hysterical and that damned TV reporter chasing me around every which way to sundown. I hate those TV people." He frowned. "They don't give a damn about real news. All they're looking for is a sensational fifteen-second sound byte. Give me a hard-bitten, cynical newspaperman anytime, though even they aren't as good as they used to be."

"You mean like Herb Springer?"

Gil looked at me for a minute and then started to laugh. And within seconds, I was laughing too. We were both trying to imagine Herb Springer, editor of the weekly *Spencer County Argus,* as a hard-bitten, cynical newspaperman. Every time I tried to stop, the vision of wispy little Herb, whose criticism never extended beyond the weather and even that was couched in apologetic tones, would flash by and I was off again.

"Touché, Jessie," Gil finally said, wiping his eyes. "You got me that time."

I dug into my purse for a tissue to wipe my eyes. How long had it been since I'd laughed that hard? I couldn't believe it, the two of us, giggling like a couple of teenagers.

"I thought you'd be at the funeral," I said, attempting to bring some decorum back to the situation, though there was nothing I would have liked better than to continue our light-hearted banter. "All the other elected officials showed up. Even Senator Arnold put in an appearance. According to Frank, it's the first time he's been seen in Riverport since the last election."

"I figured Clarence could handle the crowd just fine. He enjoys that sort of thing. Besides, it gave me a little thinking time. Was it a nice service?"

I nodded. "Biggest draw of the year. Every pew was full, and Mayor Ellwood pulled out all the stops with his eulogy. Probably the largest, and certainly the most captive audience he's ever played to. I half expected Margaret to rise up out of her casket and lead the amens."

"Jessie Schroeder. Do I detect a note of cynicism?"

I smiled. "Maybe just a bit."

"Now, tell me. What's on your mind?"

"It's Willy Bachmann." As soon as the words were out of my mouth, Gil's expression shifted, and he leaned back in his chair. I felt my own face stiffen, and took a deep breath. "I'm probably going to be on the news myself tonight. That TV woman interviewed me after the funeral. I told her Willy's not guilty."

Gil twisted in his chair, then hunched over the desk and looked directly at me, his blue eyes distracting. He was one of those rare men who focused his total attention on you when he talked.

"Look, Jessie, I know you've spent a lot of time with Willy. I've no doubt you're a big reason he's stayed off the booze and is making restitution to the folks he owes money. You gave him a job and trusted him, gave him his self-respect back. But the evidence is damning."

Gil's matter-of-fact tone was chilling. Not like Aunt Henrietta repeating third-hand tales, but the one person with the information.

"It doesn't make sense, Gil. He was really fond of Margaret, always talking about what a fine lady she was and how good she was to him. Why would he want to hurt her?"

He shrugged. "Who knows? All those years of drinking may have done something to his brain and he snapped."

"I don't accept that." The words came out harsh. "That's just a convenient excuse everyone's using for not looking elsewhere." I knew my voice had that tone to it that Frank teased me about. He claimed he could always tell when I was upset, because my lips stopped moving.

"Come on, Jessie. That's not fair. You know I have to go by the facts, not my personal feelings about a person. I like Willy. But in this case, the facts point to him."

"Sorry," I said. "It's just that I don't know where to turn. I don't have facts, but I'm certain Willy could never hurt anybody. Besides, I'm scared for him. Some trigger-happy vigilante's going to shoot him before he's had a chance to tell his side. Then we'll never know who killed Margaret."

"Sheriff." Virginia's voice broke into our conversation.

"Excuse me, Jessie." He flipped the switch on the intercom. "Yes, Virginia, what is it?"

"Clarence just called in. The graveside service is over and he's on his way back."

"Okay, tell him I'll see him in a few minutes."

I stood. "I'd better be going. I've taken up too much of your time."

He looked at me and shook his head. "Jessie," he said and then stopped and shook his head again. The look he gave me erased any doubts that his interest in me was merely professional.

I started toward the door, then stopped. I'd almost forgotten the main reason I'd come to see him.

"Could you come by my place later?" I asked. "I found something you should take a look at."

"What are you talking about?"

I shrugged. "I'm not sure, but it may tie in with Margaret's murder."

Gil ran his finger down his calendar and said, "Five o'clock okay? I'll be finished up here by then."

I was surprised he didn't pursue the question. "Fine," I said, looking at my watch.

Three and a half hours to wait.

As I walked back toward the church, I felt more confident, even though my conversation with Gil had made me acutely aware that I had no concrete proof of Willy's innocence. Just a gut belief and the leavings in my barn.

I looked at my watch again, squinting as the sun flashed off the crystal. As quickly as the flash of light, I knew where Willy could have gone. The reflection on my watch reminded me of a sundial which reminded me of Stonehenge which reminded me of the stone walls of the old cabin in Walnut Clearing. Convoluted, sure, but it made perfect sense to me. Willy had gone to Walnut Clearing.

He loved to go there, and I was pretty sure he secretly hoped I would encourage and help with the repairs on the cabin. Maybe even ask him to live there and take care of it. Why hadn't I thought of it before? I had to get there before someone else stumbled onto it.

Henrietta and George's car finally came around the corner. Henrietta rolled down her window as the car pulled up alongside the curb. Frank and Mildred emerged from the back seat.

"Well, you were smart not to go to the cemetery," Henrietta said, poking her head out from the car. "Margaret's plot is right out in the boiling sun. It was unbearable. Mrs. Pfeifer got so woozy, Harry had to take her to her car."

Frank glared at Henrietta. "You know better than that, Mom," he said. "It wasn't the heat that got to the old queen bee. She just doesn't cotton to being anywhere where she's not the center of attention, even at a burial. If I was Harry, I'd tell her to stuff it."

"Frank! That's a horrible thing to say," Henrietta said.

He shrugged. "Maybe so, but no amount of money could turn me into a lackey like Harry."

"She's lucky to have such a concerned son-in-law." Henrietta turned her face toward me. "It was just awful out there. It's a miracle the entire congregation wasn't taken with heat prostration. I have half a mind to speak to the Reverend about his bad judgment."

Frank was busy unrolling the windows of his car. He'd sweated through the back of his suit and Mildred looked like she needed to be hung up to drip dry.

"There should be a law, anybody who dies

in August has to be put on dry ice till the weather cools," Frank growled. "Let's go, ladies."

"You take it easy now," I said to Henrietta, leaning through the open window to give her a peck on the cheek. "Make sure you drink lots of liquids. I don't want you getting sick."

"Goddammedest waste of time," Frank said as we pulled away from the curb. "Plenty of pissed-off people 'cause the TV didn't come."

"Watch your mouth, Frank," Mildred said. "The heat's bad enough without us having to listen to you swear."

I decided to step in before Frank and Mildred escalated into full-scale battle. "I thought I saw Mr. Emerson's car in the procession. Did he go to the cemetery?"

Mildred turned around in her seat. "I'll say he did. Pushed himself and that floozy of a wife, if she is his wife, right up front so they could stand in the shade under the canopy. You'd have thought they were members of the family, the way they behaved. They were all over Margaret's sister."

"I don't understand the relationship between Mr. Emerson and the Bensons," I said. "Do you know, Frank?"

"Ray did some gofer work for Emerson

when he was putting together his economic development plan for the Town Council."

"Gofer work?" Mildred snorted. "To hear Margaret tell it at bridge, Ray was his right-hand man. And she made it sound like he'd get a bundle of money. Don't you remember me telling you about it, Frank?"

He ignored her question.

"But why Ray Benson?" I asked. "I don't understand. Surely there were better qualified people."

"No doubt about that." Mildred agreed immediately. "But Ray had a way of insinuating his way into anything he put his mind to. Nothing but a con man, if you ask me."

"Honestly, Mildred," Frank said. "That's no way to talk about the dead."

"Well, he was and you know it," Mildred said. "I'll bet he put together a fancy set of credentials and convinced Mr. Emerson he was the best man for the job. That Emerson may be a high-powered businessman from the city, but he wouldn't be the first to get took by Ray Benson."

Cool air was beginning to fill the car and I watched as Frank's shoulders relaxed.

"I think it's all been a waste of time and money," Mildred continued. "Emerson got the Town Council to pay him a bunch of money to tell them what they wanted to hear. If you ask me, he and Mayor Ellwood are a little too buddy-buddy."

"Nobody asked you," Frank said. "You don't know what you're talking about."

"Is that so?" Mildred shot back. "It doesn't take a genius to figure out that buying a worthless piece of land on the edge of town and putting up a sign advertising industrial plots for sale isn't going to change anything. And as far as I can tell, that's all the town got for its money."

"Leave it alone, Mildred," Frank said. "I'm tired of your yammering, especially on something you know nothing about."

"Well, I like that. I don't know what's got into you, Frank. You've been touchier than an old setting hen the last couple of days."

I leaned back in the seat. So I wasn't the only one who'd noticed Frank wasn't quite himself. I'd put it down to his worry about the murder, but maybe there was something else. I wished I'd paid closer attention to the whole Industrial Park project. I'd have to ask Gil about it when he stopped by.

"You want to come over for supper?" Mildred asked as we pulled up to my gate. "We're just having cold cuts and tomatoes, but there's plenty of it. Maybe we can get old Mr. Grump here to behave."

I answered quickly, before Frank had a

chance to erupt again. "Thanks, Mildred, but I think I'll pass this time. All the furor over Willy and the funeral has kept me away from my writing too long. I'll give you a call in the morning."

I wasn't ready to tell them the real reason for not joining them. Gil was coming at five, and I hoped he would want to stay for a while.

Genevieve met me at the door, but stalked away as soon as I tried to pet her.

"Mad at me, are you?" I asked.

She swished her tail in confirmation.

I sat down in the chair, knowing full well Genevieve couldn't resist an open lap.

As I scratched her ears, I did a mental review of the events of the past five days. Nothing fit together. It was like a complicated jigsaw puzzle. I had to be patient and keep looking. Sooner or later I'd find two pieces that fit.

The key could be in Walnut Clearing.

I followed the faint trail through the woods. The path had been little used the past year. I'd gone mushrooming for morels in the spring several times, but with limited success. Unfortunately, I hadn't inherited my dad's talent for spotting the sponge caps poking through the oak mold. About a

107

month ago I had taken Selma's children down to the creek to catch tadpoles, but that was it.

The squirrels chattered at me as I passed through their territory. People who are not used to the woods often comment on how peaceful it is. The sunlight filtered through the leaves and the humus on the ground muted my footsteps. It did look peaceful, but I knew better. The woods, like the rest of life, teemed with rivalries, intrigue, and uncertainty. Even the butterflies that floated from wildflower to wildflower were someone's prey.

I slithered my way down the small bluff that overlooked McGee Creek. The water was higher than normal for August; it had not receded totally from the storm. I could tell from the line of debris on the bank how high the creek had risen. No wonder the pier had washed out at the new bridge. The water must have come up fifteen feet.

The stepping-stones across the creek were covered with water in places and my sneakers were soaked by the time I made it to the other side. My socks squished with every step. Good way to get a blister, but too late to worry about that. I climbed the bank on the other side, using the roots that protruded to hoist myself up. The land was lower and flatter on this side of the creek, and the trees more sparse.

Deer droppings along the path showed they'd used the trail to go down to water. A few years ago a deer sighting was rare enough that Mom would mention it in her letters. Now they were commonplace, and the farmers complained the deer were pests. It wouldn't be long before the hunting season, and I'd again be bombarded with requests to hunt on my land. I wasn't opposed to hunting. The men I knew who hunted did so with care and respect. The game they shot fed their families. Still, I knew that again this year I would say no, even to Frank, who claimed I had acute Bambi syndrome.

I stepped up my pace. The trees thinned more, and then came the clearing. Every time I walked into Walnut Clearing, I went through the same ritual. I stood at the edge of the open space and looked up until the muscles in the back of my neck crimped double. When I was little, it seemed fitting that the huge black walnut tree stood alone. A monarch always stood alone. Even after Dad had explained that it was the poison the tree sent out through its roots that kept other trees and bushes from growing nearby, deep down I believed the other trees stayed back out of respect.

As a child, I knew that goblins and witches lived in the woods and they used the clearing to dance during the full moon. I would drag Frank to the glade with me and spin tall tales about the trolls who lived beneath the walls of the old stone cabin that our great-great-grandfather had built. Frank claimed he wasn't frightened, but he never looked back when we left.

Older, we'd build a fire in the old fireplace in the cabin and share dreams. Or more accurately, it was my dreams I shared with Frank. He had been happy to listen. As a young girl, my goal had been to be a cowboy, then the stirrings of adolescence had bumped that aside for a career as a beauty queen. Fortunately, that was short-lived and I moved on to "rich and famous writer." At least that one had come partially true. I was comfortable, not rich, and well-known, not famous, but who could tell? Maybe Emily's sunburnt ghost would make my dreams come true.

It took three people, fingertips-to-fingertips, to reach around the trunk of the walnut tree. The first two generations of Schroeders in Spencer County had lived in the stone cabin in the clearing, adding rooms as the families grew. I had often wondered what it would have been like if the road hadn't been changed, prompting my grandparents to build the house I now lived in and abandon the original homestead. The frame additions had long ago rotted and been torn down. All that the remained was the sturdy stone cottage William Spencer Schroeder had built in 1842.

A few late summer flowers bloomed around the edge of the clearing. Bits and pieces of walnut shells and husks littered the ground. The new crop of fruit hung heavy from the branches above. The squirrels and chipmunks would soon be in a frenzy of harvesting, eating, and hoarding the tangy nuts.

I stepped carefully through the opening that had once been the front door. A few rotting floorboards still remained, but the grass and weeds had long since taken over. I had to smile as I remembered the first time I'd brought Willy with me to the old cabin. I had wanted to dismantle one of the walls and use the stones to build a wall in the back of the garden. Enough remained of the old road to get a pickup truck in.

"Oh, Miz Jessie, this is the prettiest spot my eyes have ever seen," Willy had said. "This is pretty enough to go on a picture postcard."

He had walked around the clearing, shaking his head. "Isn't God amazing? Why if I lived here, I'd feel like I was waking up in heaven every morning."

When I had tried to persuade him to move the stones, he flatly refused.

"No, ma'am. This house was built by your forefathers. It would be wrong. This here's like an altar to your family. 'Sides maybe someday you'll decide to rebuild it. I'd be honored to help."

So the stones had not been moved, and every once in a while at the end of a workday Willy would ask if he could walk over to the clearing. He had done little things to the cabin, neatly stacking the rotten boards to the side and resetting the stones that had fallen out of the fireplace.

I poked around, trying to find signs that Willy had been there recently, but there was nothing.

"So much for that theory," I muttered and walked out of the cabin. Perched on a rock at the edge of the clearing, a sleek chipmunk studied me closely.

"I wish you could talk," I said to the chipmunk. "You could tell me if he's been here."

At the sound of my voice, the chipmunk chirped and scrambled off the stone, tail held high like the flag on a mailbox as he disappeared behind the rock. I knew if I stood still, curiosity would get the better of the chipmunk and he would reappear. When he stuck his head over the top of the rock and chirped, this time angrily, I laughed.

"What are you so upset about? Are you protecting something?" I said and walked over to the rock and knelt down. Scattered around the rock were bits of bluish-speckled paper. "What have we here?" I muttered. "Is this your hiding place?" A narrow hollow ran back under the stone.

As I tried to see into the hollow, it occurred to me what a great illustration that chipmunk would make in one of my books. Needed to make a note of it when I got back. *Emily* could spin a funny yarn about what she found in a chipmunk's hiding place.

I started to slide my hand into the crevice, but the thought of the creepy things that might be hiding in the dark stopped me. I picked up a stick to use as a probe. The chipmunk darted to and fro at a safe distance, attempting to lure me away. Chipmunks were scavengers, so who knew what I might find?

Rocking back on my heels, I studied the pieces of debris I had scraped out of the hole. More bits of bluish-white paper; the same kind I'd found in the barn. I stuck the stick back in the hollow and quickly had a mound of paper, no piece larger than my little fingernail.

As I sifted through the pile, trying to make sense out of my find, a hard brown object separated from the paper. A well-gnawed cigar butt.

I stared at the nub. How strange. No one I knew smoked cigars, at least not anyone who had business being in Walnut Clearing. I took a tissue out of my pocket, spread it out on the ground, and carefully scraped the bits of paper and the cigar butt into it. Maybe Gil could figure it out.

Gil! Oh my God, I thought. *Look at the time. He's going to be at the house before I get back.*

Stuffing the tissue in my pocket, I took off at a run down the path toward the creek.

I was sweating by the time I crossed and made it to the top of the bluff. I slowed my pace for the rest of the way, because the trees thickened and roots and vines stuck out in most unlikely places.

I tried to make sense out of what I had found as I jogged along. The chipmunk had probably found a piece of paper and dragged it back to the burrow before chewing it up. Chipmunks don't roam far. That meant the paper and the cigar butt had probably been dropped in the clearing. But why, and by whom?

It was a few minutes before five when I reached the house. The telephone started ringing as I came through the door, as if waiting for me to get back. I hoped it wasn't Gil saying he'd be late.

"Hello," I said, steadying my voice while I tried to catch my breath.

"Jessie? That you?"

"Yes, this is Jessie Schroeder."

"Hi there. This is Virginia from Sheriff Keller's office. He wants to talk to you. Hold on now while I patch you through to his radio."

A series of clicks and hums clattered over the phone line and then I heard Gil's voice. "Jessie, can you hear me okay?"

"You sound as if you're talking from inside a garbage can, but I can hear you fine."

"Listen, Jessie, I hate to tell you like this, but we found Willy."

I leaned against the wall. My heart filled with dread. I knew what he was going to say next, so I said it first. "He's dead, isn't he?"

"Yes. I'm real sorry, Jessie. They found him about an hour ago."

CHAPTER 7

They found him. The words sounded so empty. I felt tears rolling down my cheeks.

"It was an accident," Gil said.

"An accident?"

"No question about it. He fell into McGee Creek the morning of the storm. They found him down by that new bridge over the blacktop, just beyond your place. That's where I am right now. I'm going to be here for about another hour, then I'll stop by your place, if you still want me to."

I fumbled in my pocket for a tissue and watched numbly as the cigar butt tumbled to the floor and the bits of paper floated down like snowflakes to cover the floor in a blue-white blanket.

"You there, Jessie?"

"Yes, Gil, I'm still here." I took a deep breath. "You come on by when you finish."

"I'm so sorry, Jessie."

■ ■ ■ ■

Gil stood just inside the kitchen door, turning his hat in his hands and looking across the room at me.

"I guess Willy tried to ford the creek somewhere upstream from the bridge," Gil said. "He should have known better."

I have no conscious memory of my feet moving. But suddenly I was standing in the middle of the kitchen floor and sobbing into Gil's shoulder. All the pain I had been carrying — first Mom, then Alec, finding Margaret's body, and now Willy — was being wrung out of my body.

I finally brought myself under control. "Sorry. I don't usually behave this way."

Gil shifted his arms and put one hand under my chin, moving my head back until I was looking into his eyes. "Oh, Jessie." He bent down and gently kissed my lips.

I've no idea how long we stood there, maybe seconds, maybe minutes.

"Jessie," he repeated, pulling himself away. "I'm sorry. I had no right."

I reached up and touched his face. "Don't be sorry," I said. "I've wanted you to kiss me since I was a freshman in high school."

He gave me a look that bordered on sad.

"Okay, I get the message. Lighten up. Is that it?"

Damn. Now he thinks I'm being flip. Why did I say that?

I stared into his eyes. "That was a really stupid thing to say. I have this awful habit of covering my emotions with stupid remarks. Defense mechanism, I think the psychologists call it."

I couldn't tell if he understood, or if I was digging myself into a deeper hole.

"Jessie, may I ask you something?"

I nodded.

"Was it all right? I mean, is it all right? Oh damn, what I mean is, is it all right if I see you?"

I nodded again. "Yes. I'd like that very much."

I was amazed that I could feel happiness in the face of so much tragedy, but the overwhelming emotion I experienced was an almost giddy euphoria.

"Well," he finally said. "I guess I'd better go."

"No!" The word came out more forcefully than I had intended. "I mean, sit down for a few minutes. I'll get you something to drink. Finding Willy must have been terrible."

He looked at me briefly, then lowered his

gaze as if he didn't want me to see the pain that flashed through his eyes. "It's something I never get used to. Twenty years a law officer and it still gets to me." He looked over at the table. "Maybe for a bit. I could use something cool."

"I have iced tea or, better yet, I was thinking about making myself a gin and tonic. How about that?"

He shook his head. "Better not. I'll be on duty for several more hours. Iced tea sounds good. I'll take a rain check on the gin and tonic, if that's all right?"

I smiled. "Don't wait too long to claim it."

Oh my God, I had done it again, but he smiled back and said, "Deal."

"What are you going to do now?" I brought him his tea and took a seat across the table from him.

Gil looked surprised at my question. "About what?"

"About what? About Willy, of course."

"Close the file. Nothing else to do."

I stared at him. I couldn't believe what he'd just said. "You can't, Gil. Willy's not a murderer. You can't close the case."

He reached over and took my hand. "Now, Jessie, I know how you feel about Willy, but every piece of evidence points to him. He was a regular at Margaret's house, and his fingerprints were all over the toolbox. Plus, we found a key to Margaret's house in the toolbox."

"Of course there were fingerprints. It belonged to him."

"But the point is," Gil continued, "there were nobody else's. Look, Jessie, I never would have said Willy was a violent man. But we weren't there. We'll never know exactly what happened. Margaret may have said or done something that made him go off the deep end."

Gil plunged on before I could react. "Willy probably panicked when he realized what he'd done, and all he could think to do was run. It was his bad luck that the storm came up." Gil kept drumming his fingers on the table as if the cadence would bring me in step with his theory. "I'm sorry, Jessie. There's too much evidence pointing to Willy. I know how frustrating it is for you, but we can't change the facts by wishing they weren't so. I wish, as much as you, that Willy was still alive, so I could question him. I don't like pronouncing sentence on a dead man."

I couldn't believe what I was hearing. "Gil Keller, you do not make a convincing case. Sounds to me like what we have here is a verdict of convenience. And the key means nothing. She probably gave it to him so he could do work when she wasn't home. Why, he knows . . . knew," I corrected myself, "where I hide my spare key."

"Willy knew where you kept your key? Are you out of your mind?"

Gil's reaction was not at all what I expected, and his look made me squirm.

"It could have been you instead of Margaret," he continued. "Didn't you learn anything from living in the city?"

"But it wasn't me, and the reason it wasn't me is because Willy Bachmann didn't and couldn't kill anyone. And I'm getting sick and tired of everyone — you, Frank, the whole town — accusing an innocent man." I couldn't keep the bitterness out of my voice.

"Jessie, please, listen to me. Willy Bachmann killed Margaret Benson. As far as I'm concerned, the investigation is closed."

I sat and glared across the table at him. How quickly I had switched from being besotted to angry. Finally, I squeezed out a smile, although it probably looked as phony as a three-dollar bill. "Surely you're not going to close the case until you get the results of the autopsy."

"Autopsy? What autopsy?" Gil's voice

rose. "I'm not wasting Spencer County taxpayers' money on an autopsy for a man who didn't have sense enough to stay out of McGee Creek during a raging flood. Even a Mack truck wouldn't have stood a chance in that water."

I tried another smile, then shrugged my shoulders. "Suit yourself. If it was me, I couldn't close a murder case on a man who'd never had done anything violent in his life. Not unless I was satisfied I had every 'i' dotted and 't' crossed. And I'm surprised you would."

"Jessie, let's not argue. I didn't find one scrap of evidence pointing to anyone else. All an autopsy would show was that Willy was battered and drowned, and not necessarily in that order." Gil shook his head. "It wasn't a pretty sight. You know what that creek's like during a flash flood, and he'd been there four days."

I had been working hard not to imagine what Willy had looked like. I had seen whole trees swept down the creek during a flood.

"What if he was already dead?" I persisted. "What if someone put him in the water after he'd been killed? Wouldn't that show up in an autopsy?"

The expression on Gil's face indicated he had heard enough. "Come on, Jessie. There is no 'someone else.' "

"But how do you know?" I couldn't stop pushing. "Besides, by your own description, this does not appear to be a murder of passion. You said someone hit her from behind and there were no signs of a struggle. That doesn't fit with your theory that Willy made advances that Margaret was trying to fend off."

I paused to see if there was any reaction, but a stoic expression that I could not read was all he presented. I plunged on. "And why would he tear up the house? Willy was almost fanatically tidy. If he was looking for something, he would have done it in a careful fashion. I think someone else wanted something from Margaret and when she wouldn't or couldn't turn it over, she was killed and the murderer ransacked the house trying to find it."

"Jessie, you're worse than a little fox terrier I owned. Once you get hold of something, you won't let go, will you? Trust me on this. If something turns up, I guarantee I'll reopen the investigation."

I stopped myself from saying more. Gil was right. When I wrapped myself around something, it was hard to let go. "Sorry, Gil, sometimes I don't know when to shut up."

"Sure is a pretty spot," he said looking

out into the flower garden, unaware that Genevieve was stalking the perimeter of his chair in hopes of being invited up.

I wondered if he liked cats. "It is pretty, isn't it? My mom was a wonderful gardener. Even with Willy's help I have trouble keeping up with it." I couldn't stifle my sigh. "I don't know what I'm going to do now. He was so proud of the garden. We were going to enlarge the brick terrace next summer."

Gil didn't respond. His fingers started their slow drumming on the table again. For once I managed to keep quiet. I could tell he was thinking.

"You know, Jessie," he finally said, "this is the first murder case I've had since I moved back from Chicago five years ago. No one thinks twice about it in the city, but people aren't supposed to murder each other in a place like Riverport. It's been ten years, I looked it up, since there was a killing here, and that was during a drunken brawl."

"Whatever got you into police work?" I asked. "I always thought you'd become a lawyer. You were on the debate team in high school."

"I was in pre-law for a while, but never could work up a lot of enthusiasm for it. Worked as a night security guard at the University while I was in school. We had a break-in one night. I was pretty sure who'd done it — a lab tech who'd been fired. Seemed to me the evidence was plain as day, but the Urbana police wouldn't listen to me. The guy walked free with a couple thousand dollars' worth of equipment."

Gil laughed and drained his glass of tea. "Guess that's what convinced me society needed a smart guy like me to control the forces of evil. I quit school and became a cop. I'd met Elizabeth by then, and she wanted to go home. That's how I ended up as one of Chicago's finest. I finally managed to complete my degree, but it took me seven years of night school."

"Why did you decide to come back to Riverport?"

"That's the question I'd like to ask you," he said.

"Answer me, first," I said with a smile. The conversation was going far afield from Willy, but it seemed important to let it seek its own path.

"Riverport's sheriff called me with an offer I couldn't resist. He said if I'd be a deputy with him for a year, he wouldn't run for re-election and he'd support me for sheriff. The timing was right. Elizabeth had died, and the prospect of raising a teenage girl alone in Chicago was scary, so Ginny and I packed our bags. It was the right move for both of us." He stopped and smiled. "She's such a fine young woman, a lot like her mother, but with more grit. Going to be a sophomore at the University this fall."

He laughed. "When she was little she said she was going to be a cop like her dad. Now she wants to be a lawyer. In fact, she's in summer school picking up several courses. Isn't that a twist? You know, Jessie, I didn't realize how much I missed Riverport until I came back."

"Funny the way life turns out sometimes, isn't it?" I said, as much to myself as to Gil. "Here, let me get you some more tea."

"No predicting, that's for sure. I better pass. I've got to get back, but you said you had something you wanted to show me."

I rose and walked over to the drawer. Retrieving the plastic bag and the handkerchief, I laid them on the table in front of Gil, but before I could explain what I had found, the telephone rang.

Frank started talking as soon as I picked up the phone. "Jessie, you okay?" He didn't wait for an answer. "I just got in from the field, and Mildred told me they found Willy at the bridge. I know you're feeling bad. I'll be over as soon as I clean up."

I watched out of the corner of my eye as

Gil opened the Baggie and spread the contents out on the table.

"That's not necessary, Frank. Gil Keller's here. He was good enough to tell me about Willy, and he's going to be here awhile. No need for you to come, too. I'm all right."

"Sheriff stopped by? Why'd he do that?"

"I saw him after the funeral. He knew how worried I was about Willy."

I wondered if that explanation would satisfy Frank.

"Sure you're okay?" he asked.

"I'm fine. I'll call you later."

I hung up the phone. "That was Frank. Worrying as usual," I said as I walked back to the table.

"You're lucky to have him, Jessie. Lots of people don't have anyone who worries about them."

I felt my face flush. "I didn't mean to sound ungrateful. It's just that sometimes Frank forgets I'm a grown woman. He still thinks of me as his little cousin." As I sat, I pointed at the handkerchief, the cigar butt, and the chipmunk's stash. "What do you make of that stuff, Gil?"

"Looks like someone's been making confetti out of a piece of blueprint and someone else smoked a cigar. What's this got to do with anything?"

"I wish I knew. It started the night of the storm, the day Margaret was killed. I thought I saw somebody run across my barnyard. It was storming so bad and the power was out . . ." I paused. "And I was pretty scared so I didn't go out. I thought it was probably my imagination. I've never been too good with storms. In the morning, when I looked around the barn, it was obvious someone had been in the loft. A couple bales of straw had been moved and the largest piece of paper, that one with the printing on it, was on the floor along with the handkerchief . . ." Again I paused, thinking Gil would want to ask questions.

"Go on," was all he said.

"I was pretty sure it had been Willy. The handkerchief was the kind he always carried. Besides, I couldn't imagine anyone else who would think of hiding in my barn. I kept hoping he'd come back so I could talk to him, but he never did." I had to swallow hard to keep my voice from breaking. "All the time I was waiting, he was already dead."

"Take it easy, Jessie," Gil said. "Tell me about the rest."

"This afternoon, after the funeral, I walked over to Walnut Clearing." I stopped.

"Why did you go there?" Gil asked.

"I had this notion I might find Willy. He used to love to go there. He'd been using his spare time to make repairs to the old cabin. I guess I thought he might take shelter there."

"Didn't it occur to you that Willy might be dangerous?"

I shook my head. "Gil, that's the point I've been trying to make over and over again. I know Willy is . . . was . . . not dangerous. I was scared someone else would find him first and shoot him before he had a chance to explain. That was the *only* thing that frightened me!"

"Go on."

"Willy wasn't anywhere around, but there was this chipmunk." I stopped again. I didn't know quite how to explain my encounter with the chipmunk.

Gil nodded. "Go on."

"Well, this chipmunk kicked up a real commotion when I walked around the clearing, so I figured he was trying to keep me away from something. I found his cache. Bits of paper were scattered on the ground and stuffed in the hole, along with the cigar butt. It was obvious the paper was the same kind I had found in the barn, but the cigar butt had me confused. I don't know anyone who smokes cigars who would have been in the clearing. I'm afraid that's it, all I have. Saying it out loud makes it sound insignificant, but I've a feeling it's important. I was hoping you could help me figure it out."

Gil leaned over the table toward me. "Figure it out? Dammit, Jessie, how can I do that when the person who tells me doesn't have enough sense herself to be frightened, or at least careful, when a murderer is on the loose?"

I knew I had no defense, so I shrugged.

"Why didn't you call me?" Gil asked.

"I told you. I thought it was my imagination. Besides, I couldn't have reached you. All the lines were down."

"Don't you have a cell phone?"

"Yes, but I kind of let the battery run down. Then, the next day, I discovered someone had been in the barn, and I was sure it had been Willy." I shrugged again. "I don't know. I guess I was trying to protect him." I feared I was going to cry. "Oh, Gil, if I'd only checked out the barn Sunday night. I know I could have convinced Willy I could help him, and he wouldn't be dead. I thought I was so clever, keeping my secret so no one would find him before I did."

I stood up and poured myself some more tea, buying time to compose myself. I had to admit that if I were Gil, I wouldn't put much stock in the story I told. "Gil, I know what I've been saying doesn't seem to have much bearing on the case. And I know that you can't act when you don't have any solid evidence. I know all that but . . ."

"But you think I should listen to you anyway."

I nodded.

Gil rubbed his hand over his chin. "I probably should have my head examined, but I've got to admit you've aroused my curiosity. Do you mind if I go out to the barn and poke around?"

"Of course not. I'll come with you."

I could feel my confidence rise as we walked across the barnyard. Gil hadn't totally brushed off my suggestions. Maybe it wasn't too late for Willy. The barn was exactly as I had left it, except the mud had dried to hard clods. I watched Gil systematically work his way around the loft.

"Show me exactly where you found that piece of paper," he said.

"Right there in the back corner of the cubbyhole Willy had made out of the bales. And there was a big, damp spot on the floor where he must have sat down."

Gil climbed into the cubbyhole and squatted. Carefully he ran his fingers around the edges. I was dying to ask him what he was looking for because he seemed to have a definite purpose in mind, but I managed to keep quiet as he finished his search. Finally, he leaned back on his heels and held something up in the air for me to see.

I couldn't make it out in the gloom of the loft. "What is it?"

"A rubber band. Probably wrapped around the plans. When he took it off, the rubber band tore a piece off the corner. There's a little bit of something caught here where it's twisted, and I'll bet it's a fragment of blueprint paper." Gil retrieved an envelope from his pocket and carefully put the rubber band inside. "Come on, Jessie, let's get out of here. It must be a hundred degrees."

I had to trot to catch up with him as he strode across the barnyard.

"What do you think? Didn't I tell you this wasn't a simple open and shut case?"

"Now just hold on a minute," Gil said. "All I can surmise at this point is that Willy may have spent time in your loft during the storm on Sunday evening. Nothing more."

"But why was he carrying around a set of blueprints and where did they come from? Something strange is going on. I think Willy stumbled onto something. Maybe he even saw who killed Margaret and the murderer found out and killed him. Please, Gil, you've got to have an autopsy done on Willy. For your peace of mind, if nothing else."

Gil laughed.

"I don't know what you think is so funny. Murder is hardly a laughing matter."

Gil kept laughing. I couldn't help but smile myself.

"Jessie, you're enough to try the patience of Job. There was nothing bothering my peace of mind until I made the mistake of listening to you. I've got to get going. I'll call you later, if that's all right."

I stood by his car as he strapped himself in and watched him switch on his radio, wishing all the time he was not leaving.

"Virginia," he said, "this is Sheriff Keller. I'm on my way in. Do me a favor and call the Funeral Home and tell Fowler to pack up Willy Bachmann and take him over to the state lab for an autopsy. I'll do the paperwork as soon as I get back."

For once I was speechless. All I could do was lift my hand in response to Gil's good-bye. It wasn't till he was almost at the end of the lane that my voice started working again.

"Gil, Gil," I yelled, waving my arms. "Wait a minute."

The car stopped, the backup lights came

on, and he started back up the lane. I met him halfway and leaned in the window.

"I'd like it . . . that is, if you get finished in time, will you come back? I promise to get off my soap box."

He smiled that wonderful smile of his that made the crinkle lines around his eyes. "It might be late."

"That's all right, I'll wait," I said. "And Gil, whoever killed Margaret was at the funeral."

"What are you talking about now?"

"The murderer. The murderer was at Margaret's funeral. Think about it," I said. "It makes sense. We know it was someone Margaret knew, and if he or she stayed away, people would have commented on it."

Gil shook his head and he was still shaking it as he drove down the lane.

I couldn't help feeling pleased with myself. I was definitely getting his attention.

CHAPTER 8

Even a trip to Fowler's Funeral Home wasn't going to put a damper on my good spirits.

I would have to control the grin that had been breaking out randomly on my face since I had risen from my bed this morning. It wouldn't be easy. For the first time in several years, the coming days were something to look forward to and not dread.

I had actually sat down at my computer and put in a solid hour and a half before I set off on my errand. The story about Emily and the sunburnt ghost was going to be good, I could feel it, and I found myself laughing out loud as I imagined how my ghost would look when she started to peel. The spots where the skin peeled would become invisible. She'd look like a piece of Swiss cheese.

It had been past ten last night when Gil came back. He had offered to make it another night, but I persuaded him that ten was a perfectly fine time.

I thought the main topic of conversation would be Willy, but except for a quick question from me about the autopsy, we spent the next three hours talking. What about? Good question. On the witness stand I would be hard put to detail what we talked about. It was as if someone had dynamited the logjam that had held both of us captive for years.

Gil told me about his time in Chicago, first as a cop on the beat and then a detective. And the final, painful time when his wife lay dying. I spoke, without bitterness, about Alec. I felt a huge burden lifting from my shoulders and I knew what had happened was not my fault. The system had gone awry, and Alec had neither the maturity nor the commitment to try and repair it. For the first time, I said out loud that I no longer wanted it repaired.

It wasn't grim. We just talked. Two people who had spent too much time alone and now were cautiously beginning to trust in the future. How comfortable he made me feel. I felt free to say anything, knowing he wouldn't judge me. With Alec I had always carefully edited my words.

When Gil and I decided it was time to

part, he kissed me goodnight, held me close, and promised to call.

And now I needed to arrange a funeral. The parking lot was empty. I pulled into a spot by the door, right next to the handicapped spaces. How depressing to have to use a handicapped space at a funeral home.

I took a look at myself in the rearview mirror and was pleased by what I saw. A far cry from my appearance on the television news broadcast from outside the church. As Frank had said when he called, I looked as though I was preparing to rebuff an invasion of infidels. He was right. My mouth had been bracketed by lines so severe, they suggested I meant to deliver a doomsday alert.

Aunt Henrietta, however, said I looked wonderful, and how thrilling it was to see a member of the family on television, even if I was seriously mistaken in my viewpoint.

I composed my face. The funeral home's door opened into a hall with viewing rooms positioned on either side. I was surprised to find the Fowlers — Sheldon and Delores and their son and daughter-in-law, Sheldon, Jr. and Patricia — grouped in front of the double doors that led to the chapel. The men wore black suits and the women wore muted print dresses, and their faces were wreathed in expressions of concern and sympathy.

Why would anyone choose to spend his life being a mortician? Of course, someone had to do it, but what a depressing business. You could never pat your customers on the back and tell them you hoped they'd be back real soon. And morticians always appeared so solemn. Looking at Sheldon, Jr., I wondered what it had been like to grow up in a home that processed the dead on the lower level.

And why would they all be assembled? I hadn't called to say I was coming. Surely they had activities to keep them busy in other parts of the building. Maybe when I drove into the parking lot, I tripped some kind of alarm that brought them scurrying to their posts.

Sheldon, Sr. came forward to meet me, his hands outstretched, his silver mane carefully sculpted, not a hair out of place, and his face pink and glowing.

"Miss Schroeder, Jessie, how are you? What a terrible thing for you, finding Margaret the way you did. Is there something we can do for you?" he asked, carefully cradling my right hand. His hands were soft and warm. I had to wonder if that was the result of exposure to the fluids that were used in the trade.

I smiled and nodded in the direction of the other three. "I'm fine, Sheldon, and you?"

"We were sure surprised to see you on the news last night, but I must say, you made a fine appearance."

Delores joined us. "We were so excited to see you," she said. "You looked so calm. I would have fainted if someone had stuck one of those microphones in my face."

"It was loyal of you to stick up for Willy when everyone else is saying he's guilty," Sheldon, Sr. interjected. "Of course, since he worked for you, I'm sure people understand why you're sticking up for him." He patted my arm. "Fine trait, loyalty. That was your dad. Loyal to the nth degree. Never met a man who stuck by his friends like he did. You come by it naturally."

Is that how people were interpreting my stand? Dismissing it as loyalty and not taking the time to realize that I honestly believed Willy innocent?

"Willy's the reason I'm here." I decided not to get into a debate with the Fowlers. "I want to make arrangements for his burial."

"Oh?" Sheldon, Sr. looked puzzled, then smiled and patted my arm again. "Then it was you who called earlier this morning."

All I could do was stare. What was he talking about? "No," I said. "It wasn't me. I didn't call."

"How strange. I wonder who it was? Patricia took the call, but the person wouldn't leave a name. Insisted on paying the burial costs. When Patricia asked for a billing address, the person got real curt with her. Isn't that right, Patricia?" he called over to his daughter-in-law.

Patricia nodded her head vigorously as she joined us. "Said it was none of my business, to just figure out the cost."

"You didn't recognize the voice?" I asked.

"No. It was kind of muffled. I wasn't sure whether it was a man or a woman. I didn't think too much of it at first, because a lot of people who call here are upset and don't sound like themselves."

"Well, it certainly wasn't me who called," I said. "Sheldon, is this mystery person going to cause a problem about the arrangements?"

I could almost see the wheels grinding. Sheldon, Sr. was first and foremost a businessman, aware that a paying bird in the hand is better than an anonymous one on the telephone.

"No problem," he said. "I'm sure we'll be able to arrange a lovely service for you. Let's go to the office and work out the particulars." He turned to his wife. "Delores, why don't you fix us a nice cup of tea?"

"None for me. Thank you." I didn't want anything that might lengthen my stay inside the funeral home.

I let Sheldon take my elbow and steer me into the small room next to the chapel. The office was tasteful and subdued, mauve and gray like the rest of the building. I wondered if some interior decorators specialized in funeral homes.

Sheldon, Sr. showed me to an armchair beside a coffee table covered in neat little piles of catalogs. One glance at the covers convinced me I had better make my wants perfectly clear up front. No sense letting Sheldon, Sr. waste his time trying to sell me bronze caskets with velvet and satin linings.

"I want a plain wooden coffin and a simple graveside service," I said. "I'm sure the minister from the Abundant Life Baptist Church, where Willy belonged, will say a few words. I doubt that Willy has a plot in the cemetery, so I need you to arrange for that also."

Sheldon, Sr. walked to his desk and carefully twined his fingers over his front as he settled into his chair. I wondered if the change in location allowed him to assimilate the lower-than-hoped-for profit, but decided I was being unnecessarily cynical.

"We do have a bit of a logistical problem," he said.

I gave him what I hoped was a quizzical look and waited for him to explain. I knew full well about the problem, but I wanted to see how much he felt he could tell me.

"The body of the deceased is not here at the moment." Sheldon, Sr. rubbed his thumbs together and shifted his eyes away from me. "And I'm not sure when it will return."

"The autopsy, of course," I said, deciding the coy routine was a waste of time. "We'll just have to work around that, won't we?"

Sheldon, Sr. stared at me. "How did you know about the autopsy? Sheriff told me to keep it under my hat."

"He called from my house. I wasn't aware it was a secret. Why would he want to keep it quiet?"

"Guess he doesn't want folks getting all upset again. It wouldn't take much to set off a real panic if people thought there was any chance Willy wasn't the one who killed Mrs. Benson. I'm not one to criticize the sheriff, of course, but it seems like a waste of time and the taxpayers' money to send Willy over to the state lab for an autopsy."

Sheldon, Sr. sounded so peeved, I decided to ask him the question I already knew the answer to. "I wondered why the Sheriff wanted Willy taken to Springfield. You've been the coroner for Spencer County a long time. Why didn't he have you do the autopsy?"

"I asked him that very same question. He did apologize, but he wants all kinds of fancy tests done. He said it's to save the time and expense of shipping things back and forth. I don't know why he's getting so all-fired technical on an open-and-shut case."

I didn't want to think of what kinds of things would be shipped back and forth. "You know Gil. He probably wants to make sure every 'i' is dotted and 't' crossed." I suppressed my smile as I quoted from the lecture I had given Gil yesterday.

Sheldon, Sr. nodded. "Well, he is cautious to a fault, but I guess it's better to have a Sheriff who's like that than not."

"Seems like a good decision to me. Since the Sheriff never had a chance to interview Willy, I'd guess he's hoping the medical examiner will uncover something to help explain the crime." I wondered if Sheldon, Sr. had seen something to support the assertion of guilt. Would he tell me if he had?

Leaning toward him, I lowered my voice. "I think it's amazing how sophisticated the pathological sciences have become. All this DNA testing and being able to trace a single fiber or hair. Almost like magic to a layperson like myself. It must be fascinating work, and so important. I'll bet you've seen some interesting cases."

He settled back in his chair and relaxed. "I don't mind telling you that it's a lot of work keeping up with all the new techniques. And some of the things I've uncovered are not to be believed. Just when I think I've seen it all, along comes a topper. I've always thought I should write a book."

He stopped and smiled. "Hey, now, here's an idea. Why don't you stop writing children's books? We could collaborate. 'Course we'd have to change names and the place. Wouldn't want to get sued, would we? But I'll tell you, I've got humdingers we could use."

"I'll certainly keep that in mind," was all I could think to reply as I suppressed a shudder. "By the way, did you have a chance to examine Willy's body?"

"Unfortunately, no," he said. "Leastwise, not enough to reach any conclusions except probable death by drowning."

I sighed. So much for getting information.

"Terrible way to die."

Sheldon, Sr. put on his best mortician's face, sincerity radiating from his eyes. "Yes. Terrible. He never had a chance, but at least the end was swift."

I decided the conversation had gone on long enough, and rose to my feet. "Sheldon, I appreciate you making the arrangements for me. Remember, nothing fancy. Willy wasn't a fancy sort of guy. Call me when you have the details and some prices. And if the mystery person calls back, please explain that I'm handling the arrangements."

With that, I was out the door and down the hall before Sheldon, Sr. could get out from behind his desk. Escaping to the parking lot, I wasn't at all surprised to see that the sun had disappeared behind a cloud. I sat for a minute before starting the car, sorting through my conversation with Sheldon, Sr. Who had offered to pay the burial expenses?

I was the only person, other than Margaret, that Willy had worked for regularly.

One more thing that didn't add up.

CHAPTER 9

Friday promised to be one of those rare days that inspires people to unpack their bags and decide that they can survive August in the Midwest after all. A cold front had moved through during the night, dropping the temperatures and some much-needed rain. Beads of water glistened on the grass and flowers.

I should stay home and weed. Errant spikes disrupted the careful palette of color Willy and I had created in the garden. The ground ivy ran rampant. Tears formed as I thought of Willy. What or who was responsible for his death? Had it been an accident caused by his fear, or had someone orchestrated his drowning? Had an earlier incident sparked the tragedy? I felt as if I had walked in halfway through a movie. Just what had been going on in Riverport this past year and a half? Fumbling for a tissue, I blew my nose and wiped my eyes. The garden could wait. Today I would go to the newspaper office and read through the back issues.

I'd had a curious telephone conversation with Gil last night. We were both so eager to talk, we could barely take time to listen to what the other was saying. I had to admit I was pretty full of myself. After Fowler's Funeral Home, I had put in a solid four hours on my sunburnt ghost. Six whole pages, more than my total output for the previous five months. I sought praise for my prowess, but all Gil wanted to discuss was the weekend. He had decided it was time to go public.

I had to smile. It seemed forever since I'd had someone to share things with, and I couldn't get the words out fast enough. He reacted the same way. When I asked him for information on Willy and the autopsy, all I heard were vague, broad-brush responses. I had checked my irritation, giving him the benefit of the doubt. Maybe he didn't know any specifics, though my gut told me otherwise. Later, I decided, I'd pursue Willy later. And maybe Gil could find out the identity of the mysterious person who wanted to pay for the funeral.

So I said I'd love to spend Sunday with him. An actual date. I wasn't sure I remembered how to behave, it had been so long since I'd done anything that wasn't family-oriented. Alec and I had gone out a lot, but mainly to his functions, with his colleagues. Our social life had been oriented around his needs.

"I haven't had my boat out for a month," Gil had said. "I thought we could pack a lunch and go up to Frederick's Island. Would you like that? Of course, if you don't like the water, we could do something else."

"Gil, that sounds marvelous." It had been years since I'd been on the river. But growing up, Frank and I had spent so much time there that Dad used to call us his river rats. Uncle Henry had had a great boat with enough power to pull two water skiers. I even kept a special swimsuit for the river, because the stains from the muddy water were impossible to remove.

Swimsuit! Momentary panic. Which suit should I wear? Two-piece or one-piece? The two-piece was a little risqué, but it looked good on me. I dithered back and forth for several minutes and finally had to laugh. *Hell, Jessie, go for it,* I thought. *Wear the two-piece.*

As I drove toward the center of town, it seemed the cars were moving slower than usual and everyone had a wave and broad smile. The past several weeks the drivers' faces had been pinched and grim, their shoulders hunched forward to get as close to the air conditioning vents as possible. Now the windows were wide open, elbows perched jauntily on the sills.

I didn't know what I would accomplish at the newspaper, but it seemed like the logical place to begin. The *Spencer County Argus* wasn't the definitive source of information, but it would give me a starting point.

The talk by the women at the reunion, and in the car coming home from the funeral, had made me curious about the Mayor's development plans and the Industrial Park. It sounded pretty pie-in-the-sky to me, but I knew I had no right to judge if I didn't have the facts. Except for Margaret and Willy's deaths, it seemed the only other significant event of the last several years. And Margaret's husband had been at least marginally involved. If nothing else, maybe a few hours with the old newspapers would bring me back in tune with the town.

"How far back you want to go?" Herb Springer, editor of the *Spencer County Argus,* asked. "I've got copies in the office for the last five years. And Florence at the Library's got the microfilms going all the way back to eighteen forty-seven."

He stopped and looked at me. "Doing some research, are we?" he asked.

I smiled and shrugged. "You know how it is with writers. We get so involved with our work, sometimes we lose track of what's going on in the world around us. I figured the time had come for me to catch up, especially with the murders and other excitement around town. I could think of no better way than reading your newspapers."

Herb nodded vigorously. "Don't I know all about getting caught up in your work. The wife's always complaining that I'd forget to put on my pants in the morning if she didn't remind me, I get so involved in my writing. Something happens when you sit down at the old computer."

"I knew you'd understand. A year ago June should do nicely." The date rolled off my tongue so automatically it surprised me, but then I realized why. When Frank had crabbed at Mildred about her criticism of the Mayor and the Industrial Park, he'd said the Park had only been up and running for a year and it was too soon to judge. I needed to check the previous three months to see what had led up to the actual opening.

"You want to read them here or take them home?" Herb asked.

"I'll just read them here, if I won't get in your way."

"No problem. After all, it's not often I get a TV celebrity in here. That was pretty spunky of you to stand up for Willy in front of the cameras. 'Course, you're already pretty famous with those books of yours. You gotta let me run a feature on you one of these days. Folks would love to know where you get those crazy ideas for your stories."

I knew my smile was a little strained, and I mumbled something about being happy to be interviewed, but it was Willy who weighed on my mind.

"I really do think Willy's innocent," I said. "Standing up for him was the least I could do."

"Well, didn't surprise me none. Schroeders never were ones to back away from controversy. I remember many was the time when your dad stood up in front of the Town Council and gave them what for. Make yourself at home at that table in the corner and I'll bring the papers out. Think you can give me a quick statement about finding Mrs. Benson's body while you're here?"

As usual, my mouth started moving before I had formulated a plan. "Why don't you say what a shock it was, but that I'm sure Willy isn't guilty?"

Herb carefully wrote down my words, then went in the back room to get the newspapers.

I must confess my enthusiasm lessened as I studied the stacks Herb delivered to the table. The only thing that made me feel better was the fact the *Argus* was a weekly and rarely ran more than eight pages, including advertising. I didn't want to contemplate what the search would entail if the paper published daily.

"The Soap Box" was a good place to begin. The complaints, concerns, and political views of the community were aired in the column, the only requirement being that each letter be signed by the author. I smiled as I remembered the number of times I had typed up Dad's letters. Mom always complained it was downright embarrassing to be associated with him.

I was amazed to see some of the same names I remembered from my youth. Willard Munson had a diatribe on the younger generation going to hell. If I remembered correctly, he had had some pretty strong statements to make about my high school class twenty-four years ago. He lived right across from the entrance to the park. Willard was obviously still posting himself at his front window to record the nocturnal comings and goings. Esther Martin had written to cite the number of dog droppings in her yard. She demanded the Town Council pass an ordinance making it a crime to let your dog do his business on someone else's property.

A letter from Wyland Thomas, the pharmacist, in mid-July caught my attention. I didn't remember much about him except he had served on the Town Council for years and was one of the losers when Mayor Ellwood had swept into office. Wyland's letter was a meticulous examination of the city budget that had been adopted at the end of June, and he raised some interesting points. Why, for example, had the travel budget for the Council and Mayor quadrupled? Why had the Mayor's expense account been doubled? And why had a hundred and twenty-five thousand dollars been transferred from the capital improvements fund to the contingency fund with no explanation? And was that legal?

The last paragraph piqued my curiosity the most. "Why," Wyland had asked, "does the Council find it necessary to hide behind closed doors in executive sessions instead of making their decisions in public? Did they forget about the Sunshine Rule? What are they hiding from the people of Riverport?"

"Herb, have you got time for a question?" I leaned forward and called to the back of the room, pretty sure the only thing I might be taking time away from was his midmorning nap. I heard a thump as his chair settled on all four legs.

"No problem. What can I do for you?" he asked as he strolled up to the front.

"This letter in 'The Soap Box' from Wyland Thomas last summer?" I pointed to the column. "Wyland raises some serious questions, almost accusations."

Herb grunted as he scanned the item, then handed it back. "I followed up. Talked to the Mayor, even though I didn't think there was anything to the questions. Wyland hadn't taken kindly to being trounced in the election, but I figured I better see if there was anything to it. Wouldn't be doing my job if I didn't do that, would I?"

I smiled and waited.

"I was right. It was all legitimate. Council had to go into closed session to talk about real estate dealings, and the transferred funds were to pay for the start-up of the new Industrial Park. Because the new budget year started July first, they had to appropriate the money before they went public with their plans. Just the way the timing worked out."

"I see. Then it was all on the up-and-up?"

"The Mayor explained the whole thing to me, asked me to keep it under wraps till they finished their negotiations. 'Course I did. One of the cardinal rules of journalism is to respect your sources." Herb laughed. "Wouldn't do to make the Mayor mad, now would it?"

I managed to keep from commenting on the proper role of the press when dealing with elected officials. "I don't remember when the Mayor did go public," I said. "When was it, exactly?"

"Laid it all out at the first meeting after Labor Day. Said he wanted to make sure everyone was back in town." Herb shook his head. "I'll tell you, I can't remember a more exciting Council meeting. That Mr. Emerson is a real pro. He explained the whole thing. He had drawings and graphs and photographs of developments he had done in other towns. And he talked about how inspiring it was to work in a town with such visionary leadership as we have in Riverport. Here, it's all in the paper." Herb thumbed through the stack and handed me the September thirteenth edition.

The headline DEVELOPMENT PLANS

UNVEILED stretched across the top, and a three-column picture of Mayor Ellwood and Hap Emerson, grinning broadly and pointing at an easel, dominated the front page.

"I'll tell you, I was up half the night after the Council meeting writing the stories," Herb said. "Had to add an extra page to the paper to get it all in. Look, I've got a separate piece on Emerson, detailing all the things he's done in economic development." Herb looked at me. "We call that a sidebar."

"Amazing. I'm sure I'll learn a lot from the stories."

Herb beamed. "I'll keep out of your way and let you get on with it. There's at least one story each issue into November, and lots of photos. I figured something this momentous should be recorded for posterity. I probably shouldn't admit this, being in the print media like I am, but you know what they say: 'A picture is worth a thousand words.' "

I couldn't remember ever having seen Herb this animated. Clearly, this had been the story of a lifetime for him.

"Herb, one more question." I stopped him as he turned away. "Any idea how many companies have committed to the Industrial Park?"

"Committed? You mean have actually purchased land?"

I nodded.

"Well, I did hear a couple have options," he said, "but I don't think any have actual ownership. But then, Rome wasn't built in a day, was it? An operation this big is going to take time to put together."

I read through the stories, culling bits and pieces of information. The land had been purchased from old Mr. Porter's estate, one hundred and sixty acres on the northeastern edge of town. Another of Herb's sidebars explained that the property had been annexed into Riverport and that water and sewer lines were being run into the site. Just like my property, except I was on the southeastern border of Riverport. There were pictures showing the old farmhouse being razed. No great loss. It had looked abandoned even when Mr. Porter lived there. And there were many photos of the city officials in hard hats, turning shovels of dirt, sitting on huge earth-moving machines, and standing in front of charts.

Emerson and the Mayor were in most every picture, and there was one other constant — Ray Benson. I read the stories again, but nowhere in the text was he mentioned, only in the picture captions.

From a business point of view, the whole project sounded pretty iffy but, as best as I could tell, it had been set up in a straightforward manner.

I quickly scanned the rest of the papers, but nothing out of the ordinary presented itself. Ray Benson's obituary was there. In death he sounded much more appealing than in life. He must have belonged to every service organization in town, including something called the Riverport IDA. That rang a bell. I knew I had read something about it, but I was too tired to go back over the papers and find it. Maybe Herb could explain it to me. I gathered up the newspapers and took them over to the counter.

"All done?" Herb looked up. "You want to take any of them with you? Got plenty of extra copies."

"I'll be glad to pay for them."

"Heck, no. Just be that many fewer I have to haul to the landfill."

"Herb, what is this IDA that Ray Benson belonged to? It was mentioned in some of the articles I read."

"Industrial Development Authority," he said. "That's the official group in charge of the Industrial Park project." He shook his head. "I'll tell you that Mayor's pretty clever. All the big cities have them, so he figured why not Riverport. Emerson tells me we're the smallest town in Illinois to have an IDA. The truth be known, the Mayor probably wouldn't have thought of it, if Emerson hadn't been around."

Herb stopped for a minute, then shook his head. "I'll tell you frankly, I was a little skeptical of Mayor Ellwood in the beginning, but he's made a believer out of me. He's not afraid to try new things. Now if he can just get the highway thing through, we'll be sitting in fat city."

"What highway thing?"

"Jessie Schroeder! What did your dad spend the last ten years of his life working on?"

Groping through my memory, it slowly came back to me. A connector from the Interstate that would come through Riverport and cross the Mississippi on a new bridge to meet up with the north-south Interstate in Missouri.

I could see my dad pacing back and forth, ranting about the damn fool politicians who let the original highway pass ten miles south of Riverport, effectively isolating the city. "Someone in the state capital lined his pockets with gold," Dad would insist.

"Do you really think there is a chance that a connecter could be built?" I asked.

Herb shrugged. "Don't know, but I have heard some murmuring. If we could get that Senator Arnold off his duff and away from the bottle, we might have a chance."

"Wasn't he at Margaret Benson's funeral?"

"Yep. He's up for reelection in November. If you ask me, now is the time to strike. I mentioned it to the Mayor last week and he said he was working on it."

"He does seem like a go-getter," I said. "This Industrial Development Authority, where can I find out more?"

Herb looked surprised at my question. "From Flora Winters, who else?"

I put the newspapers in the back of my car and decided to walk over to the city offices to see Flora Winters, the City Clerk. I had been sitting too long. I needed to work the kinks out of my body.

The streets of Riverport sparkled. The rain had washed away the gritty dust that had covered everything like fine talc. I looked around. When I was young, I thought I would never see anything grander than Maine Street. Many of the buildings were faced in pink sandstone and the bank was banded in ornate friezes. The marquee still hung over the entrance to the movie theater, but the coming attraction was the winter season for the little theater group. A new multi-screen facility in the mall on the edge of town had sealed the fate of the theater that had seen me through my growing-up years. Some of the storefronts were empty, victims of the same mall that had closed the theater, but on the whole, the downtown still looked good.

The city offices were on the second floor of the Court House. Until a few years ago, they had been in a tiny brick building down the street, but when the County Highway Department moved out of the Court House, the County Supervisors had offered the empty space to the town for a dollar a year. Rose Markenson had her beauty shop in the old City Hall. She called it the City Hall Salon. Local wags said a more appropriate name would be the City Hall Saloon — in memory of certain previous office holders.

Flora Winters had been City Clerk as long as I could remember. Elected officials come and go, I remember my dad saying, but Flora's the glue that holds it all together. If a person needed information, Flora knew where to get it.

She was one of those women whose appearance never seemed to change. When she was forty she had looked sixty and now at seventy-five she still looked sixty. I knew her age only because Flora and her twin sister Stella had gone to school with Aunt Henrietta. Flora had a wardrobe of identical, long-sleeved gabardine shirtwaist dresses, all in muted earth tones, that she wore year round, buttoned up tight around her neck. Her only adornment was a small cameo pin anchoring the top button in place.

"May I help you?" Flora asked briskly as I came through the door of her office.

"How are you, Flora?" I said. "Haven't seen you since the church social. How is Stella's arthritis? Last time we talked, she was getting ready to take some gold therapy."

Left to her own devices, Flora would conduct the visit as if I were a stranger in off the street, instead of someone whose family she and her sister had known all their lives.

At the mention of Stella, Flora's face softened and she shook her head. "It helped for a while, but the doctor says it's progressive, so we just have to prepare ourselves for the worst."

"I'm so sorry to hear that. Please give her my best."

Flora nodded.

I took a deep breath and plunged right in. "Flora, I need your help."

She looked startled.

"I've always prided myself on keeping informed on what's going on in Riverport and Spencer County," I continued, "even all those years when I lived in St. Louis. I kept my subscription to the *Argus* —" though if I were honest, I would have confessed that I rarely took the wrapper off "— and Mom was always good about filling in the details."

Flora nodded again.

"With Mother's illness and then after she was gone . . ." I let my voice trail off. I could tell by the expression on Flora's face that she was thinking ahead to her sister's problems. "Well, I haven't kept track of things like I should. It took Margaret's death, and then Willy's, to bring me back to reality. I realize how much I've missed, including all the exciting changes Mayor Ellwood is bringing to Riverport. Since I have pretty well decided to settle back here permanently, I think it's important to bring myself up to date."

At the mention of Mayor Ellwood, the muscles in Flora's face tightened, but she made no comment. I knew better than to ask her directly her opinion of the Mayor and his activities. Flora would never breach the code of loyalty she brought to her job.

But it didn't matter. The change in her demeanor spoke louder than words.

"Anyway, I thought maybe you could fill me in on the particulars about the Industrial Park and this IDA group and anything else you think I would be interested in. I've looked through the newspapers for the past year, but Herb's stories aren't big on detail."

Flora drummed her fingers on her desk. "I can loan you the transcripts from the tapes I make at the Council meetings. Or, if you'd rather, you can listen to the tapes themselves, but they can't leave the office."

"The transcripts would be perfect," I said. "Will that include information about the IDA?"

She shook her head. "I can give you the minutes from their meetings. Unfortunately, a lot of their work is done in executive session, and that I can't release."

"I understand. Maybe you have something that explains what they do. This is a totally new subject to me. I don't even know who the members are or what their duties are."

"Why don't I make a copy of the state statutes that govern the Authority and the membership list? How soon do you want all this?"

I laughed. "You know me. Yesterday, if possible."

Flora smiled. "It'll take a few minutes, if you can wait."

"Perfect. I really appreciate your help." I looked at her. "You must think I'm crazy, but I feel like I've been in a state of suspended animation. I finally woke up and realized the world was passing me by. Now I'm trying to make up for lost time."

"No need to explain. It's good to have you perking around again. Stella and I have both been hoping that you plan to stay in Riverport. We're so proud of you. The library has all your books and we've read every one. We were just saying the other night how much your little heroine Emily reminded us of you when you were that age, all full of purpose and determination."

"Thank you," was all I could think to say. "I need to get my car. I left it over at the paper. Be just a few minutes." A thought hit me as I started out the door. "Flora, can I get copies of last year's and this year's city budget?" The assurances that Herb had given me about Wyland's comments about the city finances hadn't been convincing.

"Of course, but they make pretty dull reading."

I didn't find it curious that Flora didn't ask why I wanted all the specific information. She was one of those rare people who never pried.

I heard voices as I came back up the hall toward Flora's office.

"What in the hell does she want with all that stuff?" Mayor Ellwood's voice boomed out.

I couldn't hear Flora's reply.

"Of course, I know it's available to the public on request," the Mayor said, "but she hasn't lived here in years. I'll bet she isn't even registered to vote in Riverport. Besides, isn't she the one who's going around claiming Willy Bachmann didn't kill Margaret Benson? Sounds like a trouble-maker to me."

I decided I had better make my presence known before the Mayor dug himself in even deeper, so I backed up several steps and coughed. I couldn't help but admire the Mayor's quick recovery as I came through the door; almost immediately, he extended his hand.

"Miss Schroeder, isn't it?" he said in a hearty voice. "Flora tells me you want to do a little research on the activities of the Town Council."

I smiled and found my hand enfolded in a firm grip.

"Does my heart good to find a citizen

who's interested in his community," the Mayor continued, "though I dare say you're going to find most of our proceedings pretty boring. Any questions you have, don't be afraid to ask."

"I'll try not to bother you," I said. "I know how busy you must be."

"Nonsense, that's what I'm here for. If I'm not available to the people, I've got no business in this job. I hear tell you're thinking about staying put in Riverport. Have to get you involved."

"That's good of you," I said. "But for now I'll get out of your way and let you get back to the city's business."

I arranged the material in stacks on the dining room table. I wasn't looking forward to reading through all the paper I'd collected, but maybe, if organized, it would go faster. The transcripts and newspapers by month across the top of the table, the two budgets to the side, and the information on the Industrial Development Authority in front, to read first.

The membership list of the IDA had me shaking my head from the start. There were five voting members: Harry Williamson, William (Bud) Berry, Roland Evans, Seymour (Smitty) Schmidt, and Ray Benson. The

Mayor served ex officio, as a nonvoting member, and Harold (Hap) Emerson as executive secretary. A less distinguished bunch I had never seen. If this group was supposed to be charting the economic future of Riverport, the town faced serious trouble.

I tried to figure out some common denominator for the group. Harry Williamson worked at his mother-in-law's bank, Seymour Schmidt owned Smitty's Tavern, Bud Berry owned little except a bungalow on the edge of town and some worn-out farmland adjacent that, according to Frank, he was about to lose to the Bank. Roland Evans ran the hardware store and Ray Benson had been the town's con artist.

I pulled out the copy of the state statutes governing the IDA and started plodding my way through them. I kept going back and rereading — much of it was like reading a foreign language.

During my third reading of the section on the qualifications and membership of the IDA Board of Directors, all appointed by the Mayor, it hit me. The statute said there could be no fewer than five voting members. How could there be five members if Ray Benson was dead?

I flipped back to the membership list and

noticed a faint asterisk beside Ray's name, but there was no notation at the bottom of the page explaining it. I held the page up to the light to see if maybe something had been erased. Again nothing, but then I noticed what looked like writing on the back of the page.

There it was: *Named to replace Ray Benson, deceased, to the Industrial Development Authority, Margaret Benson.*

CHAPTER 10

A little after midnight, I carefully restacked the papers. I wasn't sure how much I had accomplished. My head felt stuffed with budget figures, legalese, and Herb's rather flowery accounts of the affairs of Riverport. Maybe overnight my brain would process the information and bring order.

The main impression I came away with was the Mayor had put out a plethora of promises without a convincing foundation. And if Hap Emerson were as successful a developer as Herb's sidebar made him out to be, what was he doing in a town as small as Riverport?

Gil had not called, which left me unsettled. I kept reminding myself that in only thirty-six hours we would spend the day together, so why should he call? Besides, this was a new relationship. I had no right to expect constant attendance, nor, I also reminded myself, should I want it. "Be patient," I said, knowing full well that patience was not one of my strong points.

The Mayor had spoken the truth when he warned me the Council proceedings were boring. But one pattern did stick out when I reviewed the transcripts of the meetings. Almost all the important decisions seemed to be made quickly, while the mundane items, like whether to open the swimming pool on Memorial Day proper or Memorial Day celebrated, were marked by marathon debate sessions. Maybe Wyland Thomas had been right when he said in "The Soap Box" that too many things were being decided behind closed doors.

My alarm went off at seven, wrenching me out of a sound sleep. It took considerable willpower to keep from hitting the snooze button. Finally, I swung my legs over the edge of the bed and set my course for the kitchen and coffee.

Once a month my favorite coffee shop in St. Louis shipped me a two-pound sack of freshly roasted Sumatra beans. Every time I paid the bill I was appalled at my extravagance, but as soon as I savored the aroma and the first sip, I knew it was worth the expense. Genevieve had learned to keep her distance until I had my first cup in hand. Only then would she remind me that she'd been neglected.

I carried my coffee out to the garden and set about organizing my day. First, a nice long run, only today I decided to vary my route. Instead of heading into the country, I would go across town and take a close-up look at the Industrial Park. Originally, I had planned to come home and spend more time at the dining room table. But I decided it would be more productive to visit several of the people who appeared to be at the center of the activity.

The Industrial Development Authority was still a bit of a puzzle to me. I wasn't totally clear whether its duties were purely advisory, or if the commission had specific and independent powers. I had gone over the Illinois State Statues several times, and it sounded as if the Authority was independent. It appeared that the IDA had its own budget, separate from the town's general fund. Maybe someone I talked to today could clear it up for me.

The Industrial Park looked even more dreary when I circled it on foot than it did from the car window. One concrete street had been laid down the middle of the site, punctuated every hundred yards or so by a fire hydrant, but not a shovel of dirt had been moved on any plot, nor did any signs announce the coming of a new business. A big billboard at the entrance proclaimed Hap Emerson the one to call with inquiries. The whole site needed a good mowing and weeds were beginning to sprout in cracks that had erupted in the new curbing. I wondered who had the contract to pour the concrete.

After I returned home and showered, I decided that Harry Williamson would be a good person to talk to. He, at least, should have some business sense from his years in the banking business, and he had been on the IDA from the start. Maybe he could enlighten me. But first, I had to detour past the Joseph farm.

I hoped to convince Otis Joseph to help with the garden and yard work. I hadn't realized how much I depended on Willy, and if I didn't find a replacement soon, the whole place would go to rack and ruin. I couldn't suppress a twinge of guilt when I realized this was the first time today I had thought about Willy. "Some friend you are," I muttered as I pulled into the Josephs' lane.

I slowed my car as I neared the house, in order to admire the huge vegetable garden that dwarfed the tiny frame house. I marveled how so many people could live in such a small dwelling. Children materialized like magic as I stopped at the gate. Viola peered out the kitchen window.

A girl who looked to be about ten came running up to the car. "Hi, Miz Schroeder. Whatcha' doing? Did you bring any of your books with you?"

"Hi, yourself," I said, embarrassed that she knew who I was and I hadn't the foggiest who she was. "No books today. I'm looking for your father. Is he around?"

She shook her head. "Nope. He's over at Gayle's place helping with the baling. Mom's here. You wanna see her?"

The last thing I wanted was to get tied up in a prolonged conversation with Viola Joseph, but before I could make an excuse and get away, Viola came out the door, wiping her hands on her apron.

"Patsy, you quit pestering Miz Schroeder and let her get out of the car," Viola yelled. "Come on in, Jessie, and sit a bit. I just put a fresh pot of coffee on."

It appeared I was stuck, at least for a while, but then it hit me that it might not be wasted time. Viola's brother was Bud Berry, one of the members of the IDA.

I felt like the Pied Piper as I went up the walk, trailed by the little Josephs. At least now I knew that the oldest one's name was Patsy.

A rich aroma of tomatoes and spices greeted me at the door. A huge pot was bubbling on the stove. "That smells wonderful," I said. "What are you cooking?"

Viola laughed. "Otis just loves homemade catsup, and we have so many tomatoes this year that I decided to surprise him. Never seen such a bumper crop of tomatoes. I heard Mildred say she thought it was all because of that global warming they keep talking about. Here, have a taste. You don't get much return on your effort, but I do have to admit it sure is good."

The children had all crowded in the door after us. "Can we have a taste too, Mama?" Patsy begged.

"No, you cannot. Now get, all of you. Miz Schroeder and I want a little peace and quiet. I'll give you some catsup with lunch. Now shoo."

"I do dearly love them," Viola said, turning to me, "but they have a way of getting underfoot sometimes."

I carefully blew on the spoonful of sauce, anticipating the tangy taste. Mom used to make catsup every year, and I had never found a commercial brand that measured up.

Viola poured two cups of coffee and carried them to the table. "There's some dry cream and sweetener." She pointed to a bowl filled with little colored packets that had originated in various Riverport fast food restaurants.

"We saw you on the TV the other night," Viola continued. "Weren't you scared? I would have just about died if anyone wanted to put me on television."

I knew there was no need to answer Viola's question. She was one of those talkers who used question marks to lead into her own statements.

"Wasn't that a lovely service for Margaret?" Viola stopped and shook her head. "Doesn't seem possible she's dead. Otis thinks it's absolutely positive that Willy killed her, but I kind of agree with you. He just wasn't the type. He never was anything but polite and nice to me, even when he was still drinking. Otis says that doesn't prove anything, but I think women have better instincts about people than men do. I think there's more going on than meets the eye."

Isn't that interesting, I thought, as Viola paused long enough to take a sip of coffee. *Maybe I'm not the only one with suspicions.*

"Strange how things happen," she continued. "That awful husband of hers dies a natural death and she's the one who gets murdered. Poor thing. She never so much as hurt a fly."

Viola's mouth was set in a grim line. "Plenty of people would have been happy to whack Ray over the head, given a chance, and I'll tell you, I would've been at the front of the line. The way he treated my Otis was just awful, and Bud too. My brother's probably going to lose his farm because of Ray Benson."

I felt my eyes widen. Frank had told me the rumors about Bud's farm, but this was the first I had heard that Otis Joseph had been involved with Ray Benson.

Viola put her hand to her mouth. "I shouldn't have said that. I promised Otis. He said he should of known better. And Bud, too. 'Course with my brother, it's not so surprising. He never had much sense about money, even when we were kids."

I reached over and touched her arm. "That's all right. From what I hear, Ray had a real knack for doing people wrong. Mildred told me he even cheated his own brother-in-law out of a pile of money. She said that's why Margaret and her sister hadn't seen each other for ten years."

Viola shook her head. "I know. I told Otis,

what's a little money compared to losing your farm to the bank or your life savings. But Otis is such a proud man and he works so hard . . ." She paused and looked out the window. "I know a thousand dollars isn't much to a lot of folks, but Otis worked long hours to earn it. He was planning on putting it down on a new pickup."

"Seems like a lot of money to me. What happened?" I hoped Viola wouldn't remember she wasn't supposed to talk about it.

She shrugged. "I don't know. Otis never told me, exactly. Ray was supposed to put it together with Bud's money and some other folks', bundling he called it, and invest it in some sure thing that Mr. Emerson — you know, the man who's helping with the Industrial Park — was putting together."

Viola looked directly at me. "I told Otis there was no such animal as a sure thing, but he wouldn't listen. Mind you, I haven't said, 'I told you so,' no need for that. What's gone is gone. Emerson claims he doesn't know anything about it, and Margaret couldn't find out anything. Least that's what she told Otis last winter."

So Otis had talked to Margaret. How recently? "Did Otis talk to Margaret often?" I asked.

"That's the funny thing. Otis probably

hadn't talked to her since January, shortly after Ray died. He'd written the whole thing off and then she called last week and said she wanted to see him . . ." Viola paused. "He was supposed to see her Monday."

"And she was killed Saturday before he had a chance." I finished the thought for her.

Viola nodded.

"Did Margaret say what she wanted?"

"All she said was maybe she had some good news for him. He wanted to come over right away, but she said no, that it had to wait till Monday." Viola looked down at her hands. "I sure hope what happened to Margaret didn't have anything to do with the money. Enough said. It's too nice a day to go on about our troubles. What's on at your place?"

I could tell from the expression on her face that the subject of Margaret and the lost money was closed, so I decided get to the original reason for my visit.

"I'm hoping Otis can give me several hours a week to help with my garden. Without Willy, there's no way I can keep up with it."

"I'm sure he'd be happy to give it a try," she said. "I'll have him call when he gets home."

"Thanks, Viola. Now I better get out of your way. I wouldn't want to be responsible for you scorching your catsup."

"Jessie." Viola followed me out the door. "Please, you won't say anything about Otis losing that money, will you? Otis would be awful put out with me if he knew I'd been talking about it."

"Of course I won't, but tell Otis to talk to the Sheriff. He should know about the appointment Otis had with Margaret. And Otis needn't worry. Anything he tells the Sheriff will be kept in confidence."

About a half mile away from the Josephs' place, I pulled over the side of the road. What in the world could Margaret have been referring to when she told Otis she might have some good news? It must have been about his lost money. Had she found a secret bank account or what?

I scrounged in my purse for some paper to jot down the high points of my conversation with Viola. If I was going to pursue this affair, I had to get organized, and I made a note to pick up a stenographer's pad to carry with me.

I chided myself for not trying harder to find out how the money was supposed to be invested. Even though Viola had claimed not to know the particulars, I suspected that little went on the Joseph house that Viola was not fully in on.

Next stop was the Williamsons. With luck I could talk to all three of them — Harry, Nancy, and Nancy's mother, Mrs. Pfeifer. I saw Nancy and her mother fairly often, but the only time I saw Harry was in the bank or trailing in attendance on his mother-in-law. Only his immense bulk kept him from being one of the invisible people.

There was one time, however, that stuck in my memory. Last fall, as I pulled into the parking lot next to Evans Hardware Store, I had seen Harry and Ray Benson talking on the sidewalk next to the driveway. Even that would not have caught my attention except that Harry was clearly agitated. His face had been beet red and he'd shook his finger at Ray. By the time I parked and walked around front, Harry was rushing down the street away from Ray so fast that his rolls of fat were gyrating in opposition to each other.

"What's the problem? You having car trouble?"

I jumped and smashed my elbow against the door as I whirled toward the voice. Spikes of pain flashed from my crazy bone as my eyes filled with tears. A face stared in at me and, gradually, Frank's features swam into view.

"Honestly, Frank," I snapped, "what do you think you're doing? Sneaking up on me! You almost gave me a heart attack."

"Don't get in a huff." He grinned at me. "What's going on?"

"Nothing's going on." I stuffed the piece of paper I'd been writing on in my purse. "If there had been a problem, I would have put my flashers on. You startled me."

"Sorry. I should have honked," he said. "What's up?"

I shrugged. "Just trying to decide which one of my errands to do next," I said. "I've kind of let things get away from me. How's Mildred?"

"Busying around like always. Why don't you come have supper with us? She was frying up a couple of chickens when I left. Nothing better than cold fried chicken on a summer evening. You haven't been over for quite a spell. Selma and the kids will be there. Charlie has to work tonight, so they're coming for the evening."

"I don't know, Frank. I'm way behind in my work."

"Now, Jessie, you know what they say about all work and no play."

"You sure Mildred won't mind an extra plate at the table?" I remembered what good fried chicken Mildred made. Besides, I

182

always enjoyed seeing Selma and the kids. I could fulfill my promise to tell Betsy and Joey a story. Their reactions would let me know if I was on the right track with Emily and the Sunburnt Ghost. Besides, it might take my mind off Gil and our date tomorrow.

CHAPTER 11

The Williamsons lived on the north edge of town on the bluff overlooking the river. Nancy's father had designed the house. He had modeled it after the Captains' houses that had been built in the days when Riverport was a major stopping point for the riverboats and barges. As a young girl, I had fancied myself strolling around the widow's walk, shading my eyes to catch a glimpse of my captain coming home. I still remember my disappointment when I learned the Pfeifers' widow's walk was only for decoration. Not even a trap door gave access.

I should have called ahead. Mrs. Pfeifer was not the sort of person one dropped in on. I needed to think of a plausible excuse. Maybe something to do with church or, better yet, the Riverport Literary Society.

Mrs. Pfeifer had been the grand dame of the Society from its beginning. She let other women serve as titular presidents, but everyone knew *she* made all the decisions. Maybe I could discuss with her my desire to become a member, even though I could think of no more deadly activity.

As I pulled up in front of the house, Harry came around from the side on a riding mower. He completely engulfed the seat, making it look like he was sitting directly on the mower. Getting out of the car, I waved. He raised the blades and drove to meet me.

"How are you, Harry? Isn't this a lovely day?"

He rolled that around for a minute and then said, "Yes, it surely is."

"Hard to believe it was ninety-five on Thursday and today it probably won't make eighty."

"You know what they say about the weather in Illinois. Just wait an hour and it'll change." Harry smiled in spite of himself.

"Too bad it didn't cool off in time for Margaret's funeral. It was beastly in the church. I'm surprised no one got sick."

Harry nodded.

"I couldn't bring myself to go to the cemetery," I said. "I heard Mrs. Pfeifer had some problems. That must have been frightening."

Harry nodded again. "Mother Pfeifer was

almost overcome. I had to take her to the car and run the air conditioning."

"Is she all right?" Getting information out of Harry was a slow process.

"Had a bad headache, but she's feeling better."

"How's Nancy?"

Harry frowned. "She shouldn't have gone to the funeral," he said.

What a strange thing to say, I thought. Nancy Williamson was one of the few in town who could truthfully call herself a friend of Margaret's. It would have seemed odd for her not to be there.

"It's always upsetting to lose a friend." I tried to sound understanding. "Nancy and Margaret were together a lot."

He didn't answer. All the time we had been talking, I had been trying to find an opening to bring Harry's membership on the Industrial Development Authority into the conversation. Suddenly I realized I had found it.

"I guess you spent quite a bit of time with Margaret, too," I said.

Harry's face flushed bright red and his mouth dropped open. He clutched at the handles of the mower with such force, his massive arms quivered.

"What . . . what . . . what are you talking

about?" he stammered.

"Didn't Margaret serve on the IDA with you? I thought I read someplace that she was appointed after Ray died. Such an important group. I assume you have many meetings."

"The IDA? Yes, of course. You're right. We do have a lot of meetings. Nancy was commenting the other night on how much time it takes."

"Must be fascinating work, charting the economic course for Riverport . . ." I paused. "And so much responsibility."

Harry nodded vigorously. I feared he would disjoint his neck. I waited patiently for him to share some of the fascinating work, but it appeared Harry had finished talking. Finally, I gave up.

"Guess I better let you get back to mowing, Harry. I'll just say hello to Nancy and Mrs. Pfeifer."

I was halfway up the walk to the front door when Harry yelled, "Nancy's round back."

Nancy was on her hands and knees in front of a huge bed of impatiens that encircled the giant pin oak shading the back of the house. The lawn continued a distance behind the house, up a slight grade. At the rear I could see a vegetable garden precisely edged with yellow marigolds. Bright red tomatoes hung heavy from their stems and cream-colored melons stuck out like polka dots from their thick vines. As I approached, Nancy rocked back on her heels, took off her gloves, and smiled. A swipe of dirt bisected one of her ruddy checks.

Every time I saw Nancy it amazed me that she was the issue of tiny, chic Mrs. Pfeifer. The only child had inherited her father's broad shoulders and rawbone physique. She was close to six feet tall and her angular features would have made a handsome man.

Mrs. Pfeifer had spent years trying to make Nancy into what she never could be. I remembered with pain the coming-out party Mrs. Pfeifer had held for Nancy on her eighteenth birthday, the only coming-out party in the history of Riverport. Mrs. Pfeifer had dressed Nancy in ruffles and bows and her blond hair had been teased and lacquered into an exaggerated flip. I often wondered if marrying Harry Williamson had been Nancy's act of revenge, or if she genuinely cared for him.

"Haven't seen much of you lately," she said. "Are you busy writing?"

"Yes, finally. I thought the words would never come again."

"I love telling people I knew you way back

when. We're so proud of you."

I looked at the mounds of impatiens around the oak tree. "Beautiful," I said. "You're giving me a guilty conscience. I should be home gardening myself, but the day is so gorgeous I just had to get out, even though that blasted ground ivy is about to take over my whole garden. By the way, how's your mother? Harry told me the heat got to her at the cemetery yesterday."

Nancy wiped her forehead with the back of her gloved hand and carefully rose to her feet. "She's fine. You know Mother. She's more easily affected by things than other folks."

What a polite way to say your mother can be a pain in the butt, I thought.

"I saw you at the church, Nancy, but I didn't have a chance to say hello. It was a nice service, and such a crowd."

"Bunch of ghouls, that's all they are." She spat the words out.

I was startled by her vehemence and didn't know how to respond.

"Sorry, Jessie," Nancy said. "I didn't mean you."

"That's all right. I'm probably as guilty as the others."

"Oh, no, Jessie. Margaret thought highly of you. She never forgot how kind you were

189

to her after Ray died. Most people just said good riddance and went about their business."

I flushed as I remembered how little I had done for Margaret. A casserole at the house and an hour's visit at the funeral home.

Enough chitchat, I thought. It was time to do some probing, but before I could ask a question, we were interrupted by a shout from an upstairs window.

"Who's out there with you, Nancy?"

Mrs. Pfeifer's voice could shatter glass, Cousin Frank claimed. I turned and walked closer to the house. "It's Jessie Schroeder, Mrs. Pfeifer," I called. "How are you this beautiful day? I was sorry to hear about your problem at the cemetery."

"Well, no thanks to that son-in-law of mine, I'm doing fine. Making me stand out in that boiling sun. He should have known better."

I glanced over my shoulder. Nancy was standing stock still, her face expressionless. I almost gave her an understanding smile, but thought better of it. I suspected Nancy had developed her own techniques to cope with her mother.

"Well, you take care of yourself," I called up. "Like I'm always telling my Aunt Henrietta, you can't be too careful in hot weather.

Be sure and drink plenty of fluids. Eight glasses of plain tap water every day and you'll be fine."

I watched as Mrs. Pfeifer disappeared from the window. The last thing she wanted was for someone to suggest she could take care of herself. I couldn't help smiling. If Mrs. Pfeifer drank eight glasses of water a day, she'd be so busy peeing, she wouldn't have time to bother anyone.

"Hot weather is hard on older folks," I said, turning to Nancy. "By the way," I said, hoping to get the conversation back to the funeral and Margaret, "I'm curious about something. I couldn't figure out what that Mr. Emerson was doing at the service."

I waited for an answer but none came, so I plunged on. "Someone told me Ray had been working with him last fall. I guess the couples could have gotten acquainted then, though the Emersons didn't look like they'd have much in common with Ray and Margaret. Did Margaret ever mention them?"

Nancy didn't answer. Instead, she looked past me, her lips set in a straight line. "Harry said he saw you on the news Wednesday night." The words came out flat and clipped.

I waited for her so say more, but she didn't.

"It was kind of embarrassing," I said. "But I really believe what I said. I'm sure Willy is innocent. Someone else killed Margaret, I just know it. You spent time with Margaret. Did she ever talk about any problems?"

"I'm sorry you had to find Margaret like you did, but she's dead and Willy's dead. Leave it alone, Jessie. Now, I have to get back to work."

I was startled at the cold finality in her voice. There was no doubt that the conversation was over.

"Well, I'd better get on with my errands," I said lamely. Something I said had caused Nancy to clam up. She knew something but, obviously, she had no intention of sharing her knowledge with me.

A throb in my stomach reminded me it was past lunchtime. All my detecting had made me hungry, and the obvious solution was a cheeseburger and an order of onion rings from Billy's Burgertown. Billy's made the best onion rings — fresh fried, each order dripping with grease.

I carried my food over to the picnic table at the side of the parking lot. It was too nice to sit in the car. I spread the onion rings on the tray and sprinkled them with salt. The rings left greasy circles on the paper liner.

Cholesterol be damned, I thought, as I took my first bite.

As my hunger abated, my brain started to process the information I had been feeding it. The pieces were still too scattered to come to any conclusion, but I had a feeling that it was all going to start to fall into place and soon.

Harold (Hap) Emerson was the real puzzle. The list of his accomplishments in the paper had certainly sounded impressive. In fact, he sounded almost too good to be true. His business was headquartered in Springfield, but his projects were all over the Midwest, including Chicago. Why would a man like that be interested in a dinky project in Riverport? Maybe Frank would have some answers for me. I'd ask him at supper.

It was coming up on three o'clock when I pulled into my lane. That barely gave me time to transcribe and expand my notes before I was due at Frank's. I was so absorbed in my thoughts, I was almost at the door before I noticed something white sticking out of the screen.

"Now what?" I muttered and pulled out the folded piece of heavy stock paper and opened it.

All I could do was stare at the letterhead:

EMERSON DEVELOPMENT CO., INC., HAROLD (HAP) EMERSON, PRESIDENT, and the words scrawled below: "Sorry I missed you. Will call Monday." The note was signed Hap and embellished with a smiley face.

CHAPTER 12

I walked over to Frank and Mildred's, still puzzled about Hap Emerson's visit. I had wanted to meet him and here he was, usurping my move. Why? I couldn't shake the feeling that there were currents churning beneath the surface, and all I could see was the faint riffle on top. Unless Frank knew something, I had to wait till Monday.

Less than a quarter of a mile of pasture separated our two houses, although a hill cut off the view. We rarely walked back and forth anymore, but Frank kept the pathway mowed. When we were children, Frank and I had lamented the fact that we couldn't flash Morse code messages back and forth. Now I was grateful for the privacy. Enough of my life seemed an open book. I didn't need my cousin in constant attendance on the comings and goings at my house.

Mildred waited at the door. "Did that Mr. Emerson get hold of you?" she asked.

"He stopped by the house, if that's what you mean, but I wasn't there. He left a note. Why?"

"He came by here looking for Frank, but Frank was out in the field. When I asked him what he wanted, he said he needed to find out something about your place. He figured that Frank could fill him in."

"Why on earth would he talk to Frank about my place?"

Mildred shrugged. "Beats me. I told him he needed to talk to you. Was that okay?"

I nodded. Another thing I didn't understand was why some people, particularly men, seemed to think that, when it came to business, no matter what kind, it automatically belonged in the masculine milieu.

Mildred pulled the screen door open for me. "I tell you, Jessie, he is just about the handsomest man I've ever seen in real life."

I couldn't help smiling. "Honestly, Mildred, I'd say you've been stuck in Spencer County too long, if you think he's that good-looking."

Mildred ignored my tease. "I kept thinking I'd seen him somewhere. You know, before he started his work in Riverport. And then the other night I finally figured it out."

"Where? Where had you seen him?"

"Promise you won't laugh."

"Why should I laugh?"

"Promise."

"All right, I promise. Tell me."

"Well, a couple of weeks ago the video store had a special offer — rent three for the price of two — so I made Frank get me *Gone With the Wind* again. He couldn't hardly object because it was free. He can't understand why I like to see movies over again. But I tell him, 'You listen to the same music over and over again, and this is no different.' "

"Mildred, what are you getting at?"

"I'm sitting there, watching the movie, and it hit me. Clark Gable. Mr. Emerson looks just like Clark Gable. Here, in my own town, is a man walking around who looks just like Clark Gable, right down to the mustache."

All I could do was shake my head. Just exactly what revelation I thought Mildred was going to share with me I couldn't say, but I knew for sure it wasn't Hap Emerson's resemblance to Clark Gable.

"You may think I'm dotty," she continued, "but the next time I rent it, I'm going to call you and make you watch with me. You'll see what I mean. He's not as handsome as Clark Gable, nobody is, but Mr. Emerson comes in a pretty fair second."

"What's all this talk about Clark Gable?" Frank joined us in the kitchen. "For the life of me, I can't understand Mildred sitting around mooning over that man. He's dead, for God's sake."

Mildred turned to me. "See what I mean? The man has absolutely no appreciation for the finer things in life."

"Fix you a drink, Jessie?" Frank asked. "The usual?"

I nodded and watched as he mixed my gin and tonic and got his beer out of the refrigerator.

"Selma called," Mildred said. "She and the kids are going to be a little late. Why don't you two go outside and let me finish up things?"

Frank and I settled ourselves in the green steel lawn chairs that had sat as long as I could remember under the huge soft maple tree in the corner of the yard.

"This spot may not be as pretty as your garden, but the breeze comes through real nice." Frank looked up at the towering tree. "One of these days this old tree is going to topple over. It's a miracle it only lost a few twigs the other night."

I debated telling Frank about my visitor the night of the storm. He would raise holy hell with me, I knew, but I'd weathered many a tongue-lashing from him, so why not?

"The Sheriff's pretty sure that Willy hid in my barn sometime during the storm Sunday," I said, then sat back and waited for the eruption.

Frank slammed his beer down on the arm of his chair, sloshing foam all over his hand. "Goddammit, Jessie, I knew it wasn't safe to leave you alone. Why won't you ever listen to me? All the time thinking you know what's best. You don't have the sense God gave a goose. You need a keeper, that's what you need."

"Now, Frank, don't get your blood pressure up. Nothing happened."

He mopped up the beer with his handkerchief and avoided looking at me. "Jessie, I don't know how to tell you this and make you understand. I'm not just being a nervous Nellie. I worry about you. You seem to have this belief that you are invincible. Jesus, you've been through hell the last two years. Why can't you accept the fact that life can be a sack of shit sometimes? I think you live in that imaginary place you write about."

Every smart remark I had been reviewing disappeared. "I'm sorry," I said.

He reached over and took my hand. "I know," he said. "You've always been different than the rest of us. But Jessie, just think about the people who love you."

His words hit a chord with me. I had felt so abandoned when Alec left me and Mom died. And why had I come running back to Riverport? Because here were people who cared. Here I felt safe.

"This is getting a little heavy, Frank," I said.

"So what else is new?"

"Did you hear the Sheriff's having an autopsy done on Willy? He decided he'd better be sure beyond a reasonable doubt that the death was accidental."

"That sounds like a waste of time and effort to me. Somehow I can't help but think that your meddling had something to do with that decision. Seems to me you're getting pretty cozy with our Sheriff."

I chose to ignore Frank's inference. Maybe I hadn't been as circumspect as I thought. "It's sound police work, that's all. By the way, Hap Emerson came by to see me today. Left a note in my door. Said he'd call me Monday. Do you know anything about that?"

Frank turned his beer can in his hands, peering into the top as if he was waiting for the answer to come floating up. He finally shrugged. "Beats me," he said. "Though there has been some talk that he's looking to buy property around Riverport."

"What do you know about him?"

Frank rotated his beer can again. "Not a whole lot," he finally said. "Makes a good couple of first impressions, but he doesn't wear well . . ." He paused. "Talks too fast."

"What do you mean, 'talks too fast'?"

Frank drained his beer and crumpled the can in his fist. "Lots of words. Fast. It's been my experience that some people talk fast because they don't have the answer, or they've got something to hide. If you talk fast enough, it's hard to keep track of what's being said. I need another beer. Can I get you anything?"

I shook my head and waited for him to come back. It was pretty obvious from his tone of voice that he had had some personal experience with Hap Emerson. I wondered, briefly, if I could get Frank to tell me about it, then brushed the doubt aside.

"Selma called again," Frank said, as he came out the door. "They're starting out. Said to be sure and remind you about the story you promised Betsy and Joey. She says the kids are driving her crazy, they're so excited."

I smiled. "I guess I'd better make it good then." I waited for Frank to get resettled in his chair. "Tell me about your conversations with Emerson."

Frank looked over my shoulder at the cornfield that stretched as far as the eye could see. "Going to be a good yield this year. Not as good as eighty-four, but then we'll probably never see anything like that again." He finally turned back to me. "First time was last fall after his talk at Rotary. He called and asked if I'd meet with him and six or so other prominent residents."

"And did you?"

"Asked him what about. He said he was trying to put together a consortium of area leaders to carry Riverport and Spencer County well into the twenty-first century. Wanted me to be a part of it."

"Sounds pretty grand," I said.

Frank produced a half-hearted grin in reply. "Yeah, I know, but I figured why not hear what the man had to say."

"And what did he have to say?"

"Well, it didn't come to anything. He was mostly looking for money. He said he needed backers to bring a start-up electronics company into the Industrial Park. Claimed we'd get a minimum return on our money of fifteen percent within twelve months of the plant being operational. He had all sorts of charts and fancy graphs.

Twenty-five new jobs, more money for the local economy. Sure looked good on paper, but when I asked to see the company's financial statements, he said he'd have to get back to me on that."

"And did he?"

"Nope."

"Who else was at the meeting? Do you remember?"

"Sure. The Mayor was there and Harry Williamson, Roland Evans, Bud Berry, Grace Michaelson, and her father. I'll tell you, old Mr. Michaelson is starting to lose it. Shame, too, because he used to be a real shrewd cookie. Oh, yeah, and Ray Benson."

I shook my head as I reviewed the names. "I can understand Harry being there because of the bank and everybody knows Roland Evans has more money put away than he can count. But why Bud Berry?"

And why you, Frank? I thought, adding another question to my list.

Frank shrugged. "I asked Roland and he said he thought it had something to do with the land Bud owns adjacent to the Industrial Park."

"Did anybody put money into the plant? I haven't seen any construction going on."

"Don't know. None of my damned business what other people do with their money."

I made a concerted effort to keep a look of exasperation off my face. Men! How could he have sat through that meeting and not been interested enough to find out if any of the others fell for the proposition? Maybe I should give Grace Michaelson a call and see what I could find out. I could tell by Frank's frown that he'd finished talking about it.

"I guess I'll just have to wait till Monday to find out what Emerson wants with me," I said.

"Don't let him suck you in with fancy promises. He's a pretty slick customer."

"Slicker than you?" I grinned.

"Yeah, he's a lot slicker," Frank said, surprising me. Then he looked beyond me, at the cornfield again.

Something was wrong. Frank seemed to answer my questions, but I couldn't shake the feeling that what I was getting was three-fourths of an answer, not the whole thing. I was almost relieved to see Selma's car pull in.

"Grandpa! Grandpa!" Betsy and Joey hurtled from the car and threw themselves into Frank's arms, knocking his cap askew. "Hi, Jessie." Betsy freed up one of her arms long enough to wave madly over Frank's shoulder. "Joey and me want you to tell us your new Emily story."

"How about after supper?"

Betsy detached herself from Frank and ran over to me. Joey stayed put, searching through Frank's shirt pocket, looking for a piece of gum. I couldn't help but speculate on how different the two children were. Betsy was a whirlwind, bouncing from person to person and activity to activity. Joey was mostly content to tag along behind her, except when his grandfather was around. It made me smile when I watched them together. Joey was a little shadow, mimicking Frank's every move.

"We don't want to wait," Betsy said. "Please tell us now."

"I think your Grandma Mildred wants to serve supper pretty quickly. But as soon as we clean up, after we eat, I promise."

That was good enough for Betsy and she rushed into the house to see her grandma.

The fireflies were beginning to wink around the yard by the time the children and I settled on the swing on the front porch. I had always envied Frank and Mildred their porch. It wrapped around the front of the house, sited so a person could sit and swing and watch the world go by. Everything peaceful. It didn't seem possible that in the last week two people had had their lives extinguished.

"Let's see what *Emily Says* this time," I said. "Are you ready?"

Betsy and Joey nodded vigorously and I began.

"Karen ran into the house," I said. " 'Emily, Emily, where are you?' Karen shouted. 'It's an emergency.' It was silly of her to ask where Emily was. Everybody knew how to find Emily, if she wasn't at school or eating dinner with her mother and father. She would be sitting at the little table in the corner of the family room with a volume of the *Encyclopedia Britannica* open in front of her. Emily loved being an authority, and she had vowed that she would learn everything in the world. Whenever she asked her father a question, he always said, 'Look it up in the encyclopedia,' so she went straight to the source for her education. She was currently on volume five. She could have gone on the Internet, but there was something satisfying about being able to turn the pages and trace a sentence with her finger.

" 'What do you want this time?' she asked Karen, who hopped up and down in front of her. Karen was always coming to Emily and demanding answers.

" 'It's Julie,' Karen said. 'She says there's no such things as ghosts, only pretend ones at Halloween. I say there are ghosts, but she says not.' Karen looked at Emily. 'Well, are there?' Karen asked. 'Are there ghosts?'

" 'Of course there are ghosts,' Emily said. 'Julie's right when she says the ones at Halloween are people dressed up in sheets to look like ghosts, but she's wrong when she says there aren't any real ghosts. I have it on good authority. Ghosts are all around us.' "

"Who is her good authority?" Betsy asked.

"What's a 'thority?" Joey said.

"An authority is an expert," I told him. "Your grandma is an authority on cooking. That's why her food tastes so good." I smiled at Betsy. "One time, a long time ago, Karen asked Emily who her authority was, but a withering glare halted her question."

Before Joey could ask, I gave him a withering glare, and he laughed.

I laughed, too, smoothing out my pretend-sneer. " 'I never divulge my sources,' Emily said, and from that day on, Karen accepted everything Emily said without question."

Both children snuggled closer and I continued.

"What most people don't know is that there are Ghost Towns all over the world. In fact, there are so many that each is given a number so the ghost mail doesn't get lost. Sally Li Mahoney lived with her mother and father in Ghost Town number forty-three, near a school in Illinois."

Betsy squealed. "Oh, Jessie, is it in Riverport?"

"Maybe. I'm not sure. Anyway, ghosts have rules, just like people do, and the most important rule, all across Ghost Land, is that ghosts must never, ever leave their homes in the daytime. In fact, it's such an important rule that the whole town could be punished if one ghost broke the rule."

"Sounds pretty serious," Betsy said.

I nodded solemnly. "Sally Li Mahoney was not a bad little ghost, but she got bored. She didn't have any brothers or sisters to play with and there was no one her age who lived close by. Sally knew about the rule, but it didn't make sense to her. All the other ghosts were happy to sleep away the daytime, but Sally couldn't sleep, so she sat at her window and listened to the children play, and she felt lonelier and lonelier. So she started sneaking out of the house. Sometimes she would peek in the windows of the school and watch the children working at their desks, but her favorite time was recess when all the children came out to play. She'd hide behind a bush and pretend she was playing with them."

"But Jessie, didn't the children see her?" Betsy interrupted. "I always see Joey when he tries to peek at my friends and me."

"No, the children didn't see her because in the daytime ghosts are completely invisible," I said, and made a mental note to clarify that in my story.

"One day Sally was watching the children on the playground at lunchtime," I continued, "and she completely lost track of the time. By then she had figured out that no one could see her, so she no longer bothered to hide behind the bush. What she didn't know was that, even though the children couldn't see her, the sun could. Sally got a terrible sunburn, and when a ghost gets a sunburn she glows like a bright red ball of fire. And when the children saw a ghost-shaped ball of fire, they all screamed and ran inside to tell their teachers."

"Did the teachers catch her?" Betsy asked.

"Sally ran back home and hid under her bed. Poor Sally. She was so sad. She had not meant to frighten anyone and now she knew she couldn't go back to school. And almost as bad was the problem of trying to explain to her mother and father how she had gotten a sunburn. It hurt awfully bad. Her mother knew what Sally had done right away. She put salve on the sunburn to make Sally feel better, then she and Sally's father tried to decide what to do. Sally was very young, only one hundred and forty in ghost years, but even a young ghost must obey the rules. They knew they had to tell the Elders."

"What are the Elders?" Betsy asked.

"The Elders are grown-up ghosts who make sure everybody obeys the rules." I smiled at Joey. "That means they punish anybody who doesn't listen to them."

"Like making them stand in the corner?"

"Yes, like standing in the corner. But the ghost Elders had a terrible problem. If the ghosts in the other Ghost Towns found out what Sally had done, there would be a big scandal. It would be on Ghost TV and in the Ghost Newspapers and the President of Ghost Land would punish the whole town. They would not be allowed to have a single birthday party for a whole year. Wouldn't that be awful? No birthday parties?"

Joey nodded. His own birthday party was next week.

"The Elders sat around a big table trying to decide what to do. Finally the Chief Elder held up his hand. 'What we need here is a little diversionary action and a little damage control,' he said."

I heard Frank snort in the background.

The kids looked puzzled, so I clarified. " 'We have to figure out how to tell only part of the truth and make it sound like the whole truth,' the Chief Elder said. 'Then maybe the President won't take away our birthday parties.' Sally sat in the corner, listening. She was getting confused. What were they talking about? She had been wrong. The sunburn was proof of that, and now that she had started to peel, it was even worse. Her skin itched something terrible, and as the sunburn peeled, those spots became invisible and she looked like a ghost-shaped piece of Swiss cheese."

Betsy and Joey giggled. They loved Swiss cheese and were always begging for some.

"Finally," I said, "Sally decided what to do. She crept out of the room and went to the kitchen. She pulled up a chair to the telephone and carefully dialed 1-800-#-1-g-h-o-s-t, and seconds later she was talking to the President of all Ghost Land. Sally's knees were shaking and her words came out in a jumble, but the President was a kind man. He said, 'Slow down, Sally, and tell me the story from the beginning.' When she had told him her story, she took a big breath and said as politely as she could, 'There are good laws and bad laws. This is a bad law. It's not fair that everybody is punished when only one ghost was bad,' and the President asked Sally what he should do. 'Well, sir, I think you should change the law,' she said, even though she couldn't believe she was telling the President what to do."

Something nagged at my mind as I talked about the number-one ghost. Damage control. Half truths. Good laws, bad laws —

"Jessie, what happened then?" Betsy tugged at my arm. "Did the President change the law?"

"Yes he did," I said. "He said Sally was a very smart little ghost, but that because she had been naughty, she would not be allowed to watch TV for a month. Then the President called in a famous doctor and asked him if he could cure Sally's sleep problem. The doctor put Sally on a supersonic ghost airplane and flew her backwards around the world twelve times to reset her body clock."

"Did it work?" Betsy asked.

"Yes," I said. "From that day on, Sally slept in the daytime and played at night, just like the other ghosts. But sometimes she would do something just a little naughty. She would set her alarm clock so she could get up and watch the children play at recess in the afternoon. But she was careful to stay out of the sun."

"Tell us another story, please," Betsy begged.

"Not tonight," Selma said. "It's time for me to take you two little ghosts home to bed." She turned to me. "I don't know how you do it, Jessie, but I think this is your best Emily story yet. I'll never be able to eat Swiss cheese again without thinking about the sunburnt ghost."

I gave Betsy and Joey a hug. I would have to simplify some of the words when I typed the story into my computer, but my sunburnt ghost had passed the test.

CHAPTER 13

The grasshoppers that had whirred around my legs on the way to Frank's were silent by the time I returned home, replaced by the steady chirping of crickets. The sun had gone down, but a faint golden glow rimmed the horizon and long-fingered cirrus clouds etched lacy patterns across the sky. I barely needed the flashlight I had brought with me.

The words "diversionary action and damage control" kept echoing in my mind. The Elders with their half truths versus whole truths. I shook my head. It was time to apply some of Emily's straight-line thinking to the situation.

Could Margaret's murder and then Willy's death be part of a horrendous damage control process? But what could be so important in Riverport that it outweighed human life? I could not shake the notion that the violence had not been planned, and something happened to cause it to erupt. But what? And why had the killer carried the wrench from the back porch into the kitchen, if the murder was spontaneous? I needed a 1-800 number to call, like my sunburnt ghost.

As I walked in the door, the telephone rang. Genevieve lifted her head from her cushion and glared at me. Obviously, the bell had interrupted her nap. My fault, of course. I picked up the phone, expecting, hoping it would be Gil telling me what time he would pick me up in the morning, but it was Aunt Henrietta who answered my greeting.

"How was supper at Frank's?" she asked.

It no longer amazed me that my movements seemed to be public knowledge. When I first moved back to Riverport, I had been almost paranoid about the open-book aspect of living in a small town. Now I shrugged and gave it no more thought than the weather.

"Lovely, and Selma's children were fun as usual," I said. It was true. Betsy and Joey were great kids, and they had responded enthusiastically to my sunburnt ghost story. This book was going to be a winner. I could feel it in my bones.

"Weather's supposed to be beautiful

tomorrow," Henrietta said. "George and I thought we'd pack a picnic lunch and go over to Geyer Springs. Why don't you come along? It's been a trying week. Do you good to get away."

What to say? There was no way I could turn down the invitation without explaining why, and I was reluctant to tell my aunt I had a date.

"Sounds lovely," I said, "but I'm afraid I'll have to take a rain check."

Before I could explain, Henrietta said, "Now, Jessie, I'm not going to take no for an answer. Can't have you moping around over that trouble with Willy. You need to get out."

"Henrietta, I'm sorry, but you'll have to take a 'no.' I have other plans." I took a deep breath. "I'm spending the day on the river with Gil Keller." Rarely was my aunt rendered speechless, but this time I had succeeded. "Henrietta, are you still there?"

"Did you say, Gil Keller? The Sheriff?" she asked in a rather stilted voice.

"Yes." I decided to take the offensive. "Doesn't that sound like fun? It's been years since I've been on the river. I'm really excited. Remember how Frank and I used to spend every hour we could out with George's boat?"

"The Sheriff?" she repeated. "I didn't realize you knew each other. I mean, do you think it's proper to go out with a man so soon?"

I had to laugh. "Of course we know each other, Henrietta. We went to high school together, remember? Besides, we're both unattached adults. Just because I'm a grass widow doesn't mean I have to be a recluse the rest of my life."

Henrietta clucked. "Listen to me. Going on like some meddling old lady. Pay no attention. It's just you surprised me. I know it's none of my business, but how long . . ." She paused. "I mean —"

"We're just friends. Don't you think it's about time I started getting out? Anyway, thanks for the invitation. Give George my best. I'll talk to you Monday."

No sooner had I hung up the phone than it rang again. This time it was Gil.

"Sorry to be so late calling you," he said. "There was a messy accident on the Interstate and we were helping the state police. We had to use the Jaws of Life to extricate one of the drivers."

"Oh, Gil, how horrible." I had this vivid memory of watching the firefighters in St. Louis demonstrate how the Jaws worked, when my ad agency was doing a public service spot for the fire department. They had used a dummy, but I had no trouble imagining what it would be like in real life.

"The amazing thing was that no one was seriously hurt," Gil continued. "Not even the driver. But it sure did make a tangle of the traffic. Anyway, are we still on for tomorrow?"

"I'll be ready whenever you say. What can I bring? Sandwiches, beer?"

"Nothing. This is my treat. Ten o'clock okay?"

"Ten is fine."

"Jessie," he said. "I'm really looking forward to spending the day with you."

"Me, too. With you. See you in the morning."

I'd thought I wouldn't be able to sleep a wink, but instead I had slept like a baby.

I remembered the island had minimal shelter for changing, so I put my bathing suit on under my shorts. I had no desire to strip underneath a towel.

As I waited for Gil, I felt unsettled. Part of it had to do with the fact that I had not been out with a man I wasn't married to for over twenty years, at least not on a date, but there was something else.

Gil had made it abundantly clear he was

convinced Willy had committed the murder. It was just a matter of tidying up the case before he filed it under "solved." He claimed he took my concerns seriously, pointing out the autopsy he had ordered, but I had the distinct impression that he was humoring me, that his patient attention to my persistent claims of Willy's innocence was part of the courting ritual. He probably would have been attentive to anything I said. But then, I couldn't imagine him doing anything that would compromise his office.

I was definitely attracted to him. He had a sexy magnetism I had not experienced in years. When he had held me the other night, I wanted nothing more than to stay in his arms and let the problems of the world take care of themselves for a change. But I had learned long ago that problems never took care of themselves. They just went unresolved. Somehow, I had to convince Gil that my doubts about the case were not flights of fancy.

"Come on, Jessie," I muttered. "Remember what Dad always said. You catch more flies with honey than vinegar. Put a smile on your face, enjoy the day and the man, and deal with Willy tomorrow."

I had to smile at that thought. I knew good and well that I was not going to be able to stay away from the topic of Willy today.

The river stretched broad and brown, spreading a mile from bluff to bluff. I had forgotten how insignificant the Mississippi could make a person feel. Gil's boat was solid, a sleek Evinrude outboard, but as we rocked in the wake of a barge moving down the river, we were but a speck on the force moving through the middle of the continent toward the Gulf of Mexico. Normally by August the current would be lethargic and the debris from upstream minimal, but storms in the northern watershed had sent a fresh supply of tree trunks and branches and other flotsam down the river. Gil steered a steady course up the channel, and I sat in the front, marveling that I had let so much time go by without seeking the solace of the river. Many times when I lived in St. Louis I had gone down to the riverfront, but there the river was compressed and I would return home unsatisfied.

I looked back at Gil and he gave me a wink. I couldn't resist a grin as I thought of the stir we'd caused at the marina. He kept his boat in a slip just north of town on the bay. I had started to help him take the tarp off, but it was quickly apparent that he had his own method for dealing with it, so I had stepped back and watched the other groups load their boats. I'd learned long ago not to mess with a person's routine. But my interest in what other boaters were doing paled by comparison to the speculation we provoked.

To say we were the main focus of interest at the marina would be an understatement. Seymour Schmidt almost dropped his beer cooler in the water when he saw me with Gil.

"Don't want to lose that, Smitty," I called to him. "How are you?"

I could see him fumbling around for my name, but before I had to remind him, he got it. "Miss Schroeder, Jessie, what a surprise," he said. "Hey, Sheriff." He turned to Gil. "Haven't seen you down here for awhile. Thought we might not see you out on the river this summer."

Gil had made some noncommittal reply and continued with his preparations, seemingly oblivious to the commotion we were causing. Seymour Schmidt, owner of Smitty's Tavern and member of the Industrial Development Authority. How I longed to go over and quiz him about the actions of the Authority, but, obviously, this wasn't the right time. Later I'd get to Smitty.

We weren't the first people to reach Frederick's Island, but Gil pulled the boat around to the back side and we slid into an inlet surrounded by wispy willow trees. As he cut the engine, I jumped out and helped pull the boat up on the sand. There was no one else in sight, and I had the feeling that anyone seeing the Sheriff's boat would give our spot a wide berth.

Gil and I were both silent as we spread out the blanket and stashed the cooler in a shady spot. I wondered if he was as nervous as I. Not that it mattered. I was skittish enough for the two of us. I had given up trying to understand how I could swing so abruptly from self-confidence to insecurity. I had felt happy and relaxed, almost languid, as we cruised up the river. Now I was as jumpy as the proverbial cat on a hot tin roof.

"Penny for your thoughts," he said as he plopped himself down beside me.

"I'm not sure they're worth even a penny," I said, resting my chin on my drawn-up knees.

"Try me."

I looked across the water at the green bluffs looming in the distance. My thoughts were such a jumble, I wasn't sure I could formulate them into anything coherent.

"Do you ever feel like you've lost control, Gil? Like a log drifting down the river, at the mercy of the current. Not knowing if you're going to go aground on a sand bar or finally make your way to the Gulf and freedom?"

"Most every day," he said. "Probably why it took me so long to ask you out."

I turned my head and looked at him, afraid I would see a condescending grin, but instead his gaze was steady as he reached out, took my hand, turned it palm-up, and placed it against his lips.

"What are you doing?" I asked. Surprising both of us, I pulled my hand away.

I turned my face so he couldn't see the tears welling up in my eyes. I heard him stand and walk away from the blanket. Then I heard the lid of the cooler open and the clatter of ice cubes.

"Here," he said, as he plopped down on the blanket across from me and handed me a can of beer. "Now, tell me what's wrong."

How the hell could I tell him what was wrong when I didn't know myself? So I settled for a shrug.

"That's not good enough," he said.

"I don't know," I said, and took a deep breath. I did know what was wrong but I was afraid to tell him. Then I made the mistake of looking at him, and I felt the tears start to reform. "I'm forty-two years old, a so-called woman of the world, and I'm scared out of my wits."

After what seemed like forever, he said, "Want a sandwich? I've got braunschweiger with mayo and mustard, or ham and cheese."

All I could do was stare. I was on the verge of a breakdown, and he wanted to know what kind of sandwich I wanted. I dredged through my repertoire of retorts, trying to come up the perfect blister to show him what I thought of his insensitivity, but all I could settle on was how much I loved braunschweiger with mayo and mustard.

"Braunschweiger, please," I said, and started to laugh. Again I said, "braunschweiger," and laughed until new tears ran down my face.

Gil sat and grinned, placidly letting me make a total fool of myself. Every time I thought *braunschweiger,* off I would go again, until my sides ached. Finally my laughter subsided into hiccups. I wiped my eyes with the hem of my tee shirt and silently accepted the neatly folded handkerchief that Gil handed me.

"You okay now?" he asked.

I nodded.

"I take it you would like a braunschweiger sandwich."

I nodded again, struggling to keep down another bout of giggles.

He handed me a neat package, wrapped in waxed paper and firmly secured with sharp butcher folds.

"Are you always so precise?" I asked, thinking about the crumpled aluminum foil I usually wadded around my sandwiches.

"I confess to a certain compulsiveness," he said.

We ate our lunch in silence, watching a huge barge labor its way upstream against the current. The wake lapped against our little inlet, causing Gil's boat to rock slowly up and down.

"Jessie, may I say something?" Gil said, after we had finished eating.

I nodded, afraid of what I might hear.

"I'm scared, too. Thought you should know that," he said.

The rest of the day passed in a blur. We took the boat out with the water skis. When I protested that I hadn't skied in over twenty years, Gil handed me a ski belt and said, "It's like riding a bike. You never forget."

And indeed I hadn't. What I had forgotten was the glorious feeling of freedom when your body bursts free of the water and you skim across the surface, twisting and bobbing over the wakes created by the boat. I skied until my shoulders and upper arms ached. I wouldn't be able to lift my hands over my head for days.

When it was Gil's turn, he showed off like a teenager, passing the tow behind his back, then kicking off one ski and making deep arcs back and forth across the boat's wake. It was obvious he hadn't been out on the river for a long time, because he had a farmer's tan. His chest, back, and legs were white, contrasting severely with his arms and face. But that didn't prevent me from admiring his body. It seemed to me that many men my age carried a little extra baggage on their bellies, but Gil's was flat and crisscrossed with muscles. His body was long and lanky. I wondered if he was a runner like myself. All in all, as my friend Sally would say, "Verrry sexxxy!"

He looked so pleased with himself that I couldn't resist temptation. When he least expected it, I abruptly changed course and he dropped like a rock into the water.

"What did you do that for?" he asked as I pulled alongside him, having retrieved the loose ski, and put the engine into idle. "I was doing great."

"Blame the Devil," I said. "He made me do it."

Gil shoved the other ski and the towline into the boat and heaved himself over the side. "The Devil, huh?"

He grinned and started toward me. Before I could squirm out of his reach, he had me by the shoulders. Then he pulled me down on top of him.

"You're going to be trouble, Jessie Schroeder," he said, silencing any reply with his lips.

Whatever my reply might have been was instantly forgotten, as I let my body mold into his. The river rocked us gently as we lay in the bottom of the boat. All I could think was how good his skin felt against mine.

"Jessie," he said.

"Yes, Gil?"

"Could you move?"

"Excuse me?"

"I need you to move. The towbar is doing permanent damage to my spine."

I hauled myself upright and laughed. "Aren't we a pair? In the movies it never happens like this."

Gil pulled himself up and rubbed his back. "Maybe not, but in the movies there is always a 'The End.' I'm hoping this is just the beginning."

■ ■ ■ ■

Gil and I were both quiet in the car on the way home, but it was not an uncomfortable silence. I yearned for the good old days, before bucket seats, when I would have snuggled myself up to him. But I was constrained to my side of the car and dependent on words to express my feelings.

"It was a wonderful day," I said, reaching across the seat and rubbing his neck. "Sorry I flipped out there for awhile."

"Not to worry. History has a habit of intruding sometimes. You have to learn to trust all over again. Not easy, but I think you can do it."

I didn't know how to respond, so I brushed his cheek with my fingers. "I think so, too," I said.

The light was fading as we pulled into my driveway. We had been together almost eleven hours. "Do you want to come in for a while?" I asked.

"Do you want an honest answer?"

"Of course."

"The answer is yes," he said. "But do you want to know what is going to happen?"

"Of course," I repeated.

"So, I'm going to kiss you good night and

228

go home and dream the most wonderful dreams I've had in years." He stopped the car by the gate, unfastened his seatbelt, and leaned over to me. "I'll call you tomorrow."

"Tomorrow," I echoed as I got out of the car. "Yes, call me. We need to talk about Willy. Oh, and I think there's some funny business going on over at City Hall with the Industrial Development Authority. I have a feeling that Hap Emerson and/or Ray Benson were working some kind of scam. I'm not sure what yet, but certain things don't add up."

"And then maybe we'll find time for a discussion on world peace and the pros and cons of capital punishment." He shook his head. "Jesus, Jessie, I'm never going to understand you."

CHAPTER 14

The air hung heavy around my body at six-thirty in the morning, as I left the house for my run. Usually, with weather like this, only sheer willpower got me out of the house, but today I was eager to go. So much to think about.

My feelings for Gil were developing too rapidly. One date, for God's sake. What did that prove?

I blushed when I thought about my hysterical performance yesterday, but he'd seemed to weather it. Then there was my reaction to the braunschweiger sandwich. *Sophisticated you're not, Jessie.*

When I stepped out of the shower and examined myself in the mirror, I looked like my sunburnt ghost. My upper legs and midriff glowed bright red, contrasting with the tan I had acquired in my running clothes. As I had expected, my arms and shoulders ached and my nose had sprouted a new crop of freckles.

I regretted my decision to pay a call on Esther and Lester Martin later on in the day. Vegging in the AC seemed like a better idea. However, the whole question of who'd killed Margaret Benson hung over me like a cloud. Maybe the Martins could provide some clues. If Esther was half as nosy as Aunt Henrietta claimed, she should be able to give a good report of the comings and goings at the Benson house. Two hours on the computer with Emily's ghost, then I'd head into town.

I was almost at the end of the lane when I remembered the coffeecake I had taken out of the freezer to give to the Martins. I backed up the car, left the motor and AC running, and used the spare key behind the drainpipe to let myself in. I felt a slight twinge as I remembered the lecture Gil had given me about leaving my key in such an obvious place. I probably should have moved it, but I found it hard to believe that anyone would think to look there. Under a flowerpot or the doormat, but not behind a drainpipe.

By eleven I pulled up in front of the Martins' house. The shades were still pulled on the Benson house next door. Probably to keep the curiosity seekers from peering in the windows. It made the house look forlorn and abandoned. The grass in the yard was brown and crumpled. I wondered what would happen to the property. Esther could probably tell me.

Lester must have been watching, because he answered the door on the first ring.

"Hot enough for you?" he asked.

"Sure is," I said, handing him the coffeecake. In my mother's day it would have been home-baked instead of something from the bakery section of the supermarket. "How's Esther?" I asked. "I know she and Margaret were close."

Lester shook his head. "I don't know if it's delayed reaction or what, but she's been real poorly the last two days. Come on in. She's on the sunporch.

"Look who's here and see what she brought us." Lester's voice boomed as he showed me onto the sunporch.

Esther was stretched out on a sofa, a box of tissues at her side. She gave me a weak smile. Lester was right. She looked terrible. She wore one of those god-awful housedresses covered with brilliant fuchsia flowers. Usually, when I saw her at church, her stout figure was neatly cinched, but today it oozed and poked at the seams of her smock.

I didn't know how to approach her, but decided the sympathetic route was best. Crossing the room, I took her hand in mine. "I'm so sorry. Are you all right?"

Esther shook her head. "It's been so awful, and people . . . people, don't . . ." She pulled her hand away and covered her face. Then she grabbed a wad of tissue and mopped her eyes and blew her nose. "You must think I'm a terrible baby to behave this way."

"Not at all. It's a terrible thing to lose a friend, especially in that way."

She pulled herself to a sitting position and patted the cushion next to her. "Here, sit down. What kind of a hostess am I, making you stand up? Besides, it's you I should be comforting. How awful for you, finding Margaret like that."

"She was a lovely lady," I said, taking my place next to Esther.

Esther allowed herself one last sniff. "Well, some people don't think so. That spiteful Mrs. Pfeifer told Grace Michaelson that she didn't understand why people were so upset, that Margaret Benson's death was no great loss to the community . . ." Esther paused for a reaction. When I nodded, she said, "Right in the market Mrs. Pfeifer said it, with me standing just one aisle over in canned vegetables."

"I wouldn't worry about what Mrs. Pfeifer says," I told Esther. "You know her. She's made a career out of criticizing the world."

Maybe I shouldn't have spoken so harshly about Mrs. Pfeifer, but it was true. Mrs. Pfeifer operated under the belief that there were two classes of people — the Pfeifers and, a distant step below, the rest of us.

"That's right," Esther said. "Just because her family owns the bank she thinks she's better than the rest of us. Never seemed right to me, that someone can get rich off other people's money."

Esther was on a roll, so I decided to let her continue.

"Bet she never knew that son-in-law of hers hung around the Bensons all the time. I asked Margaret one time how come Harry was there so much, but she just smiled that silly little smile of hers and said nothing. Maybe Harry was looking for some excitement. Lord knows that place the Pfeifers call home is like a mausoleum."

"Harry doesn't seem the type to have spent time with Ray Benson, at least from what I've heard about him," I said. This was a curious development.

Esther picked some invisible lint off her

skirt and pulled herself up straighter. "Actually, I only saw him there a couple of times while Ray was alive. But about a month and a half ago, Harry started showing up like clockwork every Tuesday afternoon at three. I told Margaret it wasn't seemly for her to be entertaining a married man, but she insisted they were taking care of business."

"Business? What kind of business did Margaret have?" The only connection between Margaret and Harry, as far as I knew, was the Industrial Development Authority. That kind of business should have been taken care of in regular meetings.

"That's exactly the question I asked myself," Esther said. "Never could get Margaret to say a word about it. Lester says it could have had something to do with Ray's estate. But I said, if that's so, why doesn't she go down to the bank?"

"Did Harry stay long?"

Esther shook her head. "Never more than half an hour or so. Lester says that's hardly enough time to get into too much mischief, if you know what I mean."

I didn't quite know how to react. It was hard to imagine Harry involved in a romantic liaison, but what had he been doing at Margaret's house? The reason *had* to be the Industrial Development Authority.

"What did the sheriff say when you told him about Harry's visits?" I asked.

"The Sheriff?" Esther looked at me, puzzled. "I didn't tell the Sheriff. All he was interested in was who I'd seen around Margaret's at the time of the murder."

I refrained from commenting. As I thought, Gil was guilty of tunnel vision. Somehow I needed to convince him that this was not a simple crime of passion. There were tentacles to this murder that spread way beyond Margaret and Willy. However, now it was time to move Esther to another subject, so I said, "Did you see Willy around Margaret's house much?"

Esther shook her head. "Everybody's been making like he practically lived there, but he only came around every couple of weeks. When Margaret needed some work done, she'd leave a message for him at the hardware store."

"I know Willy thought the world of her," I said.

Esther nodded. "Margaret said one time that she could hardly get him to take money for his work. I guess that's why she gave him things that belonged to Ray."

"Willy was a good-hearted soul. That's why I can't believe what everyone's saying about him." I decided to be direct. "Do you think Willy killed Margaret?"

"It's funny you should ask," she said. "Lester and I have been talking about that a lot. We saw you on the television news. Got to say, you surprised us when you said he wasn't guilty, because everyone else in town said it was so. What you said got us to thinking."

I sat quietly.

"Lester used to talk to Willy when he was working at Margaret's," Esther continued. "Said you couldn't find a nicer guy. And since he quit drinking, he was as dependable as the day was long. 'Course he was never a mean drunk, not like that Ray Benson. The things I could tell you about what went on in that house. Never did understand why Margaret put up with it. I guess she didn't have anyplace to go. I know it sounds cold-hearted, but it was a real blessing when Ray upped and died last Christmas."

"Esther, did Margaret ever say anything about that Mr. Emerson, the man who was doing the study for the Town Council? Someone told me Ray worked with him."

"Margaret didn't say much about him, but to hear Ray tell it, Mr. Emerson couldn't do anything without his help. 'Course Ray must of been doing some work for him, 'cause that big white Cadillac of Emerson's was parked out front every couple weeks and you'd see them driving around together. Then, after Ray died, I saw Mr. Emerson carry out a couple of boxes of stuff."

I almost held my breath as I asked the next question. "Did Mr. Emerson visit Margaret after Ray died?"

"You know, that's what's so strange. I hadn't seen him or his car since way back in the winter, and then the Tuesday before Margaret was killed, there it was again. I know it was Tuesday, because I was on my way to my hair appointment. I've had a standing appointment at Monica's every Tuesday at one, ever since Lester retired. We always drive over to Springfield for dinner and the movies on Tuesdays, and I want to look my best. Anyway, I almost hit his car when I backed out, he'd parked so close to my drive."

"Was he still there when you got home?"

Ester shook her head. "No, but I didn't get back till three. I had to stop by the drugstore to pick up Lester's prescription. Mr. Emerson's car was gone, but Harry was getting out of his car as I pulled up. Call me mean if you want, but I couldn't resist rolling down my window and asking after Nancy's health. The look on his face!" Esther laughed. "Figured it didn't hurt him to know people noticed his calls at Margaret's."

"And Margaret never told you what was going on?"

"Nothing more than he was helping her with some paperwork."

"What about Willy? Was he there during the week?"

"Well, let me think. He hadn't been there for awhile, but toward the end of the week he was there a long time." She suddenly leaned forward and yelled, "Lester!"

He must have been standing right by the door, because his head appeared around the corner, before Esther's call had stopped resounding.

"He was there all Thursday afternoon," Lester said, verifying my suspicion that he had been listening to the entire conversation. "He was planning on repainting the trim on Margaret's house this fall, after the weather cooled. He was working on her storms, re-caulking, replacing rotten boards, getting them ready. It was real hot that day, so I took him over a pitcher of ice water. I'd seen Margaret drive away, and I figured in that heat he'd be needing some water. We talked a bit, but I could tell Willy was anxious to get on with his work, so I left him alone."

Lester shook his head. "Willy was a little slow, if you know what I mean. But once he learned a job, there was no one who could do it better. Don't think I ever saw caulking so neat and smooth in my life. When the Lloyd Brothers painted our house year before last, I had to take a razor blade to scrape off the caulking they smeared on the glass."

I didn't need Lester to tell me what a good worker Willy had been. I was always in a hurry, impatient to finish one job so I could get on to the next. More than once, I had watched Willy go back over areas I had weeded, plucking out strays I deemed too small to bother with.

"And that was the last time you saw him?" I asked.

Lester nodded. "Though Esther saw him Friday."

"It was a terrible thing I did," Esther said. "It was *Friday,* not Saturday, I saw Willy. I told the Sheriff as soon as I realized my mistake, but by then everyone was thinking it was Willy who did that horrible deed." She dabbed at her eyes again.

"Now, now, Esther." Lester patted her shoulder. "You know the Sheriff said it wouldn't have made any difference."

"I know." She sighed. "Still and all, I feel

real bad about it. Anyway, he wasn't there long. I guess he just came by to get paid, because I saw him going up the street no more than ten minutes later on his bike. There was something long and skinny sticking out of his carrier. I couldn't see what, probably something of Ray's she'd given him."

Esther's words brought me to attention. Willy's bike! How could I have forgotten about that? He didn't have a car and he rode everywhere on it. He had scrounged parts off several discarded bicycles and built what he called his "Willy Bikemobile." The front tire was smaller than the back, so he could fit a deep carrier basket in front of the handlebars. He had attached a red plastic flag to a long pole on the back and there were reflectors bristling at all angles. "Don't want no cars crawling up my backside 'cause they can't see me," he had explained.

Where was Willy's bike? I'd have to call Gil and find out where he found it.

"Esther, I've got to get going," I said, taking her hand again. "Now promise me you'll take it easy."

She looked surprised at my sudden announcement. "Thank you, Jessie, for taking the time to visit. People don't appreciate how much I'm going to miss Margaret. Since Ray passed, we became real close. Why hardly a morning went by that we didn't sit at her kitchen table and have coffee." Esther groped for a tissue and I braced myself for a torrent and a prolonged stay. "You run along now," she said, surprising me. "I'll be fine. I've got Lester here to take care of me."

I had trouble concentrating on the road as I drove home, my mind was so full of questions. If Willy had come out to seek refuge in my barn the night of the storm, he would have ridden his bicycle. But where was it? He couldn't have taken it to Walnut Clearing, so that meant — I pounded my fist on the steering wheel — that meant what? Gil hadn't said anything about finding the bike along the road. I had to find out where the bicycle was hidden. And what was Harry Williamson doing at Margaret's house? Helping her with the estate or her finances? But Esther was right. Why weren't they meeting at the bank, or with the lawyer? Surely Harry and Margaret weren't having an affair! I appreciated Lester and Esther's nice words about Willy. Maybe they had offered to pay for his funeral. I should have asked.

Deep in thought, I almost tripped over

the basket that was sitting on the doorstep. "Oh great," I muttered as I looked down at a mound of ripe red tomatoes. Frank must have brought them. I could never figure out why the family thought they were doing me a favor by donating excess produce. I knew they meant well, but what was I going to do with another basket of tomatoes?

I nudged the basket aside with my foot and unlocked the door. I could hear Genevieve meowing. "What in the world are you doing in here? I thought I left you outside," I said, as she wrapped herself around my ankles. "What did you do, sneak in when I came back for the coffeecake?"

Grabbing the basket of tomatoes, I put them on the kitchen table. I should call Frank and thank him, but first I needed to get in touch with Gil.

Virginia answered the telephone on the first ring, even though I had dialed the non-emergency number.

"Virginia," I said, "this is Jessie Schroeder. Is the Sheriff in?"

"Nope. He's out at Roscoe's. The old man is raising a ruckus again. Poor old guy. He can't keep it together anymore. Then the Sheriff has to go over to Springfield. I'm afraid he won't be back till late. You want me to beep him?"

I swallowed my disappointment and tried to keep my voice as noncommittal as possible. "No, that's all right. Please ask him to call me when he gets in."

"Will do," she said. "Say, I hear you two had a fine time on the river yesterday."

Great, I thought, *the whole town knows we spent the day together.* "It was lovely," I said. "It's been years since I had a boat ride and I really enjoyed it."

"Nothing like a hot August day on the river," she said. "I'll make sure he gets the message."

"Thanks," I said and hung up before she could make any more comments about the river.

I lifted the receiver again and dialed Mildred and Frank's. A quick thank-you for the tomatoes and then I had to get to work.

"Hi, Mildred, it's Jessie," I said. "I found the tomatoes. Tell Frank thanks for dropping them off."

"What tomatoes?" she said.

"The basket I found on the stoop."

"Weren't from us, though I've got plenty if you need some," Mildred said. "I had the impression you didn't want any more."

"No, no, that's fine. Maybe they're from Henrietta. I'll give her a call. Talk to you later."

I hung up and stared at the tomatoes, ignoring Genevieve who was stalking back and forth in front of her food bowl. I doubted they were from Henrietta. She never brought anything by without calling first. Henrietta would have considered the delivery a social call, so she wouldn't have bothered if I wasn't home. So, who had dumped a load of tomatoes on my doorstep?

I looked at the clock. Almost two. Otis Joseph was due at three to look at the work I needed done in the garden, but before I changed into my work clothes, I'd heat up a cup of coffee.

Staring blankly out the window, I sipped my coffee as I reviewed my visit with Esther. Then it hit me. Her parting words about missing Margaret. They drank coffee together. The murderer had a cup of coffee with Margaret before he killed her. *Willy did not drink coffee!* In fact, he wouldn't drink anything with caffeine in it, not even soda. How could I have been so stupid not to remember that? He claimed the only stimulant he needed was the Good Book. Willy wasn't the person in the kitchen with Margaret. Now Gil would have to believe me. Should I should call Virginia back and have her beep him?

Before I could make a decision, the telephone rang. Hoping it was Gil, I jumped up, dumping Genevieve off my lap.

A hello boomed in my ear. I'd never heard the voice before, but I had no doubt who it was, even before he identified himself.

"Miss Schroeder, I hope I haven't caught you at a bad time. Hap Emerson here."

"Yes, Mr. Emerson," I said. "I found your note the other day."

"Sorry I missed you, and that's why I'm calling. I said I'd stop by this afternoon, but I got hung up in Springfield. Won't make it over to Riverport until tomorrow. Okay if I stop by then? About ten?"

"That will be fine," I said. "I'm looking forward to meeting you. I've read so much about you."

"Appreciate it," he said. "See you at ten."

I found it interesting that he hadn't told me what the visit was about, nor did he find it strange that I hadn't inquired. *Ah, the ego,* I thought. Some people just assumed the offer of their presence was enough to justify a call.

Still, I couldn't help smiling. Finally something solid to give Gil. He couldn't ignore Willy's innocence any longer. And a visit with Hap Emerson. Maybe now I would get some answers and some action.

I glanced over at the dining room table as

I walked by. The papers I had put in careful stacks were slightly askew. *Damn cat,* I thought, as I shuffled them back the way I'd had them before.

I decided to get a head start on the garden while I waited for Otis. The ground ivy was invading my impatiens patch, so I would start there. Weeding out ground ivy was immensely satisfying. The roots were shallow and it was possible to grab the end of a runner and pop it loose from the dirt, section by section, all the way back to the source. That's what I needed to do with Margaret's murder — keep going through it section by section, until I get to the source. That was how *Emily Says* would approach the problem. And I'd be willing to bet that Hap Emerson was a major player.

Otis's truck came roaring up the drive promptly at three. From the sounds of it, I could understand why he needed a new one, but, according to Viola, that wasn't to be since he'd lost his thousand dollars.

"Sounds like you've got a muffler problem," I said, as I walked out to meet him.

Otis grinned. "That ain't the only problem I got, but at least no one can accuse me of sneaking up on them. How are you, Jessie?"

"I'm fine. Had a nice visit with Viola the other day. You sure do have a lovely family."

He shook his head. "We took them over to the mall in Springfield last week to get their school clothes. Just keeping them in shoes is a real stretch. Now then, Viola said you needed some work done."

I nodded.

"Isn't this pretty," Otis said, as we rounded the corner and he saw the garden. "I've never done much work with flowers. Sure you trust me with them? This is like something out of a picture magazine. I would hate it if I did something to ruin it."

"You needn't worry," I said. "Anyone who raises the beautiful vegetables you do won't have a problem. Besides, if Willy Bachmann can learn, anybody can. He didn't know a thistle from a petunia when he started." I stopped walking and looked around. "He was so proud of the garden."

A wave of sadness washed over me. "Hard to believe a little more than a week ago, he and Margaret were both alive. Two good people. Doesn't seem right, does it?" I looked at Otis.

"No ma'am, it doesn't," he said. "How many hours you figure you're going to need me?"

Otis had come to work, not chat. I would have to figure out an excuse to talk to Viola again.

After Otis left, I took a quick shower and fixed myself a sandwich. Then I forced myself to go into the dining room and work through the papers again. I wanted to make sure I had the right questions when Hap Emerson came calling in the morning.

Genevieve tried to insinuate herself between me and my work. "Were you climbing on the table while I was gone?" I asked, and firmly removed her from the tabletop.

Finally by nine o'clock I was satisfied that I understood as much as I could about the Industrial Development Authority. I would have to find someone to explain the nuances to me. I didn't think Emerson was the one who'd do that.

I put everything in order and warned Genevieve to stay away. Not that it would do any good, but it made me feel better. I had decided to reward myself with a gin and tonic, but as soon as I walked into the kitchen the phone rang.

Thank, God, it's finally Gil, I thought. *Do I have an earful for him!*

"Hello," I said in as light a tone as I could muster.

I could tell the line was open, but no one answered my greeting.

"Hello, hello, who's there?"

"Listen to me, bitch, and listen carefully,"

a muffled voice hissed in my ear. "Quit playing your detective games or you'll end up in a pine box like Margaret Benson. We'll be watching you."

"Who is this?" I could hear my voice tremble. "What do you want?"

The only answer was a dial tone.

CHAPTER 15

Feeling numb, I stared at the telephone. The voice had been muffled. I couldn't tell if it was a man or a woman. Then I remembered the call to Fowler's Funeral Home. The voice had been described the same way.

I didn't know whether to be frightened or angry, but one thing I did know. I never could abide people who hide behind a mask of anonymity. Why didn't Gil call? The threatening phone call would make him stand up and take notice. Maybe he hadn't taken me seriously, but someone else had.

The phone rang. As I reached for the receiver, I felt a twinge. What if it was my mysterious caller again? "Jessie Schroeder," I said in as businesslike a voice as I could muster.

"My, aren't we being formal tonight?" Gil said. "Sorry to be so late in calling. The hot weather has brought out all the Spencer County crazies. I just got back to the office and found your message. What's up?"

I took a deep breath. First, I needed to find out about Willy's bicycle. Then I would share with him my theory about the coffee cup. I'd wait and tell him about the phone call last.

"Willy's bicycle," I said. "Where's Willy's bike?"

"I guess it's over at Abundant Life. Where else would it be?"

Willy had had a room at the Abundant Life Church that the minister gave him in exchange for the caretaking work he did on the grounds. Reverend Wilson said it was the best exchange he'd ever made, and he was right. Willy had kept the churchyard spic and span.

"Am I correct in assuming that you didn't find it along the road when you recovered his body?" I asked.

There was a long pause. Then Gil said, "That's correct."

I could almost hear the wheels turning in his head. "How did he get to Walnut Clearing? I doubt he would have walked. Did you check his room?" Gil was silent, so I said, "Gil, are you there?"

"Yeah, I'm here," he said, and nothing more.

"Look at it logically," I said. "If Willy came

out to my place, whether it was to hide or collect something he had hidden in Walnut Clearing, or both, he would have ridden his bike. Right?"

"Probably," Gil said.

"He would have left his bike by the road while he went over to the clearing. Then, if the storm came up, he probably left it while he took cover in the barn. We know he was in the barn because we found the scrap of paper. Then he left. If he had tried to re-cross McGee Creek, he would have had to leave his bike, and you, or someone else, would have found it. What did you find in his room? Was his bike there?"

"Wait a minute. I'll be right back."

I could hear a file drawer open and close, then a shuffling of papers.

"Clarence made an inventory," he said. "Here it is. One bicycle with padlock and chain, secured to a heating pipe by the door."

"And a set of construction plans?" I held my breath.

"No," Gil said. "That I'm sure of because I rechecked the list after you showed me what you had found in the barn and at Walnut Clearing."

"What else did you find?"

"You don't want to know."

"Yes, I do."

"Well, the place was a mess, and we found three empty pint bottles of Jim Beam. The whole room reeked of booze. I figured he tried to drown his guilt in alcohol. In that condition, he very well could have struck out on foot."

A wave of nausea swept over me. I fought to stay calm.

"Are you okay, Jessie?" Gil asked.

I swallowed several times before I answered. "I'm fine." My mind raced back over what Gil had just told me. I couldn't believe Willy would go back to the bottle. But then Gil had no reason to lie about what he and Clarence had found in the room.

"It must have been a setup," I said.

"What the hell are you talking about? A setup? The door was locked when we got there."

"That doesn't prove a thing. Did you check the bottles for fingerprints?"

"Did I what?" Gil voice began to rise. "No, I didn't check the bottles for prints. I told you the room was locked when we got there, and the man had a history of alcohol abuse. Quit grasping at straws, Jessie. I admit the question about the bicycle is an interesting one, but I don't think it has any

254

significance. He could have been too drunk to ride."

"Something is very wrong," I said. "Someone wanted to make it look like he'd been drinking."

"My God, Jessie, will you listen to what you're saying?" Gil shouted. "It was no setup. Willy Bachmann fell off the wagon because he was filled with remorse, or guilt, or both. He drank until he was drunk, then drowned. How he got to McGee Creek has no relevance."

I took a deep breath. "Yes, it does. And there's another thing that has been completely overlooked. The coffee cup in Margaret's kitchen. I assume you *did* check it for fingerprints."

"Yes, I checked it for prints."

I heard sarcasm that I'd never heard from him before.

"Margaret's were on one cup," he said, "and the other was clean. I also checked the wrench. It had been wiped clean. Do you have any other advice for me?"

I felt my throat begin to tighten. This was not the time to lose my temper, even though Gil seemed to think me a recalcitrant teenager.

"Let me tell you another thing I find interesting," I said. "The murderer seems to have had a cup of coffee with Margaret and everybody, including you, assumes that person was Willy. You're wrong. Anyone who knew Willy knew he never drank coffee or anything with caffeine in it for, not even soda. What do you say to that?" Try as I might, I couldn't resist a little sarcasm of my own. "For some reason, you seem bound and determined to ignore or make light of everything I suggest."

"Dammit, Jessie, that's not true. But I'm a cop. I have to go by the evidence. If it weren't that I'm so damned fond of you, and respect your intelligence, I probably wouldn't even listen to your theories. However, up to this point they haven't produced one bit of evidence to prove Willy is innocent."

I didn't know whether to scream or cry.

"Let's not argue, please," Gil said. "Certain facts don't add up in this case, that I grant you, but nothing suggests that someone other than Willy was involved."

"Well," I said, "someone out there seems to be taking me seriously. Seriously enough to threaten me."

"Somebody what?" His voice was sharp. "What are you talking about?"

"Just before you called, I received another call. The person said if I didn't mind my own business, I was going to end up in a pine box like Margaret Benson."

"Are you sure that's what was said?"

"Of course, I'm sure. I would hardly make something like this up."

"I'm not suggesting you made it up," Gil said, "but you've drawn a lot of attention to yourself with your statements on television and your interrogation of half the people in town. Even the Mayor stopped me the other morning and asked what you were up to. He thought maybe you were planning to write an exposé on life in a small town."

I should have been angry at his words, but they made me sad. "The voice was muffled," I said. "I couldn't tell if it was a man or a woman, but the message was quite clear . . ." I paused. "It could have been the same person who called Fowler's Funeral Home the other day."

"What person are you talking about? You didn't tell me about that."

"I didn't tell you because I didn't think it was important," I said, and repeated my conversation with Patricia Fowler, as best I could remember. "You need to talk to Patricia, Gil."

"I'll do that, Jessie. Why don't you call Frank and see if you can spend the night?"

"No, I'm not going to run over to Frank's

house. I'll be fine here."

"Somehow, I knew that's what you'd say. I can't come out myself, even though I wish I could. So I'll have the night patrol make several extra swings past your house. Don't be alarmed if you hear a car pull into your drive, and please make sure you're locked up tight . . ." He paused. "You did remove that key from behind your drainpipe, didn't you?"

After we made our goodbyes, I fixed a drink, walked outside, and got my spare key from behind the drainpipe. Then I sat down at the table. As I stared into the darkness, Genevieve crawled into my lap. My fingers gently scratched under her ears, and I slowed my mind to match the calm cadence of her purrs.

I spent a restless night, punctuated by dreams of faceless people chasing me on bicycles and flinging Jim Beam bottles at me. Finally, dawn arrived and I could leave my bed. The eastern sky was streaked with color and the bobwhites were winding down their chorus. *It's amazing,* I thought, *how dawn washes away the nighttime demons.*

I made my coffee and carried it out to the garden. The day was going to be hot, but for now a gentle breeze rustled the leaves. It would still be cool enough at ten a.m. to sit in the garden. For some reason I didn't want Hap Emerson in my house.

I had been aware of the extra circles the police patrol had made past my house during the night. Evidently, Gil took the threatening phone call seriously.

As I had suspected, Hap Emerson drove his big white Cadillac up my lane at the stroke of ten. I walked out to meet him. He came striding up the walkway toward me, his hand outstretched, as if it were attached to a line I reeled in.

"Hap Emerson," he said, grasping my hand. "Good to meet you. Saw you on the television last week. Got to say the camera didn't do you justice."

I was immediately aware of two things. First, Hap was larger but not as good-looking up close as he was at a distance, and second, he made me feel uneasy. There was something slightly off-kilter about his appearance. The right elements were there, but it was as if the assembling had been done in a hurry. His smile was too big, his teeth too white, and his handshake too hearty.

"Mr. Emerson," I said.

"Hap, call me Hap," he said, and punctuated it with a laugh. "It's a real honor to meet you, Jess. You're a celebrity. Fact is, my niece is a big *Emily Says* fan. When I told her I was going to meet you, she wanted to come along."

I managed to extricate my hand, but not before I noted that his was as cool and smooth as the skin of a nectarine. This man definitely lived by his wits and not his hands.

"Thanks for your kind words," I said. "It's good to meet you, too. You've caused a lot of excitement around here." My voice sounded thin to my ears, but I was determined to put on as hearty a front as he. "Why don't you go around to the terrace, Mr. Emerson, and have a seat? I'll bring us some iced tea."

"Aw, now, I thought it was going to be Hap. Every time you say Mr. Emerson, I look over my shoulder, expecting to see my dad."

"Hap it is," I said, with as broad a grin as I could muster.

"No need to go to any trouble on my account," he called after me.

"No trouble. Just go around back and I'll be out in a jiffy." I grimaced even as I spoke. Jiffy? I sounded as inane as he did.

Quickly filling two glasses with ice, I poured the tea and set the glasses on a tray with the sugar bowl and a saucer of lemon slices.

"Beautiful garden you have here," Hap said, leaping to his feet as I came around the corner of the house.

"Thank you," I said, setting the tray on the table. "There's lemon and sugar, if you want."

He spooned sugar into his glass and stirred rapidly, the spoon clanking against the side of the glass. He had used too much for it to go into solution and a thick white layer settled on the bottom. All his actions seemed exaggerated, and I wondered if it was a technique he had developed to keep attention on himself.

"Ah, this really hits the spot," he said, smacking his lips. "Is this sun tea? My wife makes sun tea. Claims it's the only way."

"I tried sun tea, but never seemed to get it right. I kept forgetting it, so it would brew too long and get cloudy. I'm afraid that method is for someone more organized than I am. Didn't I see you at Margaret Benson's funeral?" I asked, deciding it was time to move on. We had pretty well exhausted the subject of tea.

I watched as he carefully set his tea glass down and rearranged his face into an expression that would have made a mortician proud.

"Terrible affair," he said. "And such a lovely lady. Can't imagine anyone doing such an awful thing. I had the pleasure of working with her for awhile on the IDA." He shook his head. "She will be sorely missed. Quiet but incisive, that was Margaret."

I tried not to stare at him. No one would say Margaret wasn't a quiet woman, but incisive? Even Willy had remarked that Margaret had problems making up her mind. And that was from a man whose decision-making process consisted mainly of waiting until someone else told him what to do.

"Sheriff seems pretty well satisfied he found his man," Emerson said. "Too bad the man ended up getting himself killed, too."

I chose not to reply. I suspected that Hap Emerson was a man who could not abide silence and that he would keep talking until I interrupted him.

He hesitated a moment, then continued. "I have to tell you I was surprised to hear that you think he didn't do it. Everybody else I've talked to is certain that what's his name, Willy something, killed her." Emerson smiled. "You must know something nobody else does."

I shook my head. "No, Hap. I knew the man."

His smile broadened, but it was confined to the lower half of his face. "Well, who am I to judge? I never met him."

"Another glass of tea?" I reached for his glass.

"No, no, I've already imposed on your hospitality too much. The tea was delicious, but let me tell you why I stopped by." He settled back in his chair and crossed his legs. "As you know, I'm working with the Riverport Council to put together an economic development strategy for the town. Mayor Ellwood tells me you're showing a real interest in our little project. Can't tell you how glad I was to hear that. We need as many prominent people in the community behind us as possible."

The Mayor had not even been aware of my existence until four days ago and now I was an interested party? "I'm afraid I know very little about the project," I said, "except what I read in the newspaper. I have to confess to a real ignorance to the particulars." I smiled at him, thinking two could play his game. "In fact, until last week I had never heard of an IDA. If I'd had to guess, I'd probably have said it was some kind of medical test."

My feigned naiveté threw him off stride for a minute. I could almost see him mentally rearranging his approach.

"I'd love it if you would explain some of the details to me," I continued. "I'm sure the Mayor told you I've recently decided to make my permanent home in Riverport. I think it's important to know as much about one's community as one possibly can. Don't you agree?"

He nodded vigorously. "Couldn't agree more. Wish more people had your attitude."

I'll bet you do, I thought.

"I won't bore you with too many dry facts." He leaned forward and rubbed his hands together. "For the past twelve months I've been eating, drinking, and sleeping Riverport. I don't mean to sound braggadocio, but I probably know more about Riverport and Spencer County than most of the folks who have lived here their whole lives, and I think there's a lot of potential here."

He put his hands flat on the table and leaned forward, his voice confidential. "I'm talking outstanding potential. I'm talking development that will make this area an economic powerhouse in western Illinois."

"My, my," I said, trying to appear impressed. "That sounds awfully ambitious.

But if something doesn't happen, the town is going to die. Ever since the town fathers let the government build the Interstate so far south, it seems the life is oozing out of Riverport."

Hap gave me a curious look. "What do you know about the Interstate?"

"Not a whole lot, but my dad was the Road Commissioner for Spencer County when the Interstate was being planned. I can remember him ranting and raving about the location. But now, tell me about this IDA."

Hap chuckled. "I have to warn you, Jess, when I get started talking about my work, I tend to get a little carried away, so stop me anytime you want. Now then, IDA stands for Industrial Development Authority."

I understood the broad outlines of the Authority from my reading, but I wanted him to think I was a complete innocent.

"Well, let's see. Where to begin?" He gave me a smile much like a parent would give an over-inquisitive child. "The IDA is a not-for-profit corporation authorized by the state to assist cities and counties with economic development. It's mostly the big cities that have them, but to my way of thinking, and the Mayor agreed with me, it was tailor-made for the needs of Riverport."

I nodded.

"The question, in the beginning, was whether the Authority should be county-wide or restricted to Riverport. I think you will agree with me, Jess, knowing, as I'm sure you do, the members of the Spencer County Board of Supervisors, that the project would never have gotten off the ground with them in charge. The Mayor agreed, so we proceeded with the Riverport Industrial Development Authority."

I didn't know all the County Supervisors, but the ones I did know had been in office a long time and were a rather stodgy lot, very conservative. Just the types you wanted looking after your tax dollars.

Hap said, "I won't bother you with all the legalese, but last fall the IDA's application for incorporation was approved by the Council. The Mayor appointed the members, and the proper papers were drawn up for the Secretary of State." He leaned back and smiled, evidently thinking he was through with his explanation.

"Fascinating," I said. "Are you a member of the Authority?" I asked, knowing full well the state statutes prohibited voting membership to anyone who had not been a taxpayer in the community for five years.

"I guess you would say I'm an ex officio

member. I can't vote, but the Mayor asked me to handle the day-to-day business, much like a secretary, since I have experience in other cities."

"Makes sense," I said. "Riverport is fortunate to have your expertise to draw on."

Hap smiled broadly at the praise. I wondered how much he was being paid for that expertise. The state law allowed the Authority to hire outside personnel. None of the newspaper articles had mentioned a salary, but I was quite sure he wasn't working for minimum wage.

"But tell me, just exactly what can the IDA do?" I asked.

"About anything," he said. "The Authority can buy, sell, lease, and rent property. The Board can issue revenue bonds and make loans as long as the transaction promotes commercial and industrial development."

I shook my head. "Amazing, but I don't understand where they get the money to do all this."

He seemed tired of answering questions, but he forged on. "They're like any business," he said, his voice somewhat strained. "They generate their own money from their transactions, including fees from the revenue bonds."

"But isn't that after the fact, Hap? Any business has to have start-up funds. Where did that money come from?"

He gave me a look I couldn't quite decipher, and I decided I'd better tread more carefully.

"Sorry, guess I jumped ahead too fast," he said. "Since they're a not-for-profit, they can receive grants and gifts. The City Council provided the start-up money in the form of a grant, and they gave the land for the Industrial Park to the IDA."

That's more like it, I thought, and smiled. "I guess that gives the Council the right to monitor what the IDA does, kind of like a stockholder in a company."

Hap frowned as he considered my remark. I was pretty sure the Authority didn't have to answer to anyone but the state, so I was interested in how he was going to make the lack of oversight as palatable as possible.

"Well, not exactly," he said. "Of course, the IDA Board is always open to advice and suggestions, but they do function under state statutes and not city laws. Those statutes are quite specific and the state keeps close watch on each and every IDA. And they keep the Council fully informed, of course," he added hastily.

"In other words, the Council has no

control over the Authority?"

Hap nodded.

"Isn't that interesting," I said. "I wonder how carefully that was explained, and how many people in Riverport understand that?"

I was aware of the threat implied by that simple question, and I was pleased to see Hap squirm ever so slightly in his chair. *Let him squirm,* I thought, and abruptly changed the subject. "Forgive me," I said. "I've been monopolizing the conversation. I'm sure you had a specific reason for asking to see me."

"No problem," Hap said, and I had to admire the way he shifted gears. "I enjoy talking with someone like you, someone who's interested in her community. But I do have to confess, nice as the conversation has been, that I did have a specific reason for asking to see you. I'll be as brief as possible."

I settled back in my chair and waited.

"As a developer," he said, "I think this part of the state is grossly underutilized and is just waiting to be discovered. I am not talking only from a commercial point of view, but also from a recreational point of view — access to the river, beautiful streams, woods, rolling hills. As someone who has been out in the bigger world, I'm sure you can appreciate what I'm saying."

I nodded. What he said was true, but I couldn't figure out where he was going with it.

"In the course of my survey of Riverport and the adjoining property in the county," he continued, "I stumbled across that land you own on the other side of the road. You know, the piece that abuts the old road."

I felt myself stiffen, but managed a non-committal nod.

"To make a long story short," he said, "I have a long-time client who has been looking for a piece of land in this part of the state to build a weekend hideaway. I can't tell you his name because I'm sworn to confidentiality, but believe me, you'd recognize it in a minute. But I don't mind telling you he can afford to pay top dollar."

"I'm afraid you've caught me by surprise," I said. *Now that's a gross understatement,* I thought.

Hap held up his hand. "I'm not asking for a decision right now, Jess. Your cousin told me you probably don't want to sell, that the land has sentimental value, and I respect that. But I told him that there's no harm in talking to you, and believe me, when I say top dollar, I mean top dollar."

When had he talked to Frank about my

land and why hadn't Frank told me? Saturday, Frank had made it sound as if he'd had that one meeting with Hap Emerson. Was Frank trying to hide something, or was I getting paranoid?

"Tell me, Hap, why did you go to my cousin instead of coming directly to me?"

The look Hap gave me indicated that he was fully aware he had made a major error.

"When I asked in town," he said, "they told me Frank took care of your business affairs. I should have known better. You definitely impress me as a woman who doesn't rely on anyone else to make her decisions for her."

"An honest mistake," I said, trying to reestablish his comfort level. "Frank farms my tillable land on a share basis with me. I'm sure there are some people who assume he takes care of all the business. To get back to your offer, you're not the first person to approach me about selling that land, and I've always turned down the offers, like my dad did before me, even though several offers have been quite handsome."

I allowed myself a small sigh. "That land has been in the family for more than one-hundred-and-seventy years. My great, great grandfather settled there in eighteen thirty-three, when the family moved from Pennsylvania."

Hap was hanging on my every word. His gaze never left my face.

"Recently, I've been toying with the idea of deeding it to the county to be used as a park," I continued. "The old road could be refurbished for access. It can't be farmed and it really isn't any good for grazing, but it is beautiful. Seems a shame all the people can't enjoy it."

Hap's Adam's apple bobbed when I mentioned deeding it to the county.

"May I ask how you found out about the land, Hap? You're not from these parts."

I did not believe for a second that he'd accidentally stumbled across it during his county survey. Only those who knew the area well were aware of its existence.

Hap looked startled at the question. "Well, uh, let's see, it must have been Ray Benson. Yes, I'm sure it was Ray. I'd been talking about this client and he said he knew the perfect spot. And I must say, it's a real Garden of Eden."

"I take it, then, you've walked the land." I tried without much success to keep the ice out of my voice.

"Ray said it was okay, so I assumed he checked it out." Hap looked at me. "Looks like I assumed something else I shouldn't have."

"Did Ray Benson do much work for you?"

"Ray? Well, that's kind of hard to answer. He helped in the beginning, but he was a bit of a hot dog. Did you know him?"

I shook my head. "Not really. Just by reputation."

"Real shock when he keeled over and died last Christmas," Hap said. "Now I better get out of your hair. I've taken up too much of your time. Like I said, I'm not looking for a quick decision on the land, but I would like you to think about it. I am confident I can put together a deal you will be happy with."

"I'll think about it," I said. "But I have to be honest. I wouldn't hold out too much hope that I'll decide to sell."

"Fair enough." Hap got to his feet. "Just think about it. That's all I'm asking. Here's my card. Call me anytime. It's been a real pleasure talking to you."

I walked around the corner of the house with him and made as cordial a goodbye as I could muster. Talking with Hap Emerson made me feel like I was back in the advertising business. A person had to dig deep to find the substance. I watched as he drove up to the turn-around at the top of the lane and lifted a hand as he came back by. A big cigar was clutched between his fingers as he waved goodbye.

CHAPTER 16

Hap Emerson — what an operator! I watched his Caddy sashay out of my lane, the interior rapidly filling with cigar smoke. That cleared up one mystery: the cigar butt in Walnut Clearing.

As I stood at the sink and rinsed out the glasses and loaded them into the dishwasher, I sorted through the conversation. He had answered all of my questions, I couldn't complain about that, but the answers had been brief. I hadn't learned much new. I would love to have probed further, but that would have been a mistake. I needed to maintain at least a semblance of interested observer, rather than interrogator. I did find one thing curious about Emerson's visit. Why had he waited so long to approach me about my land when he'd looked at it last fall?

Something he had said nudged at the back of my mind, but I couldn't bring it into focus. It wasn't about the purchase of my land, that I was sure of. Something had come up earlier in the conversation, but I knew not to force it. *Patience, Jessie,* I cautioned. *It will come unbidden at some later time.*

It was too hot to go back out into the garden. Working at the computer was out, too. I knew I'd do nothing but watch it cycle in and out of its screen-saver mode. The sunburnt ghost had to wait. Instead, I walked into the dining room and, with little enthusiasm, sat down at the table and shuffled through the stacks of papers.

I decided not to reread Herb's florid prose in the *Spencer County Argus.* As I sat contemplating what course of action to follow, Hap's words came rushing back at me: "The IDA's application for incorporation was approved by the Council. The Mayor appointed the members, and the proper papers were drawn up for the Secretary of State."

That was it! The statement that had nagged at me.

I quickly dug out Flora's photocopy of the state statutes covering Industrial Development Authorities and skimmed through it. There it was: "Article 527.035 . . . the articles of incorporation shall be filed with the Secretary of State . . . he shall approve the articles of incorporation, issue a certificate of incorporation, and record the same in an appropriate book of record in his office."

Emerson had said the papers had been drawn up, but had they been filed? And if filed, had they been approved and recorded? Surely they had been, but he hadn't specifically said so.

Why hadn't I reviewed the statutes more carefully before talking to Hap? "Typical, Jessie," I muttered. "Always in a hurry." Well I hadn't, so how was I going to find out? I didn't want to go back to the Mayor's office and ask my questions. I'd stirred up enough hornets. And then in a flash, I knew how to get my answer. Just like Emily. I would get my information from a "good authority." Jim Axelrod!

Four years ago Jim had sat across from me at our twentieth high school reunion. I wasn't quite sure why I had decided to attend and, of course, Alec hadn't come with me. Nor could I remember, now, why I chose to visit with Jim. He had been a lurker all through school, living vicariously on the antics of others. Maybe I had been trying to atone for my dismissal of his existence in those long-ago years.

I had asked him about his job, and he had described — in excruciating detail — the inner workings of the Secretary of State's office where he had worked for sixteen years as an administrative assistant.

I looked at my watch. Almost one-thirty. Lunchtime would probably be over. It had been four years since my conversation with Jim. Maybe he didn't work there anymore. On the other hand, Jim Axelrod was not the type to make a career change. It was August. He might be on vacation. Only one way to find out.

Springfield information had twelve different numbers listed for the Secretary of State's office, but none of the categories the operator rattled off rang a bell. "Just give me the general number," I said. If Jim had been there for sixteen years, surely someone could track him down.

"This is the Secretary of State's office. May I help you?" The woman's voice at the other end sounded flat and bored, and I suspected that help was the last thing she wanted to give.

"I'm trying to locate Jim Axelrod. Could you give me his office number or transfer me, please?" I hoped my voice sounded brisk and efficient.

"Jim Axelrod?"

"Yes," I said. "Administrative Assistant James Axelrod."

"Could you spell that, please?"

I tried to keep the irritation out of my voice and stifled the urge to find out which she needed spelled, his name or "administrative assistant," and laboriously went through his name letter by letter.

All I got for an answer was a huff and a series of clicks. Finally, a ring. *Please let him be in.*

"You have reached James Axelrod's office. Mr. Axelrod speaking."

"Jim, this is Jessie Schroeder from Riverport."

"My, my, my," he said. "Jessie Schroeder. A voice from the past. How are you?"

"Fine, Jim. And yourself?" I longed to ask my questions, but knew certain formalities had to be followed.

"Some days good, some days not so good, but I can't complain . . ." He paused. "Say, what's it like living in murder city? I saw you on TV last week. I must admit, I had to chuckle. Good ole Jessie, I told my wife, still not satisfied to leave well enough alone. What's going on there, anyway?"

Good ole Jessie. He made me sound like some kind of eccentric, but I shrugged it off, forced what I hoped was a convincing sigh, and said, "It's been ghastly. Lots of theories, but I don't know if we'll ever get the right answer."

"That lady who was killed. I assume that was Ray Benson's wife."

"Yes," I said. "Nice lady, even though she married a real reprobate."

"You know what was really strange?" Jim said. "I probably hadn't seen Ray for five years, then a couple of weeks before he died, he showed up in my office. Looked healthy as a horse, so I was shocked when I heard he was dead. Of course, they say those aneurysms are like time bombs. Never know when they're going to go off."

I wondered if I dared ask Jim why Ray had been in his office. Hell, why not? Especially since Jim seemed to be in a chatty mood.

"What was he trying to do?" I asked. "Sell you a waterfront lot in Florida?"

Jim laughed. "There you go again, always the snappy comeback. Actually, he just came by to say hello. Said he'd picked up some plans from a buddy of his in the Highway Department and had a little time to kill. The Highway Department is right across the street from my office."

I doubted many people randomly stopped in to say hello to Jim. Ray Benson probably had a reason. I decided to let it go for now, but what plans had he picked up from the Highway Department?

"So tell me," Jim said, "how do you like being back in Riverport? I was sure surprised to hear you'd moved back. I thought after our conversation at the reunion that you were a confirmed city girl."

"It's taken some getting used to," I said. "But I don't miss the old rat race."

"Yeah, I sure understand that. Springfield's not nearly as big as St. Louie, but there are some days I miss the old hometown. The wife and I are thinking of moving to Riverport after I retire. There's something to be said for going back to your roots."

"Can't argue with that," I said. "But I'll have to say things seem to be jumping around here."

"Riverport jumping?" Jim laughed. "I guess that's one way to describe murder."

"That's not what I meant. I'm talking about the new Mayor. He seems to be a real go-getter. I hear he's even put together an Industrial Development Authority for the town. Not that I really understand what it's all about, but it sounds pretty grand."

"Some go-getter! I sent him the application form last September, and when the city returned it, it was incomplete, so I had to bump it back to them. That was a good six, eight months ago, and I'm still waiting. I admit I thought it was a pretty grandiose idea when the Mayor called me last summer, but heck, there's nothing in the statutes that prevents a town the size of Riverport from having an IDA. Fact is, I had forgotten about it until the Sheriff called this morning and asked about it."

Gil had called. Even though he'd gone out of his way to dismiss my questions about the IDA. I took a deep breath. "I'm confused," I said. "I thought they'd been meeting since last fall."

"Well, I'll tell you, just like I did Gil. They can meet all they want as long as they don't conduct any business. I don't mean to sound conceited or anything, but you're talking to the State's guy in charge of Industrial Development Authority incorporations."

Jim sounded slightly offended that I hadn't known. He probably told me all about IDAs in his long recitation at the reunion, and I'd probably stifled a yawn.

"If Riverport's IDA is up and operating, I'd know," he said. "I suspect the Mayor decided it wasn't worth the trouble."

I didn't quite know how to respond. Jim Axelrod was not the type of person to make an assertion he could not support, but the whole thing made no sense. Why would the Mayor ballyhoo the IDA if he wasn't going to follow through with it? And what was Hap Emerson's role in all this?

"Jim," I said, shifting gears, "have you ever heard of a developer named Hap Emerson? He's supposed to be based in Springfield."

There was a pause. Then Jim said, "Where'd you hear about him?"

Jim's words had taken on a measured cadence. "Mostly from newspaper articles," I said. "He was hired to do an economic development study for the town about a year ago. Today he showed up at my door with an offer to buy some of my property. I don't plan to sell to him, but I'm curious about his reputation."

"Let's just say I wouldn't want him dating my sister," Jim said.

"Is he really as much of a hot shot as the paper made him out to be?" I asked.

"Around town he's known as 'Hail Mary Hap.' If you go into business with him, you'd better start saying your Hail Marys. Yeah, he's a pretty slick operator and he's made a pile of money."

"Is he dishonest?"

"There are those who would say so." Jim spoke softly, as if he feared someone might overhear him. "But they're mostly people he's bested in business deals. Some people have sued him for false representation, but he hasn't lost in court yet. He's a smart cookie and he seems to know how close he can get to the line without stepping over it."

"What kind of development does he specialize in? Residential? Commercial? Industrial? The paper made it sound as if he was a master at everything."

"He's not really a developer," Jim said. "He's more what they call in the trade an assembler than a developer."

"You'll have to forgive my ignorance, Jim, but exactly what or who is an assembler?"

"I'll give you a generic explanation, Jessie. Mind you, I'd prefer that none of what I say be directly attributed to me."

"Of course."

"Fine." He cleared his throat. "An assembler is someone who often, but not always, learns about or receives information before the general public. Information about changing situations that could impact directly the development potential of a certain area."

"Could you give me an example?" I asked, wondering if what I had just heard was a prime example of bureaucratic double-speak.

"Let me see," he said, and I could hear his fingers drumming on his desktop. "Okay, suppose the Highway Department was planning to build a new interchange on the Interstate system. If a person found out the location before the intent to build became public information, and before construction money was appropriated, he'd be in a position to maximize the site's development potential."

"But what does that do for an assembler?"

"It's pretty simple. The assembler comes in and buys up, or more often gets options to buy, as much property as possible around the interchange location, usually for a minimal price. Minimum investment. Maximum return."

"In other words," I said, "he never builds anything. He just shuffles property, buying low and selling high."

"That's correct."

"But how does this assembler get hold of inside information? Sounds illegal to me. I'd think such plans would be kept under lock and key."

Jim laughed. "That's what the guidelines say, but a good assembler has friends in all the right places."

I remembered the big smile and hearty handshake that seemed to come so naturally to Hap Emerson. The slight underplaying of his own abilities. The feeling that he knew more than he was letting on. And the broad assurance that he would definitely make the sale of my property worth my while.

"Tell me this, Jim," I said. "Is Hap Emerson a good assembler?"

He hesitated so long, I was afraid he wasn't going to answer, but finally he said, "You didn't hear this from me, Jessie, and if you ever repeat it, I'll deny saying it. Do you understand?"

"Yes."

"Hap Emerson is one of the best, and he has friends in all the right places."

After Jim and I had said our goodbyes, with promises to keep in touch, I poured myself a cup of coffee and carried it over to the table. Genevieve immediately staked out her place on my lap. I stared out the window, not seeing anything, as I reviewed the conversation. To paraphrase Alice, it was getting curiouser and curiouser.

And what was Gil up to? He had effectively told me to quit asking questions about Margaret and Willy and the business dealings of the IDA, then he talked to Jim Axelrod about the IDA. Gil still maintained that Willy's death was an accident, but he ordered an autopsy.

I had forgotten to ask Gil about the autopsy!

"Poor Willy," I muttered. "What did you get yourself involved in and why didn't I pay attention to what you were trying to tell me?"

As I slowly scratched Genevieve's ears, I reviewed some of the things I knew. Margaret's house had been ransacked. Willy's room had been tossed, too. It didn't take a genius to figure out that someone was looking for something. The package Willy had carried away from Margaret's on Saturday was probably a set of construction plans. But where were they? Ray Benson had picked up a set of plans from the State Highway Department just weeks before he died. Were they the same plans, and what did they have to do with the deaths of two people? Where did Hap Emerson, the great assembler, fit in, and why did he want to buy my property? And why was I being threatened by somebody who obviously thought I knew more than I knew?

All the questions made my head ache. And Gil was being a major asshole. I couldn't think of a more genteel way to describe him. For all I knew, he was as big a con artist as Hap Emerson. I had more than a sneaking suspicion that Gil had played on my feelings for him to divert me from my inquiries.

What did I really know about Gil? He had been a high school hero and I had been totally star struck. Was that the problem? Was I still star struck? All I knew was that Gil owed me some straight answers. With that resolved, I stood up and walked over to the phone.

Chapter 17

"Sheriff's Office."

Virginia's slightly nasal voice grated in my ear. "This is Jessie Schroeder," I said, "and I need to speak to the Sheriff."

"Hi there, Jessie. I was just fixing to call you. Sheriff's not here, but he asked me to pass on a message to you. Hold on just a minute while I get it."

I could hear papers rustling in the background.

"His sister called him from Peoria about lunchtime," Virginia said. "They had to take his mom to the hospital real sudden. Sheriff took off like a bat out of hell, said he'd try to get back sometime tonight, but if he couldn't make it he'd give you a call. If it's an emergency, I can give you his sister's phone number."

"Just ask him to call me when he can. I hope his mom's all right."

"That's what we're all praying for," Virginia said. "Anyway, he said to tell you that Clarence is in charge and he has been apprised of the situation. He said to call Clarence if there were any problems. Let me give you Clarence's pager number. Have you got a piece of paper and pencil?"

I assured her I did and dutifully wrote down the numbers and repeated them back to her.

"Well, now, you take care," she said.

"I will, and thank you." I hung up, as frustrated as I had been before the phone call.

Now what? I'd go mad sitting around and fretting. The garden. I'd finish the weeding. Maybe if I sweated enough, I'd work some of the kinks out of my mind.

I renewed my attack on the ground ivy with an intensity that surprised even me. I ripped it out of the ground by greedy handfuls, knowing I'd have to make a second sweep to remove the bits and pieces I left behind. I was particularly anxious to get the impatiens bed cleared, because it was fast approaching hummingbird time. Every year in the waning days of summer they would pass through on their migration to Mexico and other points south, and stop to feed at the brilliant red flowers. If I hung up sugar water feeders, I could entice them to spend the entire summer with me, but I had an aversion to tampering with the natural order of things.

The thought of the ruby-throated miniatures kept me at my work. I remembered how enchanted I had been last summer, watching them dart from flower to flower, their wings moving so fast they looked like a gauze blur. Except for pictures in a bird book, I had never seen one at rest. I had followed one of the hummingbirds for ten minutes as he bounced from plant to plant, and I'd felt my own arms fatigue as I tried to imagine what it would be like never to take a rest. Then, suddenly, the bird had lifted off from the flowers and sped to the dogwood tree at the corner of my terrace. He'd landed on a branch — a tiny jewel of iridescent green and ruby gleaming in the leaves.

Bringing my attention back to the task at hand, I accumulated a huge pile of ground ivy and hauled it over to the compost heap. Willy had always refused to compost it. He insisted on burning it, even though I tried to convince him that the heat of the compost would destroy the ivy just as surely as a fire. "No," he'd say. "That's the Devil's ivy. Got to fight his fire with fire."

Devil's ivy. Willy had started calling it that

in June. I would correct him and he'd nod his head and say, "Yes, ma'am," and immediately turn around and call it Devil's ivy again. Finally one day, I had demanded an explanation, even though I knew his reasons would entail a long dissertation. Willy never indulged in idle chatter, but once a question had been broached, all restraints were off.

I rocked back on my heels. What did I really know about Willy? Not a whole lot. He had been the town drunk, benign but a bit of a pest from what I'd been told. No one knew exactly where he came from. He had drifted into town well before my return to Riverport. All I knew for sure was that he had taken the pledge, and that the smartest decision I'd made in years was to hire him. As Lester had said this morning, Willy wasn't the smartest man around, but he was steady and good, as long as he stayed off the booze.

Had something set him off again? I didn't think so.

My mind went back to the Devil's ivy conversation. It was typical Willy. Convoluted beyond description, but if a person hung in there long enough, it made sense.

I didn't have to close my eyes to remember the scene. Willy had made himself comfortable, leaning on the handle of the spade he had been using to tidy up the edging around the terrace.

"A couple of Sundays ago," he had said, "Reverend Fullerton at the Abundant Life was talking about the Devil and his ways. Now if there's anyone who should know about the Devil's ways, it surely would be me, but I figured it was a good idea for me to pay close attention because the Reverend with all his learning might just have heard about some tricks I hadn't got around to knowing. You know what they say, 'forewarned is forearmed.' "

At this point in the conversation, I was regretting my question.

"Well, the list the Reverend had was mostly the usual stuff like drinking and taking the Lord's name in vain and fornicating."

Willy had stopped abruptly and blushed bright red, but I had assured him that "fornication" was in the Bible.

"Well, anyway," Willy had continued, "the Reverend had a pretty good list and after he set it out for us, he commenced to tell us just how the Devil was able to make us do them tricks." Willy had reached down and pulled out a tiny sprig of ground ivy and waved it in front of my face. "See this?

Remember how last summer, when I first started working for you, I didn't know a weed from a flower and you were all the time having to watch me so I didn't pull out the good plants? Remember how I couldn't believe it when you told me that this here ivy, with its sweet little flowers, was bad, and how it had to be pulled or it would crowd out the flowers?"

I remembered perfectly. It was about the time I'd begun to think I'd made a mistake hiring Willy, because I was spending hours supervising him.

"I said I thought it was a sweet little plant and so pretty the way it crept along the ground and around the other plants. You got real mad at me and told me it wasn't a sweet little plant, it was a killer and it had to be pulled. I didn't believe you, but I figured I'd better do what you said or I'd get fired."

Willy shifted his weight on the shovel. "I'm kind of ashamed to tell you, but I left a patch growing back in the corner where the herbs were, just to show you I was right. Well, it smothered out the basil and that's why you had to replant it.

"The way that ivy grows is just how the Devil works. He takes something that looks little and innocent, and you think isn't that sweet, and the first thing you know it's grown out of control and wound all around your soul and smothered out the good works."

As I pondered that conversation, I looked out over the field that stretched behind the house. The alfalfa had been cut and baled, leaving tidy rows of stubble, and it occurred to me that something like the Devil's ivy had been at work in Riverport.

The sun was still pouring through the trees, but it couldn't thaw the chill I felt in my heart. Why hadn't I paid more attention to what was going on? When I thought back on it, I should have realized that something was troubling Willy the past few weeks, but I had been so absorbed in my own self that I had ignored him.

Willy had worked the Wednesday before the family reunion and the murder. We were dividing the iris bed. He'd asked if he could take the leftover rhizomes and plant them in Walnut Clearing.

"Won't that be pretty?" he had said. "Just think, a huge patch of purple flags. I think the spot just south of the cabin would be perfect, don't you?"

I had agreed and he had loaded the rootstock into a gunnysack. Now, I tried to think. Was there a freshly planted bed in the clearing? Surely I would have noticed, but my mind's eye couldn't see one. I had told him there was no great hurry. Maybe he had planned to plant the rhizomes later.

Something specific had been bothering Willy that Wednesday. Several times he had started to talk, then let his sentences dribble away to nothingness. Finally, I had said, "If you've got something to say, say it for Pete's sake, or quit your muttering."

Willy had ducked his head and apologized and worked silently for the rest of the afternoon. But right before he'd left for the day, he had tried again.

"I know you're a busy lady, but you're the only person I know who I can ask," he had said. "I could ask the Reverend, but he talks so long, by the time he finishes, I've forgotten what I asked him."

"It's all right, Willy," I had said. "Go ahead."

"Well, I've got this friend," he began.

Even though I had tried to listen, my mind had strayed toward what I was going to fix for dinner and what was on "Masterpiece Theater" that night.

Until Willy said, "I had to agree that the affairs of the dead are important and we ought to help finish up the things they didn't get done, but just 'cause someone's gone and died, if we didn't agree with what they was doing, it don't make it right now that he's dead. Do you think I'm right, Miz Jessie?"

Willy's sudden question had jolted me back into the conversation and I had tried to find a generic response that would satisfy him. "I'd say you're correct, Willy. Just because a person dies doesn't make what he or she was doing while he or she was alive any better or worse. It stays the same, and your friend should treat it the same. After all, two wrongs don't make a right."

"I just knew I was right." Willy had beamed. "I told my friend, she's got to be responsible for her own soul. We've got a duty to help the lambs that stray, but if they won't listen, if doing what they ask is wrong, even if it's a friend or a loved one, you gotta save yourself first."

God, why hadn't I listened to him? Now, I was convinced that his friend was Margaret. Why hadn't I probed a little bit? Even as I castigated myself, I doubted there was much of anything I could have done to avert the disaster. I suspected that forces were already in motion that could not be stopped.

Willy had been effusive in his thanks. "Thank you, Miz Jessie," he had said. "I know my friend will listen to me now, especially when I say you agree."

I brought my attention back to the garden. "Genevieve, will you stop that? You're worse than a little kid." Attacking the pile of ivy, the cat dragged pieces off to play with. "I guess I'd better move temptation out of your way," I said as I got to my feet.

It would take several wheelbarrow loads to move it all to the compost heap. "Maybe Willy was right," I muttered, as I loaded the weeds. "Maybe this is the Devil's ivy and should be burned."

I walked over to the toolshed to find some kerosene. The ivy was too green to burn without assistance. I felt I owed it to Willy to make sure every last sprig was destroyed. The toolshed was little more than a lean-to that had been built up against the side of the garage. I supposed there had been a reason for tacking it onto the garage, but it never had been explained to me. It was like a lot of things. Someone at one time had thought it was a good idea.

Frank had convinced me to put a padlock on the door after several of our neighbors had their outbuildings looted. Willy was forever forgetting the combination, so I had written it down on a piece of paper he kept in his billfold.

The kerosene can wasn't in its usual place,

in the corner. It sat in the middle of the dirt floor. And yet, Willy had been almost fanatical about order in the toolshed. Everything had a specific place. He would never leave until everything was clean and put away.

When I bent down to pick up the can, I saw why it had been moved. The gunnysack with the leftover iris rhizomes was jammed back in the corner in its place.

"Well, that answers the question about whether he got them planted," I muttered. "Might as well throw them away. I'm certainly not going to get to them."

The sack was heavy and when I tried to drag it out of the shed, it tipped over, spilling iris roots and dirt all over the floor.

"Dammit, Willy! Why didn't you fasten the top?"

Grabbing the top of the sack, I leaned it back against the wall, and saw more than iris clumps inside. The sacking sagged down, and sticking out of the top was something that looked like a fat broomstick. I pulled it out and carried it toward the door.

Before I made it that far, I knew what I had was a tightly rolled sheaf of bluish-gray paper, bound in the middle by a rubber band. And I knew without looking that a triangular piece had been torn off the corner of one sheet, and that the end of the roll had been nibbled by chipmunk teeth.

CHAPTER 18

I carried the package into the house as gingerly as a stick of dynamite. All my speculation about what had happened to the plans, and there they were, sitting in my toolshed. I shoved the papers on the dining room table off to the side, and removed the rubber band. When I tried to spread out the sheaf, it rolled back up again, as if it had been baked around a curling iron. Bending the papers backwards had no effect, so I gave up and weighted the corners down with books.

The plans were bound along the left edge with a dark blue spine. I went through the pages one at a time but felt almost as puzzled when I got to page twenty-three as I had when I started. Obviously a set of construction plans, it was in grade levels and elevations with match lines at the edge of each sheet. The front page had a cryptic title: "State of Illinois Highway Project No.

SJ907-2, Segment 5."

I thumbed through the pages again, more slowly this time. Each had a small box on the upper right-hand corner with numbers and letters printed on it, like the ones on the scrap of paper I had found in the barn.

"What's that?" I muttered. For the first time, I saw some words printed above the boxes in tiny letters. I finally gave up trying to read them and went to the kitchen for the magnifying glass my mom had always kept in the drawer under the telephone.

It took several readings before the actual significance of the plans became clear. The words on each page read: "Riverport Connector." I leaned back in my chair and tried to ignore the excitement that was growing in the pit of my stomach. What I had on my dining room table just might be part of a set of blueprints that could provide the economic shot in the arm that Riverport needed — construction plans for a new highway to connect the Interstate south of town with the north-south Interstate across the river in Missouri.

A new highway through Riverport had been lobbied for and talked about for more than twenty years. My dad had been a major player in the campaign and every couple of years when the surveyors showed up, he would call me to say that maybe this was going to be the time. For several years, the funding for the highway was even written into the Highway Department's capital budget, but by the end of the legislative session the money would have vanished in favor of a project elsewhere in the state, and Dad would subject me to a tirade on dirty politicians. I always told him that Riverport and Spencer County had too few people and too little economic clout to sway the politicians. After Dad died, I didn't hear anything more about it, but if these plans were valid, there was finally going to be a new roadway.

I thumbed through the plans again, trying to pick up a clue on the exact route of the highway. There were culverts and guardrails noted, but no crossroads that I could use for identification. It finally dawned on me what I was missing, and I retrieved a ruler from the kitchen. The scale marker at the bottom of each page indicated that there was thirty-two feet to the inch. That meant each page covered approximately five-hundred feet of roadway. So the twenty-three pages revealed a little over two miles.

Where were the rest of the pages?

Esther Martin said she'd seen Willy riding away from Margaret's house with a roll of something sticking out of his bicycle basket, but she hadn't said how big the roll was.

Before I could ponder further, the telephone rang.

Let it be Gil, I thought, as I hurried to the phone.

"Jessie, this is Nancy Williamson. How are you?"

"Nancy! I'm fine." I hoped my voice didn't sound as surprised as I felt.

"I'm sorry to bother you," she said, "but yesterday, when Harry dropped off the tomatoes, he should have told you we needed the basket back. Sorry to be a pest, but Mother's all in a stew about it. She got it on one of her trips to the Amanas. Harry wasn't thinking when he used it. I wonder if I could stop by and pick it up."

When *Harry* dropped off the tomatoes? Why on earth would Harry Williamson drive all the way out to my house with a basket of tomatoes? The answer came to mind even before I finished the question. So he could snoop around my house or . . .

The rest of the thought was so absurd, I couldn't finish it.

I forced myself to laugh. "So that's where the mystery tomatoes came from," I said. "I found them on the doorstep when I got home from town, and had no idea who had brought them."

"Oh." Nancy sounded puzzled. "I assumed he talked to you."

"They're beautiful tomatoes, Nancy. Thank you for thinking of me, but there's no need for you to come out. I have to go to the supermarket first thing in the morning. I'll drop the basket off."

Nancy's sigh was audible. "I know it's a bother, but I'd better come right now. I don't mean to impose, but Mother's not going to give us any peace until she has her basket back. If you're busy or something, just put it on doorstep."

Translation: Mrs. Pfeifer isn't going to give Harry any peace.

I knew how some people became more possessive as they aged. I had watched my own mother become obsessed with various objects around the house. No one could touch them, and they were never to be moved. It was as if they were her anchor to life. Mrs. Pfeifer, however, hadn't waited for the aging process to kick in before she grew grasping and selfish. It had been ingrained in her from an early age.

"No, that's fine," I said. "Come on out."

It occurred to me that maybe I could convince Nancy to visit for a while over a glass of iced tea. I was still puzzled by the

305

way she had behaved when we had talked about Margaret's funeral. Nancy wasn't much of a conversationalist, but it was possible I could get her to let something slip that might give me a clue to Harry's place, if any, in the whole affair.

My immediate thought when I hung up was that I had better put away all my papers and hide the plans. They probably wouldn't mean anything to Nancy, but I didn't want to run the chance that she might mention them to Harry. Or to someone else.

I quickly gathered up the papers and puzzled for a minute over where to stash them. I ruled out the buffet as too obvious, then decided to stick them under the sofa in the living room. What to do with the plans was more crucial. I was tempted to lock them back in the toolshed, but that option was eliminated as I heard a car pull into the lane. How on earth had Nancy driven here so fast?

Almost without thinking I thrust the roll of blueprints into the corner of the pantry, behind the shotgun.

At least they're out of sight, I thought, as I walked to the door.

"I don't think I want to know how fast you drove to get here so quickly," I said.

Nancy looked puzzled. "Oh, I thought I

told you. I was calling from my car."

"You have a cell phone?"

I couldn't imagine why anyone in River-port needed one. In fact, people groused about paying for one for the Mayor. The consensus was that it was a waste of town money, because a person could drive most anywhere in Riverport as fast as he could get a call through.

Nancy nodded. "It was Mother's idea. She gets real nervous if she can't reach me."

"Come on in," I said. "I was just fixing myself a glass of tea. Why don't you join me?"

"That sounds lovely," she said.

Nancy's response surprised me. I had expected to have to cajole her into staying. Normally, she was in a rush to get back to her mother.

I fixed the glasses of tea and added a slice of lemon and a sprig of mint to each. "Let's go sit on the terrace and admire the fruits of my day's labor," I said. Even though the plans were out of sight, I wanted to put as much distance between Nancy and the blueprints as possible.

Most people who saw my garden smothered me in quick compliments and told me I had inherited my mother's green thumb. Then they would turn to other subjects.

Nancy, however, was genuinely interested. She had to examine each planting and find out how and why I put one variety there and another here. Her knowledge was formidable. I felt like a novice as I struggled to answer her questions.

As I followed her around the garden, I was impressed again by how different she was from her mother. Mrs. Pfeifer never set foot outside her house without every hair in place and her makeup perfect. Not Nancy. As Aunt Henrietta would say, Nancy was like an old shoe — a little scuffled and run down at the edges, but comfortable. She wasn't fat, but I suspected she weighed close to two hundred pounds. The description, I knew, usually went: "She's big-boned, so she can carry the weight."

Nancy could have been a handsome woman, strong and even-featured, but she made no attempt to fix herself up. Probably the years of nagging by her mother had made Nancy turn as far the other way as possible. She wore her hair straight and cropped and, except at church, I couldn't remember seeing her in anything but a split denim skirt topped with a polo shirt in the summer and a baggy sweater in the winter. The outfit accentuated her size.

Nancy finally finished her inspection. I sat

back and sipped my tea and listened to her complimentary analysis of the garden. Coming from an accomplished gardener made it especially pleasing.

"I see you have put in some perennials," she said. "Are you tempted to plant more? All the gardening magazines tout them."

I shook my head. "Most perennials are a little too subtle for me. A few are fun, but I like a massive splash of color. Besides, they're just as much work as the annuals. The way I look at it, for the amount of sweat it takes, I want to make sure I have something that makes people sit up and take notice."

God, I sounded like one of the ladies in the gardening club.

Nancy smiled. "I have to agree with you," she said. "I've got my daisies and daylilies, and I've started a hosta bed, but I'll leave the exotics to someone else." She looked around. "What a restful spot this is."

"I don't know if it's really that restful, or whether after you've been weeding all day, anything would seem restful. Some days I'm tempted to plow it all under and plant grass."

Nancy looked shocked. "You don't mean that, do you?"

I laughed. "No, I don't mean it. Digging

in the garden is a great way to work out anxieties. Take ground ivy, for example. That was today's project. Nothing better, by my way of thinking, for working out frustrations than digging in the soil and pulling weeds, particularly a patch of ground ivy."

"I couldn't agree more," Nancy said. "I can hardly wait for spring to come each year so I can start getting my hands dirty again. Mother's always fussing about how bad my hands and nails look, and some days I do wear gloves to make her happy, but I figure there's nothing wrong with having people know you're not afraid to do an honest day's work . . ." She paused for a minute and looked at her hands, rubbing the knuckles. "Better to use them to raise flowers than some of the things people use them for," she said.

What a curious thing to say, I thought. "I don't know about your garden, Nancy, but mine seems to have a healthier growth of ground ivy than ever before," I said. "Willy used to call it the Devil's ivy, and I think he was right. He said it fooled you because it started out so little and innocent, just like a temptation, and before you knew it, the ivy took over everything."

I watched Nancy's face closely as I mentioned Willy, hoping for some response, but there was nothing. I decided to see if I could provoke a reaction. "Poor Willy," I said. "Sheriff claims the autopsy will show that Willy died by drowning, after he fell into McGee Creek. Gil's convinced Willy was drunk and it was an accident." I shook my head. "I'm having trouble believing that. I would have sworn that Willy would never touch another drop of alcohol. It doesn't make sense to me. Good worker, dependable, and honest as the day is long. Did he ever do any work for you?"

"Me?" Nancy started at my question. "No. I mentioned hiring him one time after Margaret said so many good things about him, but Mother . . . well, Mother said she didn't think it would be a good idea."

I could just imagine what Mrs. Pfeifer said, and I doubted whether it would have been anything so benign.

"I didn't know they're doing an autopsy on Willy," Nancy said. "How did you find out about it?"

"Gil told me. He seems to think it will close out the case, but I think he's being premature. It seems to me there are still a lot of loose ends that need wrapping up."

I debated how up-front I should be with Nancy. After all, she was married to the person who might be a prime suspect.

"You must be proud of Harry," I said.

"Proud of Harry?" Nancy looked startled, as if that was a statement she wasn't used to hearing.

"It's not often that a person gets to be a major player in a community," I said. "I imagine it takes a lot of his time."

It was obvious from the expression on her face that she wasn't quite sure what I was talking about. I would have to throw her a hint.

"I guess with his experience as a banker he doesn't have much trouble figuring out the regulations and powers for that Industrial Development thing," I said, "but I'd imagine some of the other people on the Authority have had difficulty. They're lucky to have Harry show them the way. I have to confess the first time I heard the IDA mentioned, I had no idea what it was."

Nancy shifted in her chair and looked down at her hands. "Harry's been a good husband and he's so patient with Mother. It's not been easy for him." She spoke so softly I could barely hear her.

I nodded. "It's not easy for a man to have to share a house with his mother-in-law. I admire him for his patience."

It's more than patience, I thought. *The man*

*obviously has a full-blown case of masoch-
ism.*

"Anyway, back to the IDA, Nancy. Maybe you can explain it to me."

She laughed. "Honestly, Jessie, you have to know about everything, just like that *Emily* you write about. You haven't changed a bit from when we were in school. But I'm afraid I can't be much help. Harry tried to explain it to me, but I've never had much of a head for such things."

I found that hard to believe. Anyone who could analyze a bridge hand as precisely as Nancy was plenty smart. "It surprised me to see that Margaret Benson had been appointed to take her husband's place after he died," I said. "Margaret was sweet, but I would have never said she had a head for figures."

Nancy looked at me sharply, but didn't answer.

"Between you and me," I said, "it seems like the only person on the IDA with any business sense at all, other than Harry, is Roland Evans, and he's never going to set the world on fire. Bud Berry, for heaven's sake! I have no idea who thought to appoint him. And Smitty may run a profitable tavern, but if it doesn't come with a liquor stamp on it, I don't think he knows what it's worth."

Nancy chewed on her thumbnail, a habit she'd had since her youth. I sensed I was making her uncomfortable, but I felt compelled to keep pressing the issue. "I suppose it makes a difference to have someone as knowledgeable as Mr. Emerson working with them. He sounds like quite an expert."

I watched Nancy closely to see her reaction to Hap Emerson, but the only thing I could detect was a slight tightening around her mouth. "Mr. Emerson impresses me as a wheeler-dealer," I said, "but then I've never had any experience with big-time real estate people. That may be the way they all act."

"I didn't know you knew him," Nancy said.

I attempted to pass Nancy's statement off with a nonchalance I didn't feel. "Oh, I wouldn't say I know him. He came to see me about buying some of my property. Claims some mystery client wants it for a weekend hideaway."

"What exactly did he say, Jessie?"

I shrugged. "He was somewhat circumspect. I told him I wasn't interested, but he said to think about it. Do you think he's to be trusted, Nancy? What does Harry say about him?"

"Harry's got the business sense in our family, so you'll have to ask him."

"It's too bad Riverport never got that new highway," I said. "I'm not an expert, of course, but it seems to me it would be a lot easier to sell Riverport to investors if there was good highway access."

I fished my sprig of mint out of the glass and nibbled on it, waiting for Nancy to comment, but she just stared straight ahead.

"I have half a notion to write State Senator Arnold and ask him why he hasn't pursued it," I continued. "Frank said he's up for reelection next November. Might be the right time to lean on him a little bit. What do you think?"

Nancy gave a tiny nod, but again offered no comment.

"Frank's sure that's the only reason he showed up for Margaret's funeral. Just like clockwork, every four years he rediscovers Riverport." I leaned toward Nancy. "I still can't believe she's dead. Just doesn't make any sense why anyone would want to kill her."

"What do you mean, anyone? Willy Bachmann killed her, Jessie. The sheriff says so, everybody says so, the evidence says so. You're the only one who's questioning it. Why can't you accept the truth?"

Nancy clenched her hands as she talked.

I leaned closer. "That's just it. The evidence doesn't say so. Whoever killed Margaret had a cup of coffee with her. Willy didn't drink coffee. He might drink a glass of ice water or lemonade, but not a cup of coffee, nothing with caffeine. Someone else was in Margaret's kitchen, and that someone else is the murderer. I'm sure of it."

"That is the most ridiculous thing I've ever heard!" Nancy's voice was sharp and thin. "You've got to stop saying things like that. Maybe someone was there earlier and had a cup of coffee with her."

"I don't think so. Esther Martin said Margaret was a fastidious housekeeper. She would never have let a dirty cup sit on her table. If someone had been there earlier, Margaret would have washed the cup immediately and put it away."

Of course, Esther had said nothing of the sort to me, but so what? I was on a roll. Before I had a chance to continue, the telephone rang.

"Excuse me," I said. "I'm expecting a call. I'll bring us more tea."

It was Frank, not Gil. I wondered if Gil was ever going to call. Cutting the conversation short, I told Frank that Nancy was visiting, and I promised to call back. As I reached into the refrigerator to get the pitcher of tea, I heard a car start up.

As I opened the door, the tail end of Nancy's car pulled out of the lane.

She had left without saying goodbye. Without her mother's precious basket from the Amanas.

CHAPTER 19

I carried the empty tea glasses into the house. Tea on the terrace seemed to be a daily event. Why had Nancy left without so much as a goodbye? I had just finished explaining my theory about the coffee cup on Margaret's kitchen table when the telephone rang. Right before that, I had discussed the highway and said I thought I'd call State Senator Arnold's office and make some waves. But first there had been all my questions about Hap Emerson and the IDA.

Which had been the trigger that sent Nancy flying from the yard?

I was disgusted with myself. I knew better than heap everything on Nancy at once. She needed to digest a statement thoroughly before being presented with a new one.

After I had rinsed the glasses and put them in the dishwasher, I reviewed the conversation. Nancy had looked increasingly uncomfortable with each subject I'd thrown out. Probably the accumulation had scared her off, not anything specific.

The muscles in my back and shoulders were beginning to tighten. It had been a long time since I'd done that much work in the garden. I'd going to feel it tomorrow morning. Running did little for the arm muscles.

Better get used to it, I thought. *You don't have Willy anymore.*

Otis Joseph was a hard worker, but I suspected he was more interested in the big picture than pulling weeds. Horsing out tree stumps was more his style.

A long hot soak, that's what I needed. Maybe a bath would soothe my muscles and my nerves.

I was halfway up the stairs when I remembered I'd left the plans in the corner of the pantry. Where could I put them where they would be safe? And why didn't Gil call?

I shook my head. *Jessie, how can you be so insensitive? His mother is sick, for God's sake. He'll call when he can.*

If someone was searching, where would he look for the road plans? It occurred to me that I was being just a wee bit paranoid. Why would anyone think I had the plans? Maybe no one would, but this whole affair was so bizarre, I wasn't ruling anything out.

I considered and rejected every spot I could think of in the house. And the toolshed was out because anyone who knew Willy knew he had access to it. The fact that no one had thought of it before made no difference, as far as I was concerned.

The car. I'd lock them in the trunk of the car. No one would think to look there.

I grabbed the plans and trotted out to the garage, darting glances every which way as I crossed the yard, knowing there was no way to conceal the sheaf of papers. I realized what a fool I must look, but that only made me move faster. In fact, I felt like a bad imitation of Inspector Jacques Clouseau in *The Pink Panther* movies, but I didn't pause to laugh at myself until the plans were safely locked in the car trunk, the garage doors secured, and my car keys tucked into my pocket. I felt decidedly creepy, and wished it was tomorrow. First thing in the morning I would take the plans to Gil's office. Even if he wasn't back yet, they'd be safe there. Then I'd return Nancy's basket and try to find out why she ran away.

Genevieve was pacing in front of her empty food bowl and casting recriminating glances in my direction when I entered the kitchen. "Sorry about that," I said to her, as I ran my hand along the cat's back, taking comfort in the reality Genevieve brought.

"I can take a hint," I said, and poured out the kibbles. As usual Genevieve let me know she would prefer something more exotic in her bowl.

As I headed once again for the stairs and a bath, the telephone rang. This time I knew who it was. I had forgotten to call Frank back.

"Sorry, Frank, I got busy," I said, before he could scold me.

"Why did Nancy Williamson stop by?" he asked. "It's not like her to make social calls."

"I honestly don't know, Frank. She said it was to pick up a basket filled with tomatoes that Harry had brought by the house yesterday afternoon. Harry had used one of his mother-in-law's precious baskets without permission, and Nancy wanted to retrieve it before her mother drove everyone mad. But then, she just upped and left without so much as a fare-thee-well and forgot the basket."

"You must have misunderstood her," Frank said. "Harry was with me yesterday. We drove over to Springfield together for the regional board meeting of Rotary. It was after five when we got home."

I stared out the window as I listened to Frank, hearing his words without understanding them. What he was saying didn't make sense.

"Someone dropped off a basket of tomatoes yesterday," I said, "and Nancy claims it was Harry. I left the house late in the morning to visit Esther Martin, and I was home by three. There were no tomatoes when I walked out the door and they were sitting on the doorstep when I got back."

"Well, he was with me all day. Believe me, there's no missing Harry," Frank said. "Besides, you know Nancy can be a little spacey sometimes. She probably had someone else drop them off and forgot, or maybe Harry arranged for it."

I shook my head, but didn't answer. Nancy had been quite specific.

"I'm sure that's what happened," Frank continued. "She probably told Harry to deliver the tomatoes and he forgot until the last minute, and had someone else do it."

"Frank, may I ask you a favor?"

I knew what I was about to do required a major leap of faith on my part. I had this nagging suspicion that Frank knew a lot more than he was letting on. What I didn't know was whether he didn't want to talk about other people, or if he was involved. But the time had come, as my dad would say, to take the bull by the horns.

"Sure," Frank said. "Ask away."

"Could you come over in about a half hour? I need to talk to you."

I listened a minute and then gently hung up the phone. Frank had said "yes." No questions asked.

It meant I had to forego my long soak and settle for a quick shower, but that was all right. I was probably too jumpy to get any benefits from a hot bath. I dressed carefully in a fresh pair of khaki shorts and a cotton sweater while I debated how I was going to present my scenario to Frank. I rehearsed it, first one way and then another, and finally gave up. *He'd have to take it as it came out,* I thought, as I pushed my damp curls into place with my fingers.

Frank was punctual, as usual, and when I let him in the door he said, "What's up?"

I shrugged. "I'm not completely sure, but I think I'm close to figuring out what led up to Margaret's murder and Willy's death. I can't *prove* who did it, but I think I know the motive."

I smiled. "I need a sounding board, Frank, and you're nominated."

He frowned. "Jessie, I've got to be honest with you. Your obsession with this has gotten out of hand. People are pretty tired of your nosing around, and I must say I am too. If you don't stop asking questions, someone's going to pop you one."

I took a deep breath. I had to be careful not to say anything that would embroil the two of us in an argument. The issue was not what people thought, but whether my suspicions had any basis in fact.

"I realize I may have gotten some people's backs up, Frank, but I think you need to hear me out before you pass final judgment. Will you do that?"

Frank nodded.

"Let's sit at the table," I said. "Want a beer?"

I pulled a mug out of the freezer, a mug that I kept iced for Frank's visits. Then I carried the mug and a glass of iced tea to the table. I would have preferred a gin and tonic, but I needed to keep my head clear.

"It's a long story," I said, "but I'll try to condense it as much as possible. Stop me if you have any questions." I took a deep breath. "I believe the events that led up to Margaret's death and then Willy's death started more than a year ago."

Frank sat silently as I began my recitation, starting with the Industrial Development Authority. "I suspect the primary reason it was formed was to serve as a legitimate front for a real estate scam, spearheaded by Hap Emerson, with the help of Ray Benson. Mayor Ellwood had to have known what was going on, and maybe some of the Council."

I paused to let Frank comment, but he just muttered a curt, "Go on."

"I think Emerson saw Riverport as ripe for the picking — a new administration and a depressed economy. He had found out that a highway was going to be built, and he realized he had a window of opportunity before the plans for the route were made public."

"Wait a minute," Frank almost shouted. "How did you find out about the highway plans? Why didn't you tell me?"

"No time," I said. "I only found out about them a few hours ago."

I told him about discovering the plans in the shed and that I was sure Willy had put them there. "Esther Martin saw Willy riding away from Margaret's house last week with a long, skinny package sticking out of his bike basket — the plans Margaret had given him to hide."

I decided not to waste time with the rest of my theory, that Willy had hidden them first in Walnut Clearing, then had moved them the night of the storm, the night after Margaret was killed. There was no longer any doubt in my mind that it had been Willy running across the barnyard, not a figment of my imagination.

"Let me see the plans," Frank said.

"No, later, after I finish," I said.

"Jessie. Now. It's important."

One look at Frank's face convinced me that he would not wait. I had seen him upset and angry many times, but this expression was different. If it had been anyone but Frank, I would have called it threatening.

"All right," I said. "Wait here. I'll get them."

I tried not to think about Frank's reaction as I dug the roll of plans out of the car trunk. Maybe I should have been more suspicious of him, but as fast as the notion came into my mind, I brushed it away. This was Frank. If I couldn't trust my cousin, who could I trust?

After handing him the plans, I sat silently as he unrolled them on the table. I couldn't see the expression on his face as he read through the plans, a page at a time, but the flush on his neck was not sunburn.

"Where are the rest of the plans and the papers that were with them?" he demanded.

"What are you talking about? What you have is all I found."

"There have to be some papers. The other

plans don't matter, but I must have the papers. Give them to me, Jessie. This is no time for games."

"Games? What the hell are you talking about?" I could feel my own face turning red. "I'm not playing games with anybody. I'm just trying to make sense out this madness. I think you've been playing games, Frank, and you owe me an explanation."

I watched as he leaned forward and hid his face in his hands. "Talk to me, Frank," I said, reaching over and touching his arm.

He rolled his head back and forth in his hands. "I'm so ashamed, Jessie," he said.

I was tempted not to respond, but decided if I didn't keep pushing Frank, I would never get the full story. "Being ashamed isn't good enough," I said. "What is going on?"

Frank lifted his head, his face gray. "I don't know where to begin."

"How about the beginning? That's always a good place," I said as gently as I could.

He slouched down in his chair and looked at his hands, as if willing them to tell his story. Finally, he looked up and said, "Okay, here goes. Do you remember me telling you about the group that Hap Emerson and Ray Benson called together to talk about planning for and investing in the future of Riverport and Spencer County?"

"Was that the meeting about putting up money for a factory in the Industrial Park?"

Frank nodded. "Yeah. The Mayor, Harry Williamson, Roland Evans, old Mr. Michelson, and Bud Berry were there. It's true I told Emerson thanks but no thanks, and didn't give him money for the factory project. But he came back late last fall with another proposal I didn't tell you about."

My heart sank. I could tell from Frank's tone of voice that that time he hadn't refused.

"Emerson said he had working plans for the construction of a new highway coming through Riverport. He told us they wouldn't be made public for at least six months, but he was willing to let us in on it, and we could make a killing by buying up property at key places along the route. He said because it was still confidential information, he would have to set up a blind limited partnership."

"What the hell is a blind limited partnership? I've never heard of such a thing."

Frank shrugged. "I'm not sure. It made sense when he explained it. Something about protecting the investors so their names wouldn't become public knowledge. We would give money directly to him and he'd handle it."

"Didn't it occur to you that what he was suggesting might be illegal?"

"Maybe."

Frank's voice was so soft I could barely hear him. *Maybe?* I couldn't believe my ears.

"Go on," I said.

"Hap had great credentials, the Mayor vouched for him, and he'd done all that fancy work setting up the IDA and the Industrial Park. And, he gave us names of people he'd worked with before. We checked some of them out, and they gave him rave references. Besides, what do I know about such things? Hap was the expert, so I figured it was okay."

"Then what happened?"

"He told us he needed a minimum of one hundred thousand dollars to make the deal work, and for that he could guarantee a tenfold return."

"How much money did you give him?" I tried to keep my voice as calm as possible.

"Ten thousand."

"Oh, Frank." I couldn't think of anything else to say.

Frank looked directly into my eyes. "I wanted to be a big man so bad. I knew where every penny of my tenfold return was going. I'd start a college fund for Selma's kids and get Mildred that fancy coat she's always dreamed of. I had so many plans. All I had to do was wait for the bulldozers to move in, and I'd be rich."

I shook my head. "Then what?"

He shrugged. "I don't know, for sure. Right around the Fourth of July, Emerson called and said there were problems. The highway project was being delayed and there were some route modifications. He said not to worry, he already held options on some of the prime property, but they were coming due soon. He needed more money in hand to renew them and secure the additional sites."

"You didn't give him more, did you?" Frank nodded, and I was only partially successful in stifling a groan. "How much?"

"A thousand. I told him I didn't have any more."

"What about the others?"

Frank shrugged again. "I don't know. Harry Williamson had sunk a lot more money than me, in the beginning, but the others I'm not sure about. Emerson sold the original partnerships in units of ten thousand dollars. You could buy as many units as you wanted, but the second time around, he took whatever we'd give him."

"You're going to need a good lawyer when

this is all over," I said.

Frank shook his head. "No, Jessie. The world's not going to know what a fool I was. I'm not going to have the Schroeder name dragged through the mud and made a laughingstock. I'll just chalk it up to experience."

I decided to table that subject for future discussions. "So it was midsummer when you found out construction had been delayed and the highway plans had been revised."

Frank nodded. "Up to then we thought it was going to enter town at the southeast corner and cut across to a new bridge at the foot of Maine Street. It was supposed to pass right next to the Industrial Park. And the timetable had construction beginning right after the start of the fiscal year, this coming November."

"Did you ever see actual plans, Frank?"

"Emerson had a big pile of plans at the first meeting, and a map of the county, and he'd drawn a line along the route. He had red dots every place he thought property would go up."

"Did you look at the actual plans to make sure his drawing was correct?"

"I didn't, but Roland Evans did. He said it looked good to him."

"But you never studied them?"

Frank shook his head.

I felt as if I was stuck in a nightmare. Cousin Frank, the world's most cautious man, had invested ten thousand dollars on the basis of a sales pitch, a line drawn across a map, and some red dots. How much more had the others handed over? How much had Harry Williamson paid?

"Let me get this straight. You invested because you had been told the highway was coming through town, but you never looked at the plans. You just depended on what Roland and Emerson said." I shook my head again and said, more to myself than Frank, "I wonder if Roland was in on the scam."

Frank didn't respond.

I picked up the roll of plans on the table. "Are these part of the original plans?"

Frank nodded. "Ray Benson had a whole set. None of us have seen the new ones."

"So, this summer Emerson found out the timetable had been delayed and changes made to the route, but he had already spent all your money. He needed more cash to renew the original options that were still valid, and to take out additional ones on property along the new right-of-way. But why did Margaret have some of the plans and not all of them? And what are the papers you're so worried about?"

And how does this tie into murder? I thought, as I waited for Frank to answer.

"She found them six weeks ago, like I told you," he said, "and that's when we found out we had been screwed. But then, a couple of days later she unearthed some photocopies of the agreements we had all signed. They were in a box Ray had hidden in the basement."

Frank gave me a wan smile. "We should have known Ray would cover his own ass. I'm sure he kept copies of everything, to make sure Emerson didn't double-cross him. Ray had the money records *and* the names and dates."

"What in the world did you think you were going to do?" I asked.

"Harry and Margaret had worked out a plan for all of us to confront Emerson and force him to return our money. We were all supposed to meet at Margaret's on Monday. Harry had found out from a buddy of his in one of the Springfield banks that Emerson had enough assets to cover it. Only Willy went berserk on Saturday and killed Margaret and everything disappeared."

So that's what the phone call from Margaret to Otis Joseph had been about, I thought. And then, sometime between the call and the murder, she decided she couldn't go through with it. I groaned as I realized the implications of Margaret's decision. The field of suspects had drastically widened. Even Frank could have done it.

"Jessie, I need those plans and we have to find those papers," Frank said.

"No!" I yanked the plans off the table and rolled them up.

"Please, Jessie."

"No. These are evidence and I'm turning them over to Gil. I don't know how or why, but whoever killed Margaret and Willy was looking for these plans. And probably those mysterious papers you keep talking about."

Frank sighed. "I don't want to have to take them from you, Jessie. Don't you understand? This has nothing to do with Margaret's murder and Willy's death. Willy killed Margaret and then killed himself." Frank stood up and started around the table toward me. "Goddammit, Jessie, all your nosing around has screwed up everything, and I'm not going to let you do it anymore. I want those plans now."

I tightened my grip. For the first time in my life, Frank frightened me, but I was determined to hang on to the plans.

"It's too late," I said. "I told Gil I had the plans, and I told him I would deliver them to his office tomorrow morning at nine o'clock. If I don't show up with them, I'll have to tell him why."

"You can be a real bitch sometimes, little cousin. Has all this kissy-face with our Sheriff made you forget that family comes first? You're making a big mistake."

"No, Frank, you made the mistake, and I'm not going to compound it."

Willy's face flashed into my mind. Leaning on his spade. Listening to me say two wrongs didn't make a right.

"I'm sorry, Frank, but I'm not going to hand over what could be evidence of two murders, just so the world won't find out you were suckered by Hap Emerson and Ray Benson. Now, I think you better go."

I held my breath, half expecting him to lunge for the plans. His hands were clenched into fists and he stared at me, not saying anything. Then his hands slowly began to relax. He looked at me for a minute, shook his head, and turned for the door, his feet shuffling over the floor. Halfway there he stopped and turned back.

"Forgive me, Jessie," he said. "I've been a real fool."

I walked over to where he stood and put my arms around him. "We all are, Frank, sooner or later. We'll work it out."

My own feet were dragging as I walked back to the table to gather up the glasses and the plans. Somehow, locking the plans back in the car trunk seemed like too much trouble, and I settled for putting them in the corner behind the shotgun again.

I tried to ignore the basket of tomatoes sitting on the pantry shelf, but knew I had to do something with them before they spoiled. They were too beautiful to go to waste. Besides, I had to return the basket to Nancy.

A sharp pain in my stomach reminded me I'd not eaten since noon. I needed some food, then I would consider what to do about Frank.

I picked out a tomato, washed it, cut it open, then retrieved some leftover tuna salad from the refrigerator. I loved fresh tomatoes and always thought it amazing that in olden times people thought them poisonous.

Wonder who was the first person brave enough to eat one? I thought, as I loaded my fork.

The fork was halfway to my mouth when I stopped. *Why had people believed they were poison?*

Maybe someone had eaten one and died.

Maybe someone had put poison into the tomato.

Maybe someone had poisoned this tomato.

"That's the most ridiculous thought you've ever had, Jessie Schroeder," I said. "You *are* paranoid."

Five minutes later I stood in front of the open freezer and tried to decide which frozen dinner to put into the microwave. The empty basket sat by the kitchen door. The tomatoes would decompose rapidly in the compost heap. Too much had happened too fast for me to assimilate it. Tomorrow would be soon enough, I decided. And Gil would be back.

Trailed by Genevieve, I wandered around the house, aimlessly straightening shades and moving magazines. The antique map of Spencer County that hung above the sofa in the living room seemed slightly askew, and I spent several minutes nudging it back and forth. My foot kicked a pile of papers as I plopped down on the sofa. It reminded me that I had shoved all my material about the IDA and the Council under there. I began to gather them up to put them back on the dining room table, but changed my mind. For the time being, I'd leave them out of sight.

As I was shoving the papers back under

the sofa, the phone rang.

"What now," I muttered, as I stepped around Genevieve and hurried to the kitchen.

"Miss Schroeder? It's Deputy Sheriff Clarence Hockmeyer." Clarence's voice boomed in my ear. "Just heard from the Sheriff. He wanted me to remind you that we'll be patrolling extra out your way, so not to fret if you hear a car passing your place pretty regular."

"Thank you, Clarence," I said. "I talked to Virginia about it earlier. How's Gil's mother doing? Have you heard?"

"He says she's out of danger. Said he'd be starting home real soon. Anyway, you call if you have any concerns, you hear?"

"Thank you, Clarence. I appreciate it."

As I looked around the kitchen, I felt an overwhelming sense of fatigue. A good night's sleep was what I needed to soothe my aching muscles and mind. I went through my nighttime routine automatically, and the clock chimed ten as I started up the stairs. I was so tired it took a concentrated effort to climb steps. I knew full well that it was mostly emotional distress, rather than physical. I made it to the top of the staircase before I remembered I had left the plans and the shotgun in the pantry.

To hell with it, I thought. The patrol would be checking the house, so all I had to do was get a good night's sleep.

Chapter 20

I don't know what woke me up. Maybe the wind. It had picked up and the curtains billowed into the room. I rolled over and looked at the clock. Only eleven-thirty. I felt as if I had been asleep for hours.

A spasm radiated down my arm as I shifted on the pillow. Between water skiing and pulling weeds, I had definitely overworked my shoulder muscles. *The price you pay for getting so lazy,* I told myself. I had closed my eyes and started the delicious descent back into sleep when a faint scratching and shuffling noise outside the bedroom door brought me fully awake.

The faint light that filtered through the window from the pole light by the barn and the waning moon was not enough to see more than the broad outlines of the room. I reached into the nightstand drawer and withdrew my flashlight. The thin and wavering beam told me it needed new batteries.

"Damn," I muttered, as I focused the light on the door and heard the scratching/shuffling noise again.

An old house has a never-ending variety of creaks and groans, but this noise was different, deliberate, not the settling of old timbers. It sounded close to the floor.

As I swung the beam along the bottom of the door, I saw something move. My first instinct was to pull the sheet over my head, but I forced myself out of bed. Silently, I tiptoed over to the door.

I don't know what I feared I would find, but it certainly wasn't a furry paw feeling its way along the crevice between the floor and the door.

"Genevieve, what are you doing?" I said, and waited for the pounding of my heart to subside.

A faint meow was my answer. When I opened the door, Genevieve shot through and immediately wrapped herself around my legs.

I reached down and picked her up, and she curled herself tight in my arms.

"What's the matter with you?" I said. "You know you can't come upstairs and share my bedroom."

Genevieve gave a deep-throated purr as she snuggled closer.

"Since you're here, you might as well stay," I muttered, fully aware that I was breaking my rule. Somehow, this night it didn't seem such a bad idea to have company.

I crawled back into bed, shifting my feet to the side to make room for Genevieve at the foot of the mattress. The only noises I could hear now were the night sounds from outdoors. I closed my eyes, willing myself back to sleep, only to immediately reopen them as the hum of an automobile engine became audible in the distance. I sat up and listened as it came steadily closer, then slowed and stopped at the end of the lane, the engine idling. A flash of light swept past the window. I smiled and lay back down. Just the deputy making his rounds.

Much as I hated to admit it, it was comforting to know someone was looking after me for a change. My confrontation with Frank had left me feeling overwhelmed with responsibility. I didn't know how I was going to proceed. I wanted so much to make things right for him, but I knew that wasn't possible. All I could hope for was to ease the problem. However, tomorrow would be soon enough to think about that. *Me and Scarlett O'Hara,* I thought as I punched up my pillow and let sleep take me away.

I felt a heavy pressure on my chest, and awoke to find Genevieve stalking back and forth across my body.

"Dammit, Genevieve, stop it," I said, shoving the cat off the bed. She landed with a muffled plop and an indignant meow. As I cursed myself for letting her into the bedroom, I heard another noise from the dining room directly below my bedroom. It sounded like a chair bumping against the table.

The windows were closed in the dining room, so the wind couldn't be responsible.

That explanation wouldn't wash, anyway. It would take a tornado force wind to move one of the heavy oak chairs. And I couldn't blame it on Genevieve, who was in the bedroom with me. I strained my ears, trying to pick up another sound, but heard only silence.

I lay rigid in bed, trying to convince myself that it was simply a normal night noise, but it didn't work. Something had bumped a chair against the table in the dining room.

Taking a deep breath, I willed my heart to stop pounding, with little success, and slowly eased my legs over the edge of the bed. My fingers trembled as I knotted the sash on my robe. I was too nervous to try anything as complicated as a bow. As I started for the door, I reached into the corner where the shotgun should have been. My hand found nothing but wall. The shotgun was in the pantry. I leaned against the wall, fighting to stifle the tears of frustration that welled up in my eyes. Every night for a week I had lugged that damned gun upstairs with me, but not tonight. I had been too tired and distracted to return downstairs and get it. I tried to sort through my options. Close to panic, I waited for another sound, but silence prevailed.

The more I tried to convince myself it was my imagination, the more certain I became that someone was, or had been, in the dining room. I wanted to barricade the bedroom door and scream, but I quickly canceled that plan. The intruder would be upstairs before I could wrestle enough furniture in front of the door. Besides, if I screamed, who'd hear me? The deputy had just made his check. It would be hours before he came back.

The telephone was in the hallway, at the top of the stairs. But who could I call who would arrive in time to help me? Frank was the closest, but even he would take at least ten minutes.

I couldn't cower in my room! Taking another deep breath, I tiptoed back to the door, pausing only long enough to slip the flashlight into my pocket. It wouldn't do much good, but maybe I could fool whomever it was into believing I had a pistol. I had seen that in the movies, but I didn't have a lot of faith it worked in real life.

I put my ear to the door. Heard nothing. Slowly, I turned the knob and eased the door open, grateful my fetish about squeaking doors made me oil it regularly. I just wished I had a similar fetish about replacing flashlight batteries.

My feet were bare. I felt my way slowly along the wall, avoiding the floorboards that would give me away. As a child I had made a methodical survey of the hallway floor and stairs, being heavily influenced by Nancy Drew. Even as an adult I regularly found myself taking a zigzag course down the hallway, avoiding boards that might give me away. I hesitated at each step to listen. All I could hear was my own ragged breath as I struggled to keep calm.

I carefully counted as I started down the stairs. The third from the top and the sixth had to be avoided. Clutching the banister, I prayed my arms would support me if my knees refused the job.

The bottom, finally. I stood with my back to the wall that opened into the dining room, trying to will enough courage to look around the corner. The front hall was completely dark, so I had the comfort of knowing I would have the dark behind me as I looked into a room that faced the barnyard and pole light.

I gave myself a count of three, but lengthened the count to ten when I realized that three did not provide enough time to convince my body to leave the safety of the hallway.

Gazing around the dining room, I quickly identified the familiar features. Nothing seemed out of the ordinary. I slid around the corner, stood motionless, then slowly turned to look into the kitchen. Any hope I may have had that I was simply a victim of my own overactive imagination vanished. A thin beam of light swept the room. Someone with a flashlight!

Suddenly, anger overwhelmed fear. How dare anyone sneak into my house! I hurried across the dining room and reached around the corner. With a flip of my finger the kitchen was flooded with light.

"What are you doing in my house?" I demanded, stepping into the kitchen.

Anything else I might have said froze in the back of my throat. All I could do was stare open-mouthed at Nancy Williamson, flashlight in hand, standing in the middle of my kitchen.

She stared back at me, her hand shielding her eyes from the glare of the ceiling light.

"Hello, Jessie," she said. "Sorry I woke you up."

I could not believe it. This woman had broken into my house in the middle of the night and now she chatted as if she'd come for more tea.

"What are you doing here?" I finally got out. "And how did you get in?"

"Sorry I left without saying goodbye this afternoon. That was rude. I was going to come back tomorrow, but after Frank called Harry, I knew I couldn't wait."

After Frank called Harry? What on earth was she talking about?

"Look, Nancy, I don't know why you broke into my house, but I think you had better go. Now!"

She glared at me. "I didn't break in. I wouldn't do a thing like that. I have a key. Yesterday, when I brought the tomatoes, I borrowed your key and had a duplicate made. You really should find a safer place to keep it than behind the drainpipe. Besides, I had to come back. You took something that belongs to my Harry, and I need it back."

I wanted to pinch myself. This had all the makings of a bizarre nightmare. I couldn't figure out what to say to Nancy next. She sounded strange, reciting her words in a sing-song voice, like a little girl in a Christmas play.

"Why don't you sit down, Nancy? I'll make us both a cup of coffee, and then I'll call your mother and Harry. They must be worried about you."

She shook her head. "Mother's asleep, I gave her a pill, and Harry's not worried. I told him not to worry. I told him I'd take care of everything."

Abruptly, Nancy took a step toward me. "I don't want a cup of coffee. Margaret made me a cup of coffee and said she could explain everything, but she lied. She made Harry believe she was going to help him, but then she changed her mind. She let that awful Willy Bachmann change her mind. She was going to ruin my Harry. I couldn't let her do that, and I can't let you do that."

"Nancy, listen . . ."

"No!" She shook her head and took another step toward me. "I thought you were my friend, Jessie. You were always so nice to me in school. You never made fun of me and Harry like the other girls, and when you came back, I thought we would be friends again."

"I am your friend, Nancy. Let's sit down and talk about it. Maybe if we put our heads together, we can figure out what to do."

"It's too late for talk, Jessie. Harry's my only friend and now everyone wants to ruin him." She started to cry. "I can't live without Harry. He's so good to me. He thinks I'm beautiful. 'My beautiful, beautiful Nancy,' he calls me."

I watched her sway back and forth as she chanted, "Beautiful, beautiful, beautiful." Then I tightened my fingers around the flashlight in my pocket as I walked toward the kitchen door. Talking to Nancy wouldn't work. Maybe, if I couldn't get her to leave, I could escape out the door myself.

"Nancy," I said, "I want you to leave now. We can talk tomorrow. I don't know what went on between Harry and Margaret, but I have a gun in my pocket. I don't want to use it, but I will if I have to."

She smiled. "Get away from the door, Jessie. You don't have a gun in your pocket. You'd never own a handgun. Remember all those letters you wrote to 'The Soap Box' when we were in high school, after the Kruegers' little girl shot her brother with a loaded pistol she'd found in her dad's closet? You said it should be against the law to own handguns."

I shrugged and took my hands out of my pockets. "You're right. Of course, I don't have a gun."

"I knew you didn't, but I do." She pulled a small handgun out of the pocket of her denim skirt. "I got it in Springfield last week, just in case I needed it. Get the plans, Jessie!" she screamed, waving the gun for emphasis. "Get the plans!"

Startled, I almost tripped over Genevieve, who was at my heels. "I don't know what plans you're talking about, Nancy."

"You think you're so smart, going around town and playing detective. Well, you can't talk your way out of this one. Frank told Harry you had the plans and were going to give them to the sheriff. Frank said you were going to tell the sheriff about the money he and Harry gave that real estate man. He made Harry cry, just like Margaret made Harry cry. I can't allow that. Get me the plans!"

My mind was spinning. Why not give her the plans? There had to be duplicate copies at the State Highway Department, so what difference would it make? I tried to convince myself that was all Nancy wanted. Surely she wouldn't hurt me. But then, never in my wildest dreams had I suspected that

Nancy was the one responsible for Margaret's death. And Willy? Had Nancy killed Willy, too? I started toward the pantry.

"Where are you going?" Nancy demanded.

"I thought you wanted the plans. They're in the pantry." *With the shotgun,* I thought, *and the shotgun's loaded.*

I could hear Nancy behind me, but I felt strangely calm. "The light's burned out," I said. "Wait here and I'll get them for you."

I walked over to the back corner and, reaching down, wrapped my hands around the shotgun and slipped off the safety. I had no doubt in my mind that once Nancy had what she wanted, she planned to kill me.

"What was that noise?"

"I opened the cabinet," I said.

When I turned around, Nancy was standing in the pantry door, the kitchen light creating a perfect backlight — an easy shot. One shot was all I needed. Not to kill, just to wound.

"Give me the plans." Nancy moved into the narrow confines of the pantry, both hands outstretched, one holding the gun, the other ready to receive the plans.

"Come and get them," I said, raising the shotgun and pointing it at Nancy.

Nancy screamed, "You lied!" and lunged. "Just like Margaret, you lied!"

A flash of light and an excruciating pain combined with a thunderous crash. As the darkness closed in, all I could think was: *It never happens like this to Emily. She gets to finish the story.*

I cautiously opened one eye. A circle of faces looked down at me and the sound of ringing filled my ears. Where was I? *I must be dead and they've all come to my visitation,* I thought. Why else would all these people be staring at me? There was Aunt Henrietta and Uncle George, Frank and Mildred, Gil, and even Clarence. It was nice of Clarence to come. He hadn't even known me that well. But why was Aunt Henrietta wearing curlers to my visitation?

"I think she's waking up." That sounded like Aunt Henrietta's voice.

"Jessie, can you hear me?" That sounded like Gil.

"Jessie, say something." That had to be Frank. He was always trying to boss me around.

I carefully opened my second eye. "Why are you all here? Am I dead?"

"Hardly," Gil said. "You've got a gunshot wound in your arm and a giant goose egg where you hit your head on the corner of the cabinet. And you sure did make a hell of a mess out of the ceiling of the pantry with your shotgun."

It was all coming back. Nancy had tried to kill me. "Where's Nancy?" I asked.

"She's in custody."

I closed my eyes again. "Is she all right?"

"Yes," Gil said. "That's enough talk for now. The ambulance will be here in a few minutes. We'll save the rest of the talk for later."

"Gil, wait a minute." I reached out my hand. "How did you know to come? I didn't call you. I couldn't call you. You were in Peoria."

"Harry Williamson called 9-1-1, and then he called Frank. You've got Harry to thank for saving your life."

CHAPTER 21

I sat with my back against the black walnut tree and looked out over the clearing and the old cabin. The doctor had told me I shouldn't leave the house for at least a week, but an overnight in the hospital and three days of confinement and ministrations by the family had made escape a necessity. If Aunt Henrietta forced one more cup of chicken soup on me, I'd gag.

The squirrels were leaping from branch to branch above, and an occasional walnut, enclosed in its thick husk, hit the ground with a thud. *Be just my luck,* I thought, *to get hit on the head with a walnut.* The chipmunk had studied me warily when I first walked into the clearing, then resumed its busy darting back and forth.

I had to admit to feeling less vigorous than I thought I would. My head still ached, especially when I turned it too fast, and the sling on my arm made me list when I walked. I had underestimated how difficult it would be to climb the bank of McGee Creek one-handed. But I had made it. The peace of Walnut Clearing began to seep into my body.

Gil had promised to meet me here at four. I could still feel his arms around me as the ambulance attendants strapped me onto the stretcher. And every time I had awakened, I could see him slumped in the chair in the corner of my hospital room, staring across at me.

I hoped he'd drive his Jeep down the old road, rather than walk the path, so he could drive me home. I was pretty sure I wouldn't be able to make it back on foot. He had fussed at me when I called and told him my plan, but the arrival of Aunt Henrietta and yet another pot of soup while we talked stopped him. He understood.

Frank had been coming to see me at least twice a day, looking worse than I did. He kept trying to apologize and explain. I finally got sick of it and told him to shut up. "What's done is done," I said.

Now, I looked at my watch. Almost four. I hoped Gil would be on time. I hadn't seen him since yesterday evening, and I was amazed at how much I missed him. Besides, he had promised he would answer all my questions. I shifted my position so I could see the old road better and leaned back to wait.

I heard the grumble of the Jeep before I saw it, and hastily ran my fingers through my hair, avoiding the sore spot just behind my right temple. I hoped I didn't look too disheveled from my trek through the woods.

Gil hopped out of the Jeep and walked toward me. He wasn't wearing his uniform, but there was something about his bearing that suggested a man of authority. God, he was handsome. He stopped a few feet from me and looked around.

"What a spot," he said. "It's been years since I've been here. Are you all right?" he asked, abruptly changing his attention to me. "You look a little pale."

"I'm fine," I assured him. "Pull up a patch of grass and join me. I'm dying to know what else you've found." I smiled. "Maybe 'dying' wasn't the best word choice."

Gil settled himself cross-legged across from me and took my hands. "Jesus, Jessie, you scared me. Please don't do that again."

"It certainly was not my intention to scare anyone, and you promised me some answers. Let's hear them."

"Well, Jessie Schroeder, you sure did stir up a kettle of fish, and you're damned lucky you didn't end up in that kettle yourself." He shook his head. "I may have to assign one of the deputies to traffic control, we've got so many experts running around town. We've got the State Police, the State Attorney's Office, and the Federal bank examiners all on the case now. Not a whole lot left for me to do, so I figured I'd take the rest of the day off. Clarence is having a high old time escorting our visitors all over town."

"Come on, Gil, I want to hear everything, and don't leave out anything," I said. "But first tell me what's happened to Nancy."

"As my nephew would say, Nancy has gone completely mental. Mrs. Pfeifer hired a big-time lawyer from Chicago. It looks like he's going to plead her guilty of murder and attempted murder by reason of insanity. The question is, whether it should be two counts of murder. Either way, she'll probably end up spending time in some posh mental institution."

"I don't understand. Why is there some question about the number of murders? Didn't she kill both Margaret and Willy?"

"Margaret for sure, but there's some question about Willy."

"Would you please explain?" I said, glaring at him.

"All right, but it's pretty gruesome."

I didn't bother to answer him, because my look gave him no wiggle room.

"Okay," Gil said, "but don't hesitate to stop me." He took a deep breath. "There was alcohol in Willy's system. The way the medical examiner explained it to me, he analyzed the heart tissue and found a substance called ethyl esters or some such thing, which forms when there's been alcohol in the body."

"I don't believe it. Willy wouldn't have started drinking again."

Gil held up his hand. "You're right. He didn't. At least, not voluntarily. The examiner found contusions and abrasions in the throat and the upper esophagus. Something was forced down his throat and the alcohol poured directly in. We found a funnel with stiff tubing on the end in Nancy's trunk."

I put my hand over my mouth as I tried to control my pitching stomach. "Oh, Gil, poor Willy."

"You okay?"

I nodded as emphatically as I could and struggled to keep control.

Gil studied my face for a minute before he went on. "This is just speculation, but Nancy evidently came to Willy's room and knocked him out somehow, then poured alcohol down his throat. She ransacked his room, trying to find the plans and the list of people who had put money in the pot. Then she loaded him into the trunk of her car and drove out to the bridge over McGee Creek. She couldn't get across because, by then, the water had risen over the bridge bed. We don't know if she just dumped him by the side of the road and Willy, in a drunken stupor, fell in himself, or whether she pushed him. It was Nancy's bad luck that she couldn't get downstream from the bridge, because then Willy would have been washed out to the river and we might never have found him."

"But why, Gil? Why?" I finally gave up and let the tears stream down my face.

He shrugged. "It was the only way she could think of to save Harry. He had made some very creative withdrawals from his mother-in-law's bank to invest in Emerson's real estate deal. When he admitted it to Nancy, after the whole deal had gone sour, she knew her mother would insist on prosecuting if she found out. And find out she would have, because a bank audit had been scheduled."

I struggled to bring myself under control. I didn't want Gil to stop talking because I was upset. I had to hear the rest of the story.

"Please go on," I said, as calmly as I could. "How does Hap Emerson and the IDA tie into all of this?"

"You look tired, Jessie. Why don't I take you home, and we can finish up later?"

"No!" I said with a vehemence that surprised even me. "Don't you understand, Gil? If I had paid attention, two innocent people might not be dead. I have to know."

"If that isn't the biggest crock I've heard in a long time. The only thing responsible for this whole sordid affair was good old-fashioned greed."

I tried to believe Gil's words, but the picture that kept flashing through my mind was Willy standing in front of me and insisting I talk to Margaret.

"Maybe you're right," I said, "but please tell me the rest."

"All right, but it's going to take a long time before we have all the details. Hap Emerson was always casting his eye around to find a new place to set up one of his real estate deals. He found out about a new highway being planned through Riverport, so he approached Mayor Ellwood. The good Mayor got swept away by Emerson's rhetoric and hired him to do an economic study. To make a long story as short as I can, Emerson convinced him to start an Industrial

Development Authority. Emerson's plan was to buy up property and options and then turn around and sell them to the IDA for a handsome profit. The reason the Council was making such hefty contributions to the IDA was to cover the purchases . . ." Gil paused. "Are you following me so far?"

I nodded.

"Of course, Emerson wasn't doing any of this with his own money, because he had found a bunch of suckers who thought they'd hit the mother lode. Ray Benson had helped him seek out the likely candidates."

I thought of Frank and cringed.

"Then this summer," Gil continued, "Emerson found out the Feds had balked on giving the matching highway funds needed for the project. Alternate plans had already been drawn up that met Federal guidelines, so the original ones were scrapped."

I nodded and took up the story myself. "Emerson had collected what he thought was all the incriminating evidence from the Benson house after Ray died. That way no one could prove he had taken their money under false pretenses. Only Ray had made copies of most of the records and squirreled them away for insurance, in case Emerson tried to cut him out somewhere along the line."

Gil nodded:

"But how can you prove all this without the records that everyone has been looking for?" I asked.

"I found them." He smiled. "All your fussing about Willy's bicycle made me think I'd better take a closer look at it. And there they were, tucked in a little metal box in the bottom of the basket."

He got to his feet. "Let's go," he said, holding out his hand to help me up. "That's all for today."

"But, Gil," I protested, struggling to stand upright. "You can't stop now. What about Margaret finding the plans and papers, and the deal she and Harry had worked out to blackmail Emerson and get the money back?"

"Not much more to tell than what you figured out yourself. Margaret got religion at the last minute and Nancy went into action, and that's it."

Gil drove slowly over the rutted road, as if he knew every jolt reverberated through my head. We didn't speak until we reached my house and Gil helped me out of the Jeep.

"What's going to happen to the other people?" I asked.